PRAISE FOR
PHEASANTS NEST

'Louise Milligan brings her trademark clarity and compassion to a page-turning novel that examines the ripple effects of a devastating crime in real time. In *Pheasants Nest*, Milligan takes the reader on an unflinching journey beyond the headlines to the heart of the crime, where Kate Delaney, along with those desperate to save her, has her own poignant (and often darkly funny) story to tell. A lively, assured debut that is a welcome addition to the Australian crime fiction canon.' **JACQUELINE BUBLITZ, author of *Before You Knew My Name***

'Milligan is a gifted writer, immersing us into a story as addictive as *Gone Girl* but with a distinctive Australian voice.' **PATRICIA KARVELAS, journalist and broadcaster**

'I loved the book. It's complex, and beautifully structured, and delivers intelligent insights into the worlds of policing and media without ever seeming to try too hard.

I consumed this novel in one sitting. In the character of Kate Delaney, Louise Milligan has given voice—and humour, and deep respect—to the ranks of women reduced every year to the stark, monochrome chalk outline that is "Victim of Crime".

It's a compelling story, written with tautness and wit. But its greatest achievement is to remind the reader that when human beings do dreadful things to each other, the pain and grief and horror do not happen in a vacuum; there is also love, and courage, and someone who will do the right thing even when it's terrifying.

Louise Milligan has spent most of her journalistic career refusing to turn away from pain. And in *Pheasants Nest*, she demonstrates with elegance and generosity what else can be seen when one squarely faces suffering, and human depravity. Namely: courage, love, black humour. All the things that are variously present in humans before they become victims of crime, but sometimes are forgotten after, in that terrible, flattening isolation of being a person to whom something unthinkable has been done.

In the characters of *Pheasants Nest*, one can clearly perceive some of the people who have most stayed with Milligan over her reporting career. In giving them depth and warmth and life beyond the chalk outline that reads "Victim of Crime, she does them—and us—a great service.' **ANNABEL CRABB, journalist, broadcaster and author of *The Wife Drought***

'Louise Milligan's journalism has always championed those who have been abused and victimised. Now she takes that same perspective into fiction, in this gripping, sinister—yet also wryly funny and realistic—crime thriller.' **JANE CARO, author of *The Mother***

'A gripping and devastating all-too-real thriller that had me on the edge of my seat, desperate to know how it was going to end.' **SARAH BAILEY, author of The Housemate**

'Anyone familiar with Louise Milligan's work will not be surprised to find her first novel is nuanced, considered and deeply concerned with the darkest places a human soul can go. But it's the style, pluck and heart in these pages that make what should be an unbearable story unputdownable. *Pheasants Nest* is simply unmissable.' **HAYLEY SCRIVENOR, author of *Dirt Town***

'When writers of truth write fiction, a profound understanding of the world echoes on every page. Louise Milligan's extensive experience as an investigative journalist provides an insightful backdrop to the story of the kidnapping of Kate Delaney after a night out with friends. Milligan's use of shifting perspectives allows the reader to see how the crime plays out through the eyes of everyone involved. Laced with clever insights and wisdom, *Pheasants Nest* propels the reader on a rollercoaster ride of peril and nail-biting tension. At the same time, the characters seem so real, you want them for your friends. Some of them, at least. It feels like everything Louise Milligan has learnt, has led to this novel.' **VIKKI PETRAITIS, author of *The Unbelieved***

'A crime novel that could only be written by a fine journalist—so original, funny and true. *Pheasants Nest* is a pleasure all the way.' **DAVID MARR, journalist and author of *Killing for Country***

Louise Milligan is a multi-awardwinning investigative journalist for ABC TV's *Four Corners*, the Australian national broadcaster's flagship current affairs documentary program. She is the author of two bestselling non-fiction books: *Cardinal: The Rise and Fall of George Pell* and *Witness: An Investigation into the Brutal Cost of Seeking Justice*. Her books have been awarded multiple prizes, including the Walkley Book Award, the Davitt Awards' Best Non-Fiction Crime Book, the Melbourne Prize for Literature People's Choice Award, the Victorian Premier's Literary Award's People's Choice prize, the Sir Owen Dixon Chambers Law Reporter of the Year Award, a Press Freedom Medal and a shortlisting for the Stella Prize. Louise's journalism, particularly her coverage of historical institutional child abuse and the experience of women in the criminal justice system and parliament, has broken national and international news, sparked government inquiries and led to profound cultural change and law reform. She started her career in newspapers and is a former High Court correspondent and political reporter. Born in Ireland to an Irish mother and Scottish father, Louise moved to Australia as a child. She lives in Melbourne with her husband and two children. *Pheasants Nest* is Louise's first novel.

LOUISE
MILLIGAN

Pheasants Nest

This is a work of fiction. Names, characters, places and incidents are products of the author's imagination or are used fictitiously. Any resemblance to actual events, locales or persons, living or dead, is entirely coincidental.

First published in 2024

Lyrics from 'Under The Milky Way' by The Church reproduced by permission of Steve Kilby.

Allen & Unwin
Cammeraygal Country
83 Alexander Street
Crows Nest NSW 2065
Australia
Phone: (61 2) 8425 0100
Email: info@allenandunwin.com
Web: www.allenandunwin.com

Allen & Unwin acknowledges the Traditional Owners of the Country on which we live and work. We pay our respects to all Aboriginal and Torres Strait Islander Elders, past and present.

A catalogue record for this book is available from the National Library of Australia

ISBN 978 1 76147 034 9

Set in 12.25/20 pt Minion Pro by Bookhouse, Australia
Printed and bound in Australia by the Opus Group

10 9 8 7 6 5 4 3 2 1

The paper in this book is FSC® certified. FSC® promotes environmentally responsible, socially beneficial and economically viable management of the world's forests.

FOR MY DARLING MOTHER, MARY.

AND FOR ANYONE WHO EVER LOVED.

1

COLD

KATE DELANEY'S EYES snap open and the first thing she notices is the cold. It's a familiar cold: the sharp sting of a thousand acupuncture needles plunging into her skin at once. She knows that cold. Southern Highlands cold. She's approaching the Southern Highlands.

She's lying on the back seat of a car. His car. Shudder. The Guy. The Guy doesn't get to have a name.

She looks ahead and sees his frosted blond hair glinting, his arms at the steering wheel, snaked with veins, buffed at the gym. His wrists and fingers tap-tap the wheel in time to the music in manic delight. Pearl Jam.

It would be kind of funny if it wasn't so grim. Kate loathes Pearl Jam—nineties commercial grunge. On the car CD player, the nasal whine of Eddie Vedder's voice, warbling that he's still alive.

Kate Delaney is still alive but her stomach churns with the understanding that she mightn't be for long. She's hundreds of kilometres from where she started from in Melbourne that night. If Pearl Jam is to be one of the last sounds of her thirty-something years . . . it feels like one of those postmodern jokes she once scoffed at over cheap shiraz.

She glances down at her stockings: black opaques, torn at the knee, her blood like treacle in the moonlight. It hurts to move and she's afraid to move in case he realises she's awake and does something . . . else.

Instead, she stares out the window. There are the windmills near—what was the place? Gunning. Normally busily spinning away, but now, in the small hours of a Sunday morning, they simply sway ominously in the gunmetal sky like a drunken KKK crew, arms akimbo, pointed hoods flopping lazily to the side.

Soon she'll be passing Goulburn and the Big Merino. The thought of it draws a half-smile to her chapped lips, despite everything. One particularly chilly winter she had bought a red scarf at the shop inside the giant concrete ram, knitted from, of all things, possum fur. It was deliciously cosy and not as unstylish as it sounded. Nevertheless, when she wore it to Fashion Week, Sylvia, her best and most fashion-forward friend, collapsed in giggles on discovering its provenance. Kate felt quietly and smugly subversive. *Fuck you, fashionistas, I'm wearing possum fur. And I got it at the Big Merino.*

Kate Delaney knows this drive so well. She has travelled from Melbourne to Sydney countless times, and it is far from lost on her that the part of the drive that always struck her as unutterably creepy is where she now finds herself. She always felt foreboding when she drove that stretch.

There is the Belanglo State Forest to the left, where serial killer Ivan Milat murdered and buried seven backpackers.

Not so far away, someone took to hanging stuffed animals from trees along the side of the road. It was speculated that this had something to do with a sinister paedophile ring, but nobody really knew. It took years for all the animals to be removed and it had made Kate wince every time she'd seen them, many decapitated, most dirty, with synthetic, rain-matted fur.

Then there was the time she was driving along and saw a car puttering along at maybe ten k's an hour in the stopping lane. She and her friends had turned back to see no one visible at the wheel.

Kate, her then-boyfriend Michael King and their mate Steve felt too sick to speak. They slowed down and gawped, too scared to drive back to the Toyota to see what had happened. Suddenly, a police car zoomed up. Told them to move on, nothing to see here.

They discovered not half an hour later from a cop contact of Kate's that a guy had set out on the Barton Highway from Canberra, dosed himself up with enough OxyContin to knock over a horse and kept driving on the Hume until he lost consciousness. By the time they had seen him, he was slumped to the side, his foot at a miraculous angle on the accelerator that kept him at such a slow speed and didn't veer him into oncoming traffic. Kate, Michael and Steve spent the rest of their road trip in silence.

The culmination of this strangely gothic drive was the Pheasants Nest Bridge. A place name without an apostrophe. A place name, thought Kate Delaney, bound up in a mistake. Didn't the nest belong to the pheasant? Kate had a horror of missing apostrophes. Every time she saw the sign on the entrance to the bridge, she vowed that when she returned, she would bring a marker pen and add the punctuation herself.

But who was she kidding? Kate Delaney wouldn't get out of the car at Pheasants Nest. She sensed the darkness of this place, even in the daytime. Pheasants Nest made Kate Delaney shiver.

Back in 1990, the bodies of two teenage boys had been found inside the bridge's huge concrete pylons. They had climbed into the tunnel in the undercarriage of the bridge and plunged to their deaths in the shafts.

But most of the lives that finished off at Pheasants Nest did not end accidentally. Most of the people who ended their days at Pheasants Nest were jumpers.

The Pheasants Nest Bridge and the surrounding bridges that lined that stretch of the Hume were notorious for jumpers.

If you lived near the coast in Sydney, you threw yourself from The Gap at Watson's Bay. But if you were a westie, particularly an outer-westie, your jump of choice was Pheasants Nest.

And as Kate Delaney had sped past those bridges, those forests, she'd never failed to feel overcome by the road that ran along at the top of the gum trees and the unspoken sadness that surrounded it. The ghosts clamouring for attention out of the bleak stillness of the bush.

2

BAR

IT NOW SEEMS like days ago that Kate first noticed him across the bar. It has really only been a matter of hours, but she's been unconscious for many of them. It has left her confused and hazy. How many hours? She doesn't know. Time seems elastic and imprecise. It's still quite dark, so she figures it's only four or five am. She isn't sure what he's been up to in the interim. Has he stopped anywhere? Has he been caught on CCTV? Will they be able to trace him? She hopes so, but doesn't know.

He had looked at her across that bar in Northcote in a puppyish way at first. Kate was out with a group of girlfriends—Sylvia, Adie, Brigid and Sophie. He was there with another guy that she was sure he would describe as his 'wing man'. He was on the cusp of middle age, but obviously placed a lot of pride in his appearance. Not particularly tall but buff in the way that only someone who spends hours in the gym several times a week can be.

A tattoo of a yin and yang sign on one of his biceps. Strawberry blond hair tipped in the style of Australian cricketers. Fitted aqua shirt made of some sort of unspeakable synthetic fibre that strained slightly and deliberately at the buttons, tucked into pale Levi's that left a bit too little to the imagination.

It occurred to her later that he probably thought the shirt matched his eyes, which were glassy slits the colour of pale sea-water. They crinkled in the corners in what was, *prima facie*, an agreeable way. But upon closer inspection, they fixed on things a little too hard. The laugh was a little too practised—he threw back his head as he did shots with his friend at an angle that was somehow too acute. Slapped his mate twice on the shoulder and winked in a way that he'd seen in a TV show. *This is how the agreeable guy acts. You know, Joey, from* Friends.

Anyway, Kate didn't quite clock all of this as he stood at the bar and glanced repeatedly in her direction, throwing the odd good-natured '*What?*' her way when she found herself frustratingly unable to not look back at him, but she clocked enough to know that this fellow was not, in any sense, her type. So, when it was her round for drinks, she deliberately went to the other end of the bar and turned her back to him.

Kate Delaney was difficult to miss in a room. Tall, with masses of red curly hair that she usually blow-dried into a sixties style. Pale skin, hazel eyes. A peppering of tiny freckles on the bridge of her nose. She liked to wear mini shift dresses in the style of Mary Quant. Tonight's was navy with a white collar, with black tights to give it an edge. Huge red handbag. Crocodile knee-high boots with blocky heels. She was not to every man's taste—her teeth were a little gappy, her loose-jointed elbows somehow awkward, her knees scarred with too many childhood scrapes—but those that did find her attractive found her devastating. And when she walked into a room, well, there she was. Unmissable.

And this guy did not plan on missing Kate Delaney on this night. As she ordered the drinks, she felt a tap on her shoulder.

'Can I buy you one of those?' he asked, in a voice that she instantly pitied for its nasal high pitch.

'Nope, I'm fine thanks—just here with them-there ladies,' she said, grinning in her sweetest way, giving him a playful, let-us-have-our-fun wink.

'Huh, okay.' He looked at her, again with that fixed gaze, set jaw. She suspected he was a tooth-grinder. Insecure but pumped up.

She walked back to her friends and downed several more glasses of wine. The room was getting warmer, the girls were getting funnier. Tonight's topic of conversation: why couldn't you be the person you were with the guys who really loved you (but who you didn't love) all the time? Because that was the *SuperYou.*

What was it about going out on a date with a guy who was nice and smart but just not quite right, but who was clearly smitten, that turned you *immediately* into the SuperYou, funnier than Tina Fey . . . But as soon as you spent five minutes in the company of a man you were actually into, the one-liners washed out to sea. You became inarticulate as a bloody baboon. It was one of life's great tragedies. Sylvia mooted that they get together and write a self-help book entitled *Unleash the SuperYou*, only they all realised, shrieking and choking on their drinks, that they had no bloody, bloody idea how to do it.

At which point Kate and Brigid decided they needed to go to the bathroom. As she got up, Kate felt that familiar warm rush to the head of a couple too many wines. A not altogether unpleasant feeling, but one that signalled she should probably think about calling it a night soon. And yet she knew that she was kidding herself that she would leave. She reapplied red lipstick in the dirty, speckled mirror that was bolted on to the wall and gave herself a shake, bursting out of the toilet door with Brigid to her left. To her right, she heard the nasal voice.

'Nice arse, sweetheart. I'd like to get a piece of that.' She felt his hand brush against it in a proprietorial way.

Kate felt the familiar Celtic temper flood her veins. She was five wines down (or was it six?), and she had heard this sort of thing before. Her friends were the types to shrug and walk. Not Kate Delaney.

At times her retorts had had great comic effect. She'd never forget the time when, at a rave party, a sleazy guy, E'ing off his dial, came up to her and asked her in a schmaltzy whisper, 'If you could have anything in the world, right this minute, what would it be?' And Kate Delaney had turned to this orange-hued man and said, 'Anything? Right now? Okay, I'd wish that you would stop going to the solarium.' She could practically see the MDMA doing a triple pike and turning its effect inside out, right there in his addled brain, right there on the spot.

He had looked like the sort of guy who fancied himself and his prospects with women rather highly, particularly when they were much-younger, naïve-looking girls at dance parties. Collateral damage.

So again, on this particular September Saturday night in Northcote, she decided to resort to comedy. To *Unleash The SuperYou*. She circled behind him, pointed to his bottom and shook her head, tut-tutting to Brigid, who was pressing her lips together in comically anxious anticipation.

'Saggy arse, love. So much for all those hours at the gym,' she said, as Brigid cackled. It was true. His arse was flat. Kate and Brigid then bolted over to the table, grabbed Sylvia and the other girls and their handbags and coats and shot out the door in fits of laughter, adrenaline pumping through them like soda, running down the street like schoolgirls in their mothers' heels.

Kate felt catapulted back into those teenage nights when you'd pour out half a bottle of Bacardi, fill it with coke and push each other in shopping trolleys while listening to The Clash on a ghetto blaster.

And that was Kate Delaney's Big Mistake.

—

Kate Delaney is now trying to mentally squeeze Pearl Jam out of her brain. *Need to replace song. Choose The Stone Roses.*

Although it isn't really on, it is just in her mind, 'I Wanna Be Adored' instantly makes her feel hopeful.

Even decades later, The Stone Roses are cool. She closes her eyes and it hurts. '*I wanna, I wanna, I wanna be adored, I wanna, I wanna, I wanna be adored,*' she chants in her mind.

Outside, the trees are laced with night fog. Infrequent streetlights whiz by. The car smells of the cloying pine-tree air freshener that dangles from his rear-view mirror. Those things always made her car sick when she was a kid. She begged her dad never to buy them again. Whenever she's in a taxi now and sees one, she's instantly catapulted back onto windy country roads, rolling around in the back of an unairconditioned Valiant station wagon on a forty-degree day.

Underneath the seat, she can see a bong rolling around on the carpet. Why is it that bong smokers always think they can cover up the smell of dope with artificial air fresheners?

Her bones hurt. *I wanna, I wanna, I wanna be adored . . .*

In the boot of the car, she hears her phone ringing again. Her boyfriend, Liam. He must be out of his mind with worry.

The tapping on the steering wheel suddenly stops. In the rear-view mirror, she sees The Guy's eyes dart around a bit. He turns down Pearl Jam.

'Huh,' he says, pulling over the car and stopping the engine. The electronic trill of Kate's ring tone echoes out into the still night. 'Huh.'

'Fuck's sake.' He veers into the service lane with an alarming screech. She's thrown forward with the force of the jolt as he comes to a stop. She snaps her eyes shut again and tries not to breathe.

He gets out and slams the door shut and even the tough-guy way he does that is deeply annoying.

The gravel crunches under his shoes. He whistles through his teeth and walks around to the boot.

And Kate Delaney watches through her eyelashes as her phone, still ringing, hurtles like a comet through the freezing night sky and into the bushland below. Thwack.

First thought: Did she back up her contacts?

Second thought: Will she ever need them again?

Third thought: Rookie error, loser. They'll know her phone came at least this far.

—

In Melbourne, Liam Carroll looks at his phone and wonders what the hell is going on. Where is she?

3
LIAM

KATE DELANEY HAD met Liam Carroll a few months before.

Liam was a medical negligence plaintiff lawyer with a shock of almost black hair that he could never quite keep neat, and large, simultaneously bashful and knowing eyes. He was smart/self-deprecating, dogged/uncertain, meticulously competent/perennially late.

His voice sounded like honey. He laughed at her dumb jokes.

Each of them had been dux of their forgettable, suburban Catholic colleges and they bonded over their shared historical nerdiness with a faux Smiths song they called 'Duces of Fair-To-Middling Schools'.

Liam, in suitably dour Morrissey tones: '*I would go out tonight . . . but I have a very important exam to study for in the morning . . .*'

Kate, without pausing for breath: '*Please, please, please, let me, let me, let me, let me . . . get . . . an A+ for my English Literature essay.*'

—

Liam Carroll had recently made partner at a Melbourne CBD firm called Le Carre & Company, founded by a flamboyant solicitor called Steven Carver, who had changed his name by deed poll to Sebastian Le Carre—Sebastian, after the foppish antihero in *Brideshead Revisited* (he'd always imagined himself as a character in an Evelyn Waugh novel) and Le Carre, because he just thought it sounded fancier.

Sebastian Le Carre founded the practice as a determined sole practitioner in 1980 and it had grown, thanks to his legal skills, marketing smarts and then-pioneering use of the 'no win–no fee' model, into one of the biggest plaintiff law firms in the country.

Le Carre was a brilliant lawyer with a wry sense of humour and, his mother always said, 'a front the size of Myer'. He was a man of contradictions. He had a penchant for made-to-measure suits in chalk-striped flannel, and would present designer jewellery to his largely female workforce as bonuses when they won an important case. But he was also known for his big heart and his extensive pro bono work for impoverished litigants with important causes, even when he could really be doing with a big pay day.

The Le Carre women were a flashy flock, who shared their boss's love of the finer things in life as much as they did his championing of the underdog. They'd stride in packs along William Street in Melbourne's legal district, clad in red-soled Louboutins, with their big hair, glossy lips and laughs like drains. The private school types from the more staid establishment firms would roll their eyes. 'And there go the Carredashians,' they'd sneer.

The Carredashians were also known as the Carrecrashians. The firm had a thriving motor vehicle accident injury practice. They didn't think of themselves as ambulance-chasers, but nor did they give a rat's what anyone thought of them. And their clients loved them.

Kate Delaney thought them somewhat fabulous and had been invited on their infamous champagne-fuelled benders once or twice.

'Our firm's name is Le Carre & Company,' one of them said to Kate, taking a sip of Bollinger, 'but the defence lawyers like to call us, "Le Carre and *Cunts*". And our care factor?' She pinched her thumb and forefinger into at little circle. '*Zero*. What do we say, ladies?'

'Total cunts and proud of it,' her colleagues chimed.

'No fucks to give.'

Kate choked on her bubbles.

—

Liam Carroll was the favourite pet of the Carredashian crew. 'I'm the firm's token white privileged male,' he would quip. 'Don't hold it against me.' His schooling was too pedestrian, his upbringing too lower middle-class and his overall demeanour far too shambolic for him to truly be considered privileged. But the Carredashians played into his joke.

They loved his awkward bashfulness, tried in vain to jazz up his wardrobe, felt *simpatico* for his overall sense of decency—something Sebastian Le Carre always made sure his people possessed.

Liam lacked the superiority often seen in men in the law. He wasn't a smug skirt-chaser. He didn't spend all of his conversations reminding you, in case you hadn't noticed, about just how accomplished he was. He didn't belong to old boys' networks and found them, frankly, irritating. He was the sort of guy you could go to with your problems. He was an incredibly driven lawyer, motivated by the human tragedy that is inescapable in a medical negligence practice to try to somehow make his clients' lives less awful. To make the bastard insurance companies pay. And he was smart enough to realise that sometimes things just didn't work out. And outcomes were far from ideal. That life was nuanced. And that sometimes his clients got a really shitty deal.

—

The Carredashians heartily approved when Liam took up with the journo with the sixties-style dresses, the mane of red hair and the preoccupation with social justice.

'She's *luxe*, Liam,' they trilled.

'Go *you*.'

Liam had met Kate Delaney when she was covering a coronial inquest into a child's death. The little boy had died in suspicious circumstances at an isolated country hospital. Liam was representing the boy's parents, who were accusing the doctor of negligent conduct.

Kate had discovered after the inquest that there were many other children who had died at the hands of the same doctor during a period of ten years. Liam had been a huge help to her during her investigation. He was one of those lawyers who just got how journalists operated—didn't see them as a hindrance. Understood that careful cooperation would only help his clients.

They would text at all hours as she stumbled upon the next break in the story. At first, he just admired her tenacity. She was, in journalistic parlance, a terrier. But the more that time wore on, the more Liam noticed that he couldn't stop thinking about her. That he looked forward to her late-night texts and felt a little rush when the notification light popped up on his phone. That he'd pour himself a glass of wine and settle down to help with her constant questions. That her turn of phrase and general impertinence made him smile.

Four months after they first met, when Kate's series of stories was finally published and the creepy doctor was struck off and their work relationship on that story was done, he invited her out to a bar to celebrate. For an hour or so, they studiously avoided each other's gazes and nervously bantered about politics. Then Liam had awkwardly summoned some courage.

'I just want to lie down next to you and hold you. Would that be okay?'

'Umm, sure,' she replied, pretending to be nonchalant, hoping he wouldn't notice how furiously her heart was racing.

And then he kissed her, in a lift, and as the floor rose beneath them, she knew she was gone. Every time she stepped into a lift after that, she closed her eyes and felt warm.

—

He came, like her, from generations of mad Catholics.

He even knew the words to her favourite prayer, 'Hail Holy Queen'. They had both been forced to say it every school morning of November, the Month of Mary.

They'd recited it together, in fits of mirth, that night when they got to his apartment. She'd sat on his knee, eating oysters he had pre-arranged in the hope she might come back ('Too much?' he'd wondered, but needn't have). They'd kissed each other's eyelids and drunk too much champagne.

Hail Holy Queen, mother of mercy,

Hail our lives, our sweetness and our hope.

To you do we cry, poor banished children of Eve,

To you do we send up our sighs, mourning and weeping in this valley of tears . . .

And they'd both fallen off the sofa, laughing so hard at the melodrama of it all.

Playing to his crowd, Liam had pointed out to her the Child of Prague statue standing on his bookshelf. She gasped. He was the only person Kate had ever known in Australia who even knew about the Child.

The original Child was a small, wooden, magnificently dressed infant Christ, festooned with a golden crown. It was first owned by a Spanish Contessa and was now housed in Prague, in the Church of Our Lady of Victories, which was owned by the Order of Discalced Carmelites.

But in Ireland, where Kate lived until she was nine, the Child had spawned endless cheap imitations, made out of plaster and crudely painted with gold.

When Kate was twenty-one, visiting Dublin with her then-boyfriend, her Great-Auntie Maggie had given her an oversized Child the size of a cricket bat.

Kate was, by that time, well and truly lapsed in the faith of her childhood and living a life that would have made Auntie

Maggie's toes curl. It hadn't been that long since Auntie Maggie had stopped buying her inappropriately childish sundresses and pressing a fiver in her hand for sweets.

'Now,' Auntie Maggie had said in that whispering-sighing way she'd had, every word a slightly plaintive exhalation, 'this is for the night before you get married.'

Kate's eyes widened and she kicked her non-Catholic boyfriend under the table as he suppressed a smirk.

'Your Mammy had one, too. I brought it home from Lourdes—' Auntie Maggie paused meaningfully on the name of the French town, her eyes welling up, her veined hands shaking.

Lourdes was the site where Our Lady had appeared to the fourteen-year-old Bernadette Soubirous and it had become the beloved destination of Catholic pilgrims. Auntie Maggie told stories of 'cripples' rising from their wheelchairs to walk, cancer patients going into remission.

Apart from holy statues like the Child, she brought home little plastic packages tied up with cobalt bows. In them were Lourdes sweets which contained in their centre *real water from the holy grotto*. A tiny Kate had gulped before biting into the blessed confectionary, wondering what miraculous future awaited her. Auntie Maggie had been to Lourdes seventeen times.

Maggie possessed an almost child-like naïveté. Her hair bore the hallmarks of too-tight rollers that had been set overnight and the too-dark brown dye she bought at Penneys. She was an endearingly terrible cook and a lifelong spinster who absolutely adored children. Maggie's sister had twenty-seven grandchildren and Maggie had always made it clear that Kate was her favourite one of them. Her little brown brick 1930s public housing flat was crammed with crucifixes and holy water fonts and rosary beads. It always seemed to have a faint odour of overcooked cabbage that was slightly on the turn. On her windowsill, which looked out onto the dirty grey water of the Dodder, was a bank of porcelain swans.

Each week, Maggie would wash down the statue of Our Lady in the stone grotto in the middle of the flats, polishing the Blessed Virgin's crown and laying daffodils or carnations at her feet.

She attended mass three times a week at the austere church on the bottom of the arch of the old stone bridge adjacent to the flats. When Kate was dressed like a little Catholic bride on the day of her First Holy Communion, Auntie Maggie had told her, with tears in her eyes and without a skerrick of exaggeration, that it was *the most important day of your life.*

'So,' Auntie Maggie said, placing her hand on Kate's and gesturing to the Child of Prague, 'you put this out the night before you get married to make sure it doesn't rain on the day—but mind, first, you have to chop off his head!'

'Jesus, Mary and Holy Saint Joseph, what?' Kate said.

'That's what you need to do. That's the tradition. It worked for your Mammy. It will work for you, too, please God. *Now.*' Auntie Maggie had, like many Irish women of that generation, a habit of punctuating her sentences with a little pause for breath and then, 'Now', as if she was going to say something else, but never did.

Kate stared into the large cornflower eyes of the Christ child and imagined the statue unceremoniously beheaded in the garden. 'Are you sure, Auntie Maggie?'

'Oh definitely,' her auntie said, cocking her head to the side. She had always reminded Kate of a bird. 'Of course.'

—

There were three problems.

The first was that at twenty-one, Kate Delaney was a university student, who had no intention of getting married. The second, unbeknownst to her dear aunt, was that Kate had not gone to mass in five years and was an avid non-believer who was doing Nietzsche and the death of God in Philosophy. The third was that Kate and her then-boyfriend were about to go backpacking around Europe. And the Child of Prague barely fit in her already overstuffed rucksack. Kate liked clothes too much to ever be a sensible packer.

So, as she left Dublin Airport, Auntie Maggie's favourite great-niece took a deep breath, mentally did a sign of the cross, asked the secular universe for forgiveness and threw the Child in a dustbin. As she turned around to walk away, looking back wracked with the requisite Catholic guilt to see the gold crown poking awkwardly out of the chrome bin lid, she consoled herself with the possibility that a deeply superstitious Dubliner might find the statue and seen it as a Sign from God.

Kate Delaney told Liam the story that night in his Northcote apartment years later. Liam was of Irish Catholic descent, but his family were very much Australian. They were the sort of Catholics who discovered that you had been born in Dublin and insisted on telling you their distant relative had been in The Troubles. Those sorts of Australian Catholics didn't know about the wedding superstition. Liam just thought the Child of Prague was endearingly kitsch, which appealed to his slightly gothic sensibilities. He'd picked it up at a garage sale in the suburbs.

Liam: 'But that's the Baby Jesus! You can't behead the Baby Jesus!'

Kate, suppressing a giggle: 'They behead the Baby Jesus. They can't exactly have it rain on their wedding day.'

'And you threw the Child in the bin at Dublin Airport!'

'I threw the Child in the bin.'

Liam shook his head in mock disapproval.

Outside his apartment, the Melbourne drizzle turned to what Auntie Maggie used to call 'wet rain', plopping hard and loud on the roof.

Kate walked over to Liam's bookshelf and picked up his Child.

'I think you're going to have to smash the head of this statue to make the rain stop,' she said in a low voice, eyeing him levelly.

'You think?'

She nodded.

His brown eyes softened. He looked her in the eye, took the Child, opened his hand and let the holy statue drop onto the floor.

A little miracle happened. Instead of the entire thing smashing to smithereens, the only thing to break off was the head, which came clean off at the neck.

And as tiny shards of cheap plaster infant head scuttled across polished concrete, Liam Carroll put the headless child back on the bookshelf. He took Kate's face in his hands and, as he pressed his forehead on hers, she smiled a gappy smile.

Then Kate Delaney and Liam Carroll stumbled their way through his apartment and onto his roughly made bed.

They didn't stop the rain.

But that was where, as much as they could, in the months since then, they had stayed.

That is, until Kate decided to go out on the tear with her girlfriends, and pissed off The Guy.

—

Now Kate was lying bleeding in the back of the car, speeding through the Southern Highlands, trying not to stir; The Guy was thumping the steering wheel; her phone was lying in the scrub beneath a canopy of trees; and Liam Carroll was pacing up and down on polished concrete wondering why his girlfriend hadn't yet come home. Why she hadn't sent any of her playful texts. Why she hadn't answered her phone, when they hadn't even had a bad word. And why her phone was going straight to message when he called her at four am.

4

GONE

BY THE TIME the first strobes of sunlight started to peek through the clouds, Liam Carroll was sweating.

Her phone had been off for hours now.

A lesser part of him, the part he didn't much like, had at first wondered if she'd gone off with someone else.

But that didn't make sense. They were still drunk on love. It still hurt when they were apart for too long. The silliest things still made their pulses quicken. She still hadn't gained back the weight she'd lost from the first buzz of infatuation.

He was, at times, prone to very dark periods, for which he had had to be medicated, and the provenance of which he had never fully explained to her. She still smarted whenever the sadness she had come to recognise flickered in his eyes. She would stroke his brow and kiss his lips and try to make him better. And when all else failed, she would take off her clothes, and then his. And he would. He would feel better.

Liam Carroll had been a late bloomer. Studious and shy in his teens, he only really came into his own in his mid-to-late twenties. He never really had the party-and-drug-fuelled youth that many of his peers had experienced. He had always been too scared to try heroin, but that feeling of reciprocal mad desire coursing through his veins that he had when he was with Kate Delaney, well that was how he imagined it felt.

Where the hell was she?

He glanced again at his watch: seven am. It was surely an acceptable time to message Sylvia, even though Sylvia had been out the night before with Kate, and likely had a hangover.

Hey Sylvia, top of the morning—sorry for the early text.
I don't suppose Kate came and crashed at your place?

Nope! She insisted on walking back to yours.
You know what she's like. Can't bloody keep her away
from you. You two are incorrigible. ☺

Wait, what? Hang on. Isn't she with you?

No, she isn't. That's why I'm texting. I'm really
fucking worried. She hasn't answered her phone.
Hasn't texted. And her phone's gone straight to
message for hours

Maybe she went back to her place? Maybe she just went home, passed out and her phone died?

Maybe. I'm going to head over there now.

Okay. Let me know as soon as you get there

Will do. Where was the last place you saw her?

Walking out of the bar we went to after the pub. On High St

Don't stress

☹ Speak soon

—

Liam scrambled into clothes, doused his face with cold water and then padded into the kitchen to fish for the key to Kate's place that she had left in an old-school milk bottle on the shelf above his stove.

In it was a little note.

Hello kind sir,

If you are reading this, it means that I am a complete dunder-head and have locked myself out of the house (again). My excuse for my pathological vagueness is that my mind is preoccupied with Terribly Important, Big Picture Ideas. Please dash across to mine at earliest opportunity and rescue me from my latest plight. I assure you, I will find devastatingly appealing ways to repay your kindness.

Best,
Madam

Liam smiled and, despite his worry, felt that familiar hot feeling wash over him. He'd get over there and find that she'd just decided to go home instead, and walk in to see her waking up with a sore head and a dead phone. They'd watch reruns of *The West Wing* and order Lebanese comfort food and Coke Zero Sugar. He'd tell her how he wasn't sure if he was fit enough these days to start his dream career as a White House staffer who marched endless corridors and discussed, in rapid fire, strategies for breaking a filibuster. She'd complain that she couldn't keep up with the dialogue. She'd tell him, again, that CJ was her spirit animal. They'd scoff at the way Josh and the rest of them would all gaze into the distance and talk about democracy and how implausible all that cheesy idealism now seemed. They'd wish, again, that Josiah Bartlett was really President. It would be beautiful.

He almost ran a red light on the way over there. A beefed-up guy in a souped-up Commodore blasted his horn.

'Watch where you're going, fuckstick,' the guy yelled out of his window.

'Fuck you, cunt,' Liam yelled back, pretending to be tough. Sometimes 'cunt' really was the only appropriate word. He sped up and tried to lose the guy, who was trying to get alongside him to continue with the road rage.

'Listen, mate, I'm sorry,' he called, when they stopped at the lights. Liam wasn't a very successful tough guy. And he was stressed and exhausted. 'I've got an emergency. I'm worried about my girlfriend.'

'Okay, whatever,' Mr Beefy replied, and thundered off.

Liam rounded the corner into Kate's street.

He glanced up at the rounded balcony of her art-deco apartment to see if there were any signs of life. She would often go out there on weekend mornings with a coffee because, at this time of year, autumn, it was covered in cerise bougainvillea. She'd planted it against her mother's advice that the thorns would drive her mad. She had, inevitably, scratched her arms. But she just loved the colour. The plant was going gangbusters. There was no sign of Kate.

He let himself into the building and hopped up the creaky parqueted stairs two at a time.

Her lock was always jammy.

'Come on, key, just help me this time,' he muttered, his fingers reddening with the effort. She seemed to have a method to get in, but he hadn't mastered it yet. Finally, after several tries, the barrel turned. Thank fuck.

Silence. The air in the apartment had that feeling of being both cold and stuffy that suggests no one has been in it for a while.

'Kate. Kate! Kater! Katie!' he called, trying not to sound panicked. She hated being called Katie. He blamed the worry.

He opened the door to her bedroom. Unusually, her quilted Dutch blue duvet lay perfectly flat on a made-up bed. She'd fluffed up the pillows in a rare moment of calm domesticity. There were three pink peonies in a little vase, starting to brown at the edges because she had been spending all her time at his. Some books lay stacked on the bedside table: F. Scott Fitzgerald's *The Beautiful and Damned*. The latest Franzen. A get-even biography from an unspeakably boring former Minister for Infrastructure she must have been hate-reading for work. He noticed a small trail of ants running over the table. The balcony that led out to the bougainvillea was empty and still, save for the solitary high-pitched chatter of a mynah bird that was perched on the wall, surveying the ground below for unsuspecting pedestrians to swoop at.

No Kate.

The blood began to drain from Liam Carroll's face. His mouth went dry.

No Kate.

He looked again at the first text from Sylvia.

Nope! She insisted on walking back to yours. You know what she's like. Can't bloody keep her away from you. You two are incorrigible. ☺

Fuck, fuck, fuck.

He texted Sylvia.

She's not here. Kate's not here. No sign of life at all.

Okay. Breathe. I'm going to put something up on Facebook. You call the cops.

The room started spinning. How had they arrived at 'call the cops' so quickly? How could he be someone who was now calling the cops?

Palms dripping, he clumsily dialled triple-zero.

'My girlfriend. She didn't come home last night.'

'Okay, sir, what's your name?'

'Liam. Liam Carroll.'

'Where are you?'

'Well, I'm in North Carlton.'

'Speak slowly if you can. I'm here. What's your girlfriend's name?'

'Kate. Kate Delaney. Actually, Katherine Mary Delaney. She's, she's tall. And she's got lots of, lots of long red hair. And, you know, Irish. But, you know, Australian now, with an Australian accent. And she has this really cute, you know, gap in her two front teeth. Hazelish eyes. Long eyelashes. And she's a newspaper journalist. And she's a bit disorganised, but she's never once done anything like this. I'm totally oversharing here but fuck it—sorry for swearing, sorry, I need to tell you what's going on—we are really in love.'

He heard the word coming out of his mouth that he'd still been scared to say to her, even though he'd rehearsed it in his head and knew she did, too.

'And she texts me all the time. And she went out last night with her girlfriends and they thought she was walking back to my place, you know, you know, late, and she didn't come back, and her phone went dead and she's not here. She's not here. She's really not here.'

'Rightio, sweetheart,' said the folksy operator, 'now just slow down, I can hear that you're a bit breathless there. She's not where, sweetie?'

'Here. At her apartment. She didn't walk home to my place after being out in Northcote and there's no sign of life at her place. I'm at her place now. I raced over here this morning as soon as I realised she was missing. She clearly hasn't been home. It's stuffy—you know that sort of stuffy, where no one's been in for a while? *That* stuffy. Kate hates that stuffy. She's got this really overdeveloped sense of smell and look, it doesn't matter, but she would have opened a window or something. Or burned one of those candles she likes. And there is no scent of lemongrass in here and she would have burned that, sorry, she would have burned that lemongrass candle. And I called her best friend, who she was with, and she said that Kate was going to walk to mine. That was the last they saw of her. This is not like her at all. You need to do something. Quickly. Please. Sorry, sorry, I'm just really worried now.'

Liam could hear in his own incoherent babble that rather than sounding like the in-control lawyer he was capable of being, the guy whose lesser self revelled, at times, in scaring the shit out of newbies on the defendants' side, he sounded about fifteen. There was a ringing in his ears. He kept being struck by how empty her apartment was. Maybe he should go back to his place. That's where she had intended to go. He wrapped up the triple-zero call, with the operator promising to send police to his apartment. He grabbed his coat and headed back down to the car.

His phone started to ping. Sylvia had obviously posted on the socials.

Mate, is Kate okay? Have you found her?

You alright? Kate there yet?

Sorry, haven't seen her, sure she'll turn up, she's scatty, you know.

Heart emoji, heart emoji, heart emoji.

He damned to hell the well-meaning but useless heart emojis as he started up the engine to go home.

5

COPS

AT A FEATURELESS red brick police station, a building with the sort of vaguely nineties architecture that you immediately can't remember a single thing about, Detective Sergeant John Dooley was trying to get up to date on his interminable paperwork.

He glanced out to the foyer, where a large woman with curly purple hair and no bra was loudly telling anyone who would listen that she was being stalked by aliens. Slumped on the grey plastic moulded chairs fixed into grey tiles with dirty grouting were a surly moustachioed drug dealer who had come in to report for bail, a harried mother seeking an apprehended violence order against her partner and a few impatient randoms wanting forms signed.

One of the randoms was upset about the state of the toilets. Dooley didn't blame her. They were so dirty as to be mentally scarring. He didn't know why they didn't get cleaned more often. It was like punters were being punished just for the mortal sin of going to the toilet in a police station. Dooley didn't like that. It didn't sit well with his very fixed moral compass. But he didn't dislike it enough to kick up a stink. That would be extra work.

The narky woman came and pressed the buzzer and, as the on-duty constable was in one of the meeting rooms taking a preliminary statement, Dooley put his pen in his top pocket and strode out into the foyer.

Dooley was at times an officious man with rusty, curly hair the texture of a broom. He was covered so densely in freckles that they joined up. His shoes were so highly polished they looked like glass. He prided himself on his superlative policing and hid his weariness at how horrible humans could be to one another with a brusque way of speaking that brought to mind the quick snap of an elastic band.

'I'm sorry, ma'am, I know it's pretty gross. But we're not allowed to give the public access to our toilets back here,' Dooley explained. 'If I made an exception for you, I'd have to make an exception for everyone.'

Dooley was one of those guys who says, 'I'd have to make an exception for everyone.' A rules guy. John Dooley never met a rule he didn't love keeping.

The woman flicked her hair and pleaded. 'The smell is so bad in there it makes me dry retch,' she beseeched.

'I'm very sorry,' Dooley said. 'Is there anything else?'

'I'll just hold it in, then,' the woman said. 'But I'll be writing to the Chief Commissioner.' She tottered on her high heels back to the moulded plastic chair, crossing her legs and grimacing.

'Good idea,' Dooley said, nodding and swiping the security pass on his lanyard and going back to his office. He genuinely hoped the Chief did something about that filthy loo, but didn't have a lot of hope.

'Another option is to head out to the shopping centre behind us. Apparently, they're really clean,' he said as the door shut behind him, sounding the sort of beep that those doors do.

Issues like this were, of course, on a policing scale, so minor as to almost go unnoticed. What irritated Dooley far more was the amount of paperwork you had to do on a job these days. Dooley got it, he was a process-driven man, but he just felt like he spent his entire life filling out forms.

The other thing that John Dooley found most difficult about policing was bearing witness to the way that men treated women. The tide of domestic violence cases that flowed into this station every day filled him with despair. He was a gay man who had never had so much as a party snog with a woman. He adored his mum. And his aunties. And his sisters. They had always understood and accepted that he could be, simultaneously, a fairly conservative stickler for rules and someone who sang Celine Dion into a hairbrush when he'd had a few at Christmas.

John's dad didn't get that so much. But his son liked women, saw them as his equal, hated with every fibre of his being the macho types who thought it was their right to punch on their girlfriend or wife just because they disagreed with them, or offended their manliness, or whatever the hell it was that motivated them to think that a dispute could be solved with aggression. He had no truck with these people. It annoyed him, reading the papers, when they reported the latest homicide against some poor woman and the stories were about how the bloke had seemed such a good guy, but had 'snapped' after he lost custody of the kids. Snapped so badly that he just had to end a woman's life? No, thought John Dooley. That was horseshit.

He wished all the people who gave these guys excuses for their poor behaviour could spend a few days doing his job and realise what animals the bastards were.

Dooley really struggled to keep his cool when he went out to homes to deal with those situations. The sorts of situations cops once upon a time wrote off as 'domestics' but which John Dooley always took very seriously.

He did keep his cool, though. John Dooley was a keep his cool kind of guy.

—

Back in the open-plan office behind the grey-tiled foyer of misery, Dooley made himself a cup of tea. Very milky, but very strong. He trusted pretty much no one to get his tea order right. Waiting for someone to come back with a cup of tea set his teeth on edge. *This will be wrong.* They always returned with something that was appropriately milky, but weak and watery, or, alternatively, not milky enough. Or they left the tea bag in. *Don't leave the tea bag in!* he would feel like screaming at them. *Not with the milk! What kind of barbarian are you?*

He settled down to his desk, opened up his computer screen, and dunked the one sweet biscuit he allowed himself each day into his cup. He watched the tea drenching the Hob Nob, then raised the soft biscuit up to his mouth. Nice.

But policing was all about interruptions. And today's came from Macey James, an earnest young detective senior constable who Dooley liked a lot.

Macey plonked herself on his desk, giving him a fixed look.

'You heard, Sarge?'

'Heard what, Macey?'

'About the girl. Well, the woman, to be clear. I think she's going to land on your desk.'

'What girl–woman?' Dooley asked.

'I think this is going to be a big one,' Macey said.

'Go on, Macey.'

'She's a journo. A pretty one. Not that it should matter, but you know, and I know, *it matters*. Reasonably well-known, as far as newspaper reporters go. She's gone missing. Like, totally, *zip*, in the middle of the night. She was out in High Street, Northcote, with her girlfriends. Didn't come home. The boyfriend reported it. She didn't come home to him. I know women don't come home all the time. But she's apparently not the type to not come home. And it's all over the socials already.'

Macey James leaned over Dooley's computer and tapped out 'Kate Delaney' on the keyboard. Up popped a newspaper dinkus of a striking redhead who looked like she was trying to be serious but had a mischievous glint in her green eyes.

'Didn't come home to the boyfriend?' Dooley repeated, sizing up the picture.

'Nup,' Macey deadpanned.

'Who is the boyfriend?'

'Well, he's a lawyer. Medical negligence. Name's Liam Carroll. You know, you see him on the TV a bit? Goes after dodgy doctors. Le Carre & Company. You know them? They advertise? No win, no fee?'

'Oh yeah,' Dooley replied. 'They got a good lump sum for my auntie Joan when she had a shitty knee replacement from that ortho surgeon who got struck off.'

'Yeah, that's them. So, the boyfriend hasn't been on the scene with Kate that long—a few months, it seems. No priors or anything. Seems pretty harmless, from what I can glean.'

'Seems pretty harmless?' Dooley tries not to scoff. 'Yep. They all do.'

6
SUSPECT

BY THE TIME Liam Carroll got back to his apartment, the cops had arrived and Sylvia was sitting on the building's front stoop. Sylvia Estrellita was a Filipina-Australian whose real name was Crystal; she was named so, to her great embarrassment, because her mother had always loved bling. Sylvia's mum, Gloria, had been an excellent seamstress—she was a garment outworker who was paid by the piece. Gloria had sewed all day and night as little Sylvia sat at her feet, playing with scraps of fabric, making up stories about princesses and celebrities in her head. Sylvia had grown up to be obsessed with clothes. She was now a fashion reporter and Kate was her best friend.

Liam could see that Sylvia had been biting the skin off her lips, and there was a little blood shining through. She'd dipped into her emergency stash of Marlboro Lights and was smoking furiously for the first time in forever. She was wearing a tan denim boiler suit tucked into knee-high gold cowboy boots.

Gold cowboy boots! he imagined Kate saying. *I mean, who wears gold cowboy boots to a police incident on a Sunday morning? I mean, I love her, but for fuck's sake, Sylvia.*

When she snapped eyes on Liam, Sylvia came rushing over and threw her arms around him, trying not to blow smoke in his face and giving him one of those awkward hugs that kind of hurt.

'Tiger's going to be okay. She's going to turn up,' she said, squeezing his hand.

Liam stared blankly. He had by that point lost the power to form words.

'Liam Carroll?' the male detective said, coming up to shake his hand as he nodded slowly.

'Detective Sergeant John Dooley. This is Detective Senior Constable Macey James. It's alright, mate. Do you mind if we come inside? You can come in, too,' he said, nodding to Sylvia.

'Now Liam, we're just going to ask you a few preliminary questions before we get started. This is not a formal interview or anything. We just want to try and work out what's going on and get Kate home as soon as possible. We okay with that?'

'Of course, Detective Sergeant.'

'Listen, call me John.'

'Okay John.'

'John' had a thick moustache that made him look like one of those cops from the seventies. *Cops still have those moustaches?* Liam wondered. *Don't they realise it's a bit . . . dial-a-cliché?*

'Was there anything that was worrying Kate, before she went missing?' Dooley asked, breaking Liam's thoughts.

'Not really, John. She just seemed herself.'

'I see that she is a journalist. Had she upset anyone? Received any threatening messages, prank calls? Anything like that?'

'She often jokes that she's running out of people to, well, pardon my language, but people to piss off,' Liam said. 'You know, I suppose it comes with the territory in that line of work. But they were people like, well, you know, white-shoe-brigade doctors who she had exposed for harming patients—you know, they didn't like her. I remember there was one guy who would inject a completely useless concoction into people's knees, telling them it was a sophisticated medical breakthrough. Would cost twenty thousand a pop. Completely fanciful. No medical benefit. One of the poor patients got necrotising fasciitis and lost a leg. The Medical Board took away the doctor's medical registration after Kate exposed him. So, of course, that doctor was not exactly Kate's number one fan.' Liam knew he was babbling, knew the relevance of any of this was questionable at best, but he didn't seem to be able to stop. 'Medical negligence cases are how I first got to meet Kate, so she's talked to me about a lot of them. But dodgy doctors aren't exactly the types to—'

'No, they're generally not, Liam. But we have to keep an open mind. Did her work ever bring her into contact with known criminals?'

'Not recently, no. She used to be a court reporter, but that was a while ago.'

'Stressful line of work, though, journalism. A bit like ours.' Dooley turned to his partner and she nodded. 'Kate wasn't feeling depressed or anything like that, Liam?'

'No, not at all, John.' Liam shook his head. 'She was in a really good frame of mind. I mean, yeah, she's a heart-on-her-sleeve type. She feels things. But she wasn't depressed. She's actually enormously resilient.'

From the corner of the room, Sylvia agreed.

'Tiger's had to do some pretty depressing work,' Sylvia said. 'But it makes her feel, I don't know, like she's doing something worthwhile. It makes her weirdly happy, I suppose because she's helping people. She's not a suicide risk, if that's what you're implying, officer.'

'Tiger?' Dooley said.

'Oh, that's just what I call her. You know, "I love you like a TIGER",' Sylvia said, curling her hands like paws and adopting the politically incorrect faux-Pakistani accent of a character in a nineties comedy show. 'That's what we would say to each other, "I love you like a Tiger." And then she just became my Tiger.'

Dooley pursed his lips. 'Okay, thanks for that, Sylvia. We'll talk to you later.' He turned back to Liam.

'Now Liam, I have to ask you this, and I don't want you to think anything of it. It's just me doing my job, you understand that, don't you?'

A little lawyer light went off in Liam's head. Christ. *The boyfriend did it.* He turned to Sylvia and looked back at Dooley, trying to regain his composure. Thinking about how not to seem too slick. But then, not seeming like a hot mess. It was a cold day and he was not a sweaty man, but he could feel a trickle running slowly down his lower back. What did an innocent man look like? Honest. Just honest, Liam.

'Yes, of course, officer, ahem, John. I totally understand.'

'Now you and Kate, you hadn't had any, you know, fights, lovers' tiffs, anything like that, you know, in the lead-up to this event?'

This event. Cop speak. What event? There was no event. He just didn't know where she was.

'Um, no. Not at all. We were—are—how do I say this? Mad for each other. Not mad, you know what I mean. Not mad. We're crazy about each other. Not crazy. I'm sorry, I'm sorry, I'm so tired. I didn't sleep last night. We get along like a house on fire. You know, we finish each other's sentences. We haven't got to the fight stage, really, yet. Not that there is a fight stage, *per se.* We just don't fight. We do . . . other things.'

He sensed that Dooley was doing that thing he knew cops did. And what Kate had told him journalists did. He was allowing Liam to nervously fill the silence. When Liam caught Sylvia grinding her teeth and tapping her cowboy boots on the floor, she gave him a quick, forced, smile.

'What other things do you do, Liam?'

'Well, you know, we go out for dinner and we cook for each other a lot. We're both foodies, you see. And sometimes we go to, you know, antique fairs and stuff. We—well, really, I—like antiques. She kind of puts up with it. She's not really into clutter. And we like bookshops. And we like movies. And plays, we sometimes go to plays. We're busy. We like to be busy. And sometimes we both go and sit in that beautiful reading room at the State Library. You know, that big old reading room? And it's the coolest thing, having a girlfriend who just wants to hang out with you silently in the reading room at the State Library and occasionally peer at you over the top of her book. And you know she's yours. And she knows you're hers. And we have, you know—' he blushed crimson '—we have sex quite a bit. A lot. We find it hard to keep our hands off each other, when we're together. You know, we're crazy about each other. Not crazy-crazy. Normal crazy. Not . . . crazy.'

Dooley was pacing around, looking a bit distracted. 'You have sex in the reading room of the State Library, Liam?'

'Oh no, no, no. I mean, don't get me wrong, I can't lie. I can't say I haven't thought about it. I may even have sent her the odd drunk text fantasising about it. And she was totally into it. She's cute . . . funny, like that. You know, ha-ha funny? Not weird funny.'

Liam was acutely aware that he was rapidly sliding into what is known in the profession as being a shit witness.

''Kay. You'll be cool to hand us your phone, right, Liam?'

'My goodness, yes, of course. Just don't, you know, no judgement, on our, our silliness. Not that there's anything wrong with it. I bet you'd hate, you know, your texts with your wife to be seen by a, by a law enforcement official.'

'I'm what's technically referred to as a homosexual, Liam,' Dooley said, eyes glittering for a nanosecond, 'And, well, I tend to not put things in writing. Occupational hazard. You'll understand that—you're a lawyer, aren't you?'

Dooley didn't like lawyers. Like many cops, he found it hard, from years of battling with them and being cross-examined by them, not to adopt an unconscious bias against them. He thought they were generally smart-arses who were slippery with the truth and who messed up his cases.

'Oh, good Lord, sorry, I did not mean to be presumptuous. Got it in one. And yes, I'm a solicitor, yes. Officer of the court. And as a lawyer, I know to be careful with texts. I guess there just wasn't—isn't anything to worry about with Kate. I just, I love her. I just want to know where she is, Detective—I mean, ahem, John. I just want to know where she is.'

'It's okay, mate,' Dooley said, good cop again. 'That's what we want, too.'

Liam's eyes welled up with tears. That was two strangers he'd told in the space of an hour or two that he loved the woman he hadn't yet had the ticker to tell.

As he choked back a sob, he remembered a recent text where she had been complaining about a photograph of herself from when they had first met. She had lost weight since that time and hated the photo. *But that's when I [. . . insert words here I'm too embarrassed to say . . .]*, he texted back to her. *I thought you were the most beautiful woman I had ever seen.* The missing words were *fell in love with you, Kate. That's when I fell in love with you.*

He snorted again and realised that he was in danger of being what Kate liked to describe as an ugly crier. She thought she was an ugly crier because her skin was so white that when she burst into tears her nose would go red and her eyes would get all puffy.

Sitting in the corner, Sylvia clocked what Liam had said. She knew that Liam and her best friend had yet to formally declare their love for each other, despite it being glaringly obvious to anyone who cared to pay attention that they were smitten. She clasped her hands and then drew a little love heart in the air.

Dooley began pacing around Liam's apartment in the way that cops do, or at least, in the way that Liam had seen them do on TV shows. In the middle of the polished concrete floor was a large square rug. Liam's eyes followed Dooley as he came to a spot on it and pointed at a small brownish red stain.

'What happened here, Liam?'

'Oh, that was the table. She hated it, I mean Kate hated the table. The coffee table,' Liam replied.

'What coffee table and why did she hate it?'

'Well, I bought it at an antique fair, and I thought it was pretty cool, but it was kind of rusty and she said that it was, well, she said it was—you know, in her words, "A) way too shabby chic for this apartment, and B) the rust is absolutely going to ruin that nice rug, Liam." And you know, I like old things, but I find shabby chic, well, you know, a bit embarrassing and twee. You know, like those people twenty-odd years ago who purposefully sanded the paint off the edges of dressers instead of just buying an old dresser?'

'Oh yes, those people, complete nightmares,' Dooley said.

Liam swallowed and pretended not to notice that Dooley was ever so slightly taking the piss out of him.

'And I like this rug. And so, well, I put the coffee table out in the hard rubbish, and it was gone in a nanosecond, because I suppose there are still a lot of people out there who don't mind shabby chic.'

'I suppose there are,' Dooley said.

'Anyway, err, John, the upshot of all of that is that what you are looking at on the carpet is a rust mark from a poorly executed furnishing decision. Just rust.'

'A poorly executed furnishing decision.'

Dooley repeated the phrase again. 'A poorly executed furnishing decision,' was what his mouth said. But Liam registered his eyes, which fixed on him and said, 'You stupid hipster, I see you.'

Dooley got down on one knee and squinted his eyes, labouring the gesture for effect in a way that Liam found unbelievably irritating. He pointed at the floor, clicked his fingers with a sharp snap and turned to his partner. 'Senior Constable?'

Macey James walked over and snapped several photos of the rust stain with her smart phone. She pressed her lips together and nodded to Dooley.

Dooley nodded back. 'Let's get forensics to have a look at that.'

'Got it, Sarge.'

Dooley smiled stiffly and started pacing again. He stopped at Liam's bookshelf and gestured to the headless Child of Prague statue.

'What's this then, Liam? Was there some sort of altercation here?'

Despite the tears stinging his eyes, Liam suppressed an almost-laugh. Dooley narrowed his gaze.

'Something funny there, mate?'

'Oh, well, you see, John, that's the Child. The Child of Prague.'

'Yes, Liam, my surname's Dooley. I know it's a Child of Prague statue. Pretty sure my nan had one.'

'Well, if your surname's Dooley, you might know about the superstition—about the rain and weddings—and beheading the Child of Prague.'

'I do not know about that superstition, Liam,' Dooley said. 'Tell me more.'

Dooley glanced at Macey James, who had sat silently in the corner across from Sylvia. Macey gave him a meaningful look.

'Well, you know, Kate's Irish. You know, like, proper Irish? She came to Australia when she was a kid. And in Dublin, believe it or not, they have this tradition. Where, you know, the night before the wedding, they leave out the Child of Prague statue, so it doesn't rain.'

'So, it doesn't rain?' Dooley countered. 'I did not know that about my people.'

My people. Liam could just see Kate's eyes rolling now. Dooley's people were probably one step removed from even Liam's people. The sort of people who thought the Irish still repeated *to be sure, to be sure* at the start of every sentence, the sort of people who drank Guinness with a shamrock poured into the froth once a year at a fake Irish pub and who traced their heritage to Donegal on Ancestry.com. And who, Kate would say when they found out that you were from Limerick, told you that they had once been to Kinsale.

Liam wished Kate was here right now, to explain it. To set him straight. But of course, she wasn't. That's why they were here. Because Kate wasn't here.

'But you and Kate, you're not married, right, Liam?'

'No, no, we actually did this . . . Well, *I* did this . . . [You did this?] Yes, I did this, the night we . . . the night we first, you know . . .'

'The night you first had sex, Liam?'

God, he wished Dooley would stop saying his name like that. Sylvia was sitting in the corner, sliding onto the floor, rolling her eyes back into her head, with her fingers in her ears, silently mouthing *la la la*. Sylvia could swear like a sailor, but she struggled to even say the word 'sex'. She had gotten through her entire sexual history on the back of euphemisms.

'Yes, the night we first had sex. Kate had this *way*. You know, it was raining. Well, it was raining soft. And then it started raining hard. And she told me the story about the Child of Prague. And how she threw one in the bin at Dublin Airport. And she felt guilty about leaving it there, because of her Great Auntie Maggie, and—'

'How did the Child of Prague lose its head, Liam?'

'Well, I smashed it. Because,' he said, taking a deep inhale of mortified breath, 'she asked me to.'

'She *asked* you to?'

'Yes. Well, this is a while ago now. Yes, she asked me to. To stop the rain. She was just being silly and kind of sexy. You know, in an understated way. She told me I needed to behead the Child of Prague to stop the rain.'

'Jesus Christ, peeps,' Sylvia muttered under her breath. 'You complete fucking *nutters*.'

'No need for that,' snapped back Macey James, breaking her silence for the first time. Liam noticed she was wearing little diamante crucifix earrings.

'And look, this has nothing to do with why we're here—why you're here—it's completely irrelevant, quite frankly, and we're wasting time, with the greatest of, uh, respect, Detective Sergeant—John. But because she told me to, I dropped the statue on the ground here, and the head, well, it broke clean off and while the head smashed up into little pieces, the body stayed intact.'

'The body stayed intact? And what happened then, Liam?'

'Well, we had sex, for the first time. We went, well, we kind of stumbled into my room, and we had sex.'

'You had sex?'

'Yes, and it was wonderful. I mean, Kate is wonderful.'

'Horses for courses, I suppose, Liam. Horses for courses.'

Liam was sweating now. He didn't want to look at his watch, but this was getting ridiculous. Time was ticking by. And they were talking about the Child of bloody Prague. And, seemingly, implicating the most sweetly innocent story (granted, it had shades of mental, but cute mental, not sinister mental) into some sort of fucking domestic violence narrative. He realised he was swearing like a trooper in his head. The more he panicked, the guiltier he realised he sounded. *The boyfriend did it.*

'So, where's the head, Liam?'

'Well, as I was just, ah, explaining, the head smashed into little pieces. And we joked about how it was this weird sort of miracle. But I wonder, I mean, given that this is a thing, you know, in Ireland, beheading the Child, well, maybe it's a design feature?'

'A *design feature*?'

'Yeah, you know, a design feature. Like, the thing is designed to smash at the neck, and the head, you know, disintegrates, but the body is made of something—' he gestured in the air '—stronger.'

'I see.' Dooley looked at the floor. 'You didn't use this thing, this statue, to hurt Kate in any way, did you Liam? This statue wasn't broken in some sort of altercation?'

'What? No! Jesus. No. No. Please. Like I told you. I love her. I wish I had told her that before she . . . I can't even say the word . . . disappeared last night. I wish I'd told her that I love her. I'd never do anything to hurt Kate. Or anyone.'

Liam Carroll was beginning to feel like he was John Proctor in some twisted Irish Catholic post-post-postmodern version of *The Crucible. Because it is my name! Because I cannot have another in my life!* Or a character in Kafka. Or just something that wasn't what this was—him desperately needing them to stop going on about a beheaded religious keepsake and to start looking for Kate.

He thought about the headline that might appear in the tabloids: *High-profile Lawyer Boyfriend in Bizarre Headless Statue Ritual Implicated in Melbourne Woman's Disappearance.*

In truth he wasn't that high-profile, really, he just worked for a media-savvy law firm, but as Kate would say, they'd take a stick to it. They'd beat it up within an inch of its life. Then chase him down the street: *What do you have to say for yourself, Mr Carroll? Did you use that statue to harm Kate Delaney? Where's Kate, Mr Carroll?*

'Liam Francis Carroll was one of Melbourne's most successful medical negligence lawyers,' Sandra Sully would tell her viewers, adding his middle name in the way they always did for criminals. 'But that all came crashing down after he smashed a religious statue before, he says, having sex with his girlfriend.'

Kate's beautiful face would feature in an oval frame. They would choose her most flattering picture. The tabloids loved nothing more than a pretty victim of (potential) homicide. Potential. Potential. Christ on a ship, he needed to get these cops back on track.

'So, where's the head, Mr Carroll?' It was the first time Macey James had asked a question.

'Well, the head, Senior Constable,' she hadn't exhorted him to call her Macey, 'the head—or the pieces of the head—well, they were just thrown out the next day. It was, you know, unsalvageable. But I—we, well, we kept the body as a keepsake. Look, I know this sounds very strange to someone who doesn't get it. But that's what happened.

'That night, well, we had had oysters and champagne, and without sounding all, you know, Hallmark or whatever, it was really, really romantic. We connected. And the whole thing with the statue was just one of those things that people do. You know, our little funny secret that no one else gets? You know—' he realised he kept saying 'you know' '—I am not a guy who fights with people much at all. I'm pretty bloody conflict-averse. And that's because I have anxiety, and look, that's my cross to bear, but Kate, she understands. She makes me feel better. I really need you to find her, officer. I really need you to help. All her friends do. Her mother would be beside herself, if she was still here. Kate needs us to find her.'

Macey James nodded and even smiled, not as brusquely as when she had first arrived. He felt that he was perhaps starting to win her over. As weird as she clearly thought his relationship with Kate was.

'Okay, mate,' Dooley said, cutting in. 'I think it might be time to wrap it up for now.'

'But, what—' Liam started.

'Oh, just for now. Just for now. We're going to go back to home base at the station and we're going to start making some other inquiries.'

Macey James took a couple of photos of the bookshelf with a camera. Then she snapped on some latex gloves and pulled out a plastic pouch. She carefully slid the Child of Prague statue into the evidence bag.

'But you haven't asked anything about the night—where she was, what she was doing, her movements?'

'Well, you say that you weren't with her last night, so we'll need to direct those inquiries elsewhere,' Dooley said.

'Sylvia was there,' he started. 'She can help you.'

'Oh yes, we'll talk to Sylvia. And everyone. She's kindly given us some numbers of the other friends they were with. We're going to start giving them a bell this arvo.'

'This arvo?'

'Well, time is marching on, Liam.'

'Yes, time is marching on, um, John,' he said, staring at the pattern on the rug he'd lugged home from a trip he'd done to the Middle East. 'Time is marching on.'

'I'm sorry,' Dooley said. 'I know this is all very difficult.'

—

Liam let the two detectives out of the apartment and slumped on the sofa.

'Fucking hell!' he said to Sylvia. 'What the fuck are we going to do? We're dealing with Keystone Cops here.'

'Give them a chance, Chicken,' Sylvia replied, quietly. 'They say they want to find Tiger as much as we do. They say they are going to make calls.'

'They think I bashed her with a Catholic holy statue of the infant baby Jesus, Sylvia! I mean, for fuck's sake!'

'Look, I know this is a difficult time for you and this is not very opportune, but . . . you—you know—you did the thing, you did *the thing* for the first time after she asked you to smash a Child of Prague statue?' Sylvia started snorting. She was so spent she was laughing kind of deliriously now. 'What kind of sickos are you two?'

He started laugh-crying, despite himself. 'It was really beautiful, okay?' he said, managing to adopt the sort of faux saccharine voice of a daytime matinee idol. 'It was a beautiful moment. Okay? Listen to me. It is true. I am crazy statue-smashing lover-boy. Same guy who fantasises about having sex with his girlfriend in the reading room of the State Library. Guilty as charged. But she asked me to! Your best friend is all those things, too!'

They both laughed briefly, then sourly, and then Sylvia started sobbing.

'I miss her so much,' she said, and Liam winced as she licked snot away from her mouth. 'I mean, it's only been a day, but I miss her. I need to find her.'

'*We* need to find her,' Liam said, straightening his back and suddenly finding his inner lawyer. 'Or we need to help those cops do it. Because I don't have a huge amount of confidence that they'll find her on their own.'

He picked up his phone, which had been face down on the coffee table, and turned it over. Two hundred messages and fifty missed calls.

'Don't ever let it be said that Sylvia Estrellita doesn't do social media comms like a pro,' Sylvia said, flashing at him a Facebook post on her own phone of Kate looking impossibly gorgeous. 'I took that picture of her. I refuse to ever take a bad photo of anyone. Ever. It is written. Do you like the filter? Cute, *non*?'

Liam sighed. 'Cute.'

Sylvia walked over to the window.

'Quick, Liam, come look.'

Outside, down on the street, a handful of television cameras and newspaper snappers were gathering. Liam could see a journo he'd dropped a medical negligence story to strolling across the nature strip on his phone.

Sylvia carefully opened the window, and they stood back at an angle where they couldn't be seen. A stiffly coiffed commercial television reporter was doing a piece to camera in that sing-song way they did.

'Kate Delaney is a much-loved, award-winning newspaper journalist, Peter,' the reporter said, nodding sagely, thickly powdered cheeks contoured just so. 'And she is missing. A Facebook page set up to discover her whereabouts has, in a matter of a few short hours, received thousands of likes, well-wishes, and theories about her disappearance. And, well, at this stage, Pete, it's a heartbreaking mystery. Back to you.'

7

CRIME

KATE DELANEY AWAKES to find that, despite her fear, she's somehow managed to sleep. She's still in the back of the car. But it's now daylight.

She supposes that daylight seems like a risk for him and wonders what she can do to somehow capitalise on this.

She's so dehydrated now that her mouth has taken on the consistency of a dried sea sponge.

And the pain is so bad.

Idiot-head has stopped maniacally drumming the steering wheel, so that's something. He's talking to himself in a way that attempts to convey everything is completely normal here.

'Oh-kay, now we just need to take this turn-off here and we'll be on the right road to where we need to go . . .'

But his voice sounds too forced. Because this situation is not normal at all. He has kidnapped a woman and she's lying, bound, on his back seat. She has joined the inauspicious club known as rape victims. She's bleeding. She's a long way from home. People—most particularly Liam—will have noticed she hasn't returned. And The Guy's going to have to work out what the hell to do with her.

He glances in the rear-view mirror and catches her looking at him.

'Aw, g'day, Blue,' he quips, using the Aussie vernacular for red-heads that is, for Kate, like fingernails on a blackboard. 'How's tricks?'

'Tricks?' she barely manages from her sandpaper mouth.

He lets out a snicker that he wants to sound good-natured, but again it sounds fake.

'Probably wrong choice'a words, eh? Aren't up to too many tricks at the moment, are we? Some might say tricks got you here in the first place.'

He is such a monumental fuckwit.

How does one play this scenario? Kate wonders. Her mind goes to the countless hours of Scandi noir she's watched. Does she scoff at him—maybe fire a well-aimed ball of spittle in his direction? But those tough girls always seem to get bopped off. Does she feign Stockholm Syndrome and be sweet and compliant, hoping to trick him in some way and plan an escape? The thought of being nice to this pathetic man-child leaves her cold.

She wonders if they have discovered her missing yet. Has it broken in the news? Who has been assigned to cover her story? Have they started spooling through her social media and pulling out photographs? Constructing a narrative about who she is and what possible reason any person has to kidnap or (let's be frank) kill her? She tries not to let out the whimper that's building in her sternum, at the thought that he might. Kill her, that is. He might kill her.

She remembers as a young journo once covering the murder of a young woman in a tiny and isolated town. There was a coronial inquest in the town, a creepy place with a shallow gene pool that was famous as the site of a notorious colonial gaol. It was the first time Kate Delaney had been absolutely convinced of the presence of ghosts. At night, walking along the freezing roads, she often had this chilling sensation of hands running down her back. One night, she was sure she heard the plaintive sound of a young woman singing outside her motel room. When she peered out the window, she saw nothing. She had to call her best friend on the courts round, an avuncular teddy bear of a man, to come in and have a hot chocolate with her to stop her heart from racing.

It was one of those towns full of people with bad dentistry and priors and burner mobile phones, who had solid motives to disappear. Accordingly, there was a rich vein of potential suspects for the murder of the young woman, whose body had been found washed up on the silt-bed of a dried-up lake like a modern-day Laura Palmer from *Twin Peaks*. 'She's dead, wrapped in plastic,' one of the wags from the tabloids had kept whispering in court. Even though she wasn't. Wrapped in plastic, that is. No one had bothered to wrap this poor girl in plastic. They just left her naked like a mouldy Barbie a little girl had left in the bath.

Journalists, including Kate, had flocked to the town for the inquest, and the locals hated them, egging their cars and cursing at them when they went to the local pub, for bringing down the name of their town. Each morning during the inquest, which had made not only national but international news, Kate was flabbergasted to listen to the local radio news bulletin. They'd mention the meat raffle at the town's RSL, the upcoming agricultural show. Not once did the bulletin ever mention the inquest.

By contrast, Kate and her colleagues from the other national media had churned out a constant stream of stories, filled with speculation about the multiple Persons of Interest named by police. The young woman had played the field and the details of lovers she had jilted and why they might be to blame were raked over in scarifying detail. At the inquest Kate would often look at the parents of the victim, feeling desperately sorry for this kind couple, retired teachers, who now found themselves without their only child and who had to read about the minutiae of their daughter's sexual exploits. The kind of stuff no parent needs to know.

But the point was, Kate Delaney remembers now, that all of the speculation was wrong. Because the killer happened to be an opportunist. A psychopathic shearer who had been travelling through town and just felt like killing a woman. He wasn't a Person of Interest. He wasn't on anyone's list. The invasion of the poor victim's privacy turned out to be unnecessary. The crime was a one-in-a-million.

Just like this one, Kate Delaney clocks. *This crime is one-in-a-million.* But the journos won't realise that. They'll go for all the usual tropes—the clichés that are clichés for a reason. The clichés that usually turn out to be bang on. Her heart sinks. *They'll land on Liam. The boyfriend did it.*

—

Back in Northcote that night, The Guy stood outside the bar she'd bolted to with Sylvia, Sophie, Brigid and Adie after she'd offended his manliness at the pub with her quip about his saggy arse.

He was a patient man when he wanted to be. He'd walked from bar to bar, right along High Street, until he saw Kate Delaney's auburn hair, shining like a beacon, through a window. She was laughing at one of her friend's silly jokes. He saw the bright red lipstick and the gap in her two front teeth.

'Huh,' he muttered to himself, watching their little circle clink glasses.

He watched as they eventually hugged and kissed goodbyes, filing out one by one, and rubbed his sweaty palms as he saw that Kate was on her own. Then he followed her till he got to a place where he could circle in front of her. It was the quietest part of the street, away from the bars and the restaurants, and, crucially, people. The long incline of the hill that led down to Liam's place.

'Well, hello there, lady,' he said, standing squarely on the pavement.

Kate's eyes widened as she realised who it was. *Saggy arse guy.* Fuck.

She moved to the left and he stepped with her, then she moved to the right and he did the same, like they were two people doing that awkward dance on the street when they are trying to avoid each other but keep bumping into each other. Except this wasn't awkward or accidental. It was unambiguously menacing. Each time she bumped into him, it was like slamming into a brick wall—he was like someone who had a trainer punch them in the stomach at the gym and didn't flinch.

Bam.

Bam.

Bam.

'Not so cheeky now, are we?'

'Look, mate, we've all had our fun—' Kate began.

'That wasn't fun, Sunshine.'

'Okay, look, I'm really sorry. No, I am, I'm sorry. I'd had a few drinks. I was being silly. But I'm tired,' she said, trying now to fob him off politely, trying not to make a scene.

'And I've got to get to my boyfriend's place—he lives just over there . . .' She motioned in the direction of Liam's flat, emphasising the word 'boyfriend'.

As she fumbled unsuccessfully in her handbag, trying to reach for her phone to call Liam, and looking around to see if someone, anyone, was close by, she twisted her ankle slightly and her boots scuffed along the pavement as her knees buckled.

She straightened herself up and walked bang into him again.

Bam.

Bam.

She glanced around desperately. Not a soul in sight. Northcote was unusually silent. Should she raise her voice? Should she shout out for help? But she didn't. Her heart rose in her chest, but her voice said nothing.

She started walking. He grabbed her arm to keep her from fetching her phone again and clasped her wrist really, really hard. She expected it to be bruised the next day from the force of his grip. He kept walking alongside her. He didn't say anything now. But periodically, he would lean in and breathe on her neck in a way that made her feel like she had hundreds of tiny baby Huntsman spiders crawling all over her.

They got to the really quiet part of the street, where there were no shops or businesses. Then he looked around to confirm that no one was watching and in a jerking motion, he pushed her roughly into a side street, nearly winding her in the process.

Her heart began to beat so violently, she thought she might pass out. How was this happening?

'Please stop,' she whispered.

He didn't. He held a knife to her throat, and he turned her around and shoved her navy dress up around her waist, and he pulled down her tights and her underwear, and then he roughly penetrated her.

What is it with fuckwits like this and anal? she found herself thinking as pain jolted through her body like an electric shock. It was like her mind, or even her soul, was floating above her body, hazily looking down on the horror scene below. How can you adequately describe the moment of the worst terror most women can imagine? You can't. It seems like you're watching a film of your own life. You can't compute it, neither in that moment nor afterwards.

—

As her forehead thumped on the pavement, in time with his violent shoving, and her thighs grazed against the cobblestones, she dissociated with thoughts of how she was now someone who might have been in one of her stories. She thought about how she might describe what was happening to her now. What she might sanitise for the sake of taste and decency and loved ones, and what she thought her readers would need to know. Kate Delaney was becoming a capital-V Victim and, as someone who had catalogued the victimhood of so many others, she couldn't help but mentally catalogue her own.

Then the faces of other victims whose stories she'd covered began to slot into her mind, and illuminate, one after another, like they were in one of those slide carousels people used to have in the seventies.

Little boy with enormous blue eyes and a snotty nose and Thomas the Tank Engine t-shirt whose mother's boyfriend had tortured him. *Flash. Click.*

Grandmother in lilac crocheted cardigan who perished from malnutrition at a low-rent nursing home. *Flash. Click.*

Nineteen-year-old bashed to death by her boyfriend who had come of age at a time when the only photos of her were selfies with duck-faced lips, orange perma-tan and over-plucked eyebrows. Kate had endlessly searched the girl's socials for a picture to go with her story that didn't make the poor thing look comical and vain. *Flash. Click.*

As these victims revisited her in her own moment of trauma, Kate Delaney reflected, *I'm one of them now.* Broken glass in the alleyway sliced through her stockings and cut her knees. A cockroach scuttled into a bin. A possum hurried along the top of the fence. A streetlamp glowed, nauseously yellow. The moon dipped behind clouds.

Instead of doing the expected thing and screaming her lungs out, she lost her voice. How could Kate Delaney lose her voice? But she did. She was so petrified she could only silently mouth her screams. She was close enough to the back of Liam's apartment building he'd almost have heard if she'd cried out. She closed her eyes and imagined Liam running to her, scooping her off the ground and making it all okay. Well, not okay, but somehow better. Safe.

But she didn't scream, and Liam didn't come to take her home. With her blind panic came maddening inertia, like her limbs were encased in molasses. Her strength had sapped away from her. She'd let him do it and she hoped that he'd just leave her there, and she could limp home to Liam.

He didn't leave her there.

He stood over her, rubbing his damp palms together, nervously.

'Leave me alone,' she tried to mouth, but the words barely formed. She realised she had gravel in her mouth.

He didn't leave her alone. Before she had time to do anything, he suddenly reached into a rubbish skip that was on the side of the laneway and yanked out a broken chair.

Then he banged her over the head with it, just once, but that was enough. Everything was suddenly black. The next time she came to was in the Southern Highlands in the small hours of the morning in a car she assumed he had gone home to collect.

—

When The Guy returned, he found her unconscious, with her handbag lying next to her on the road. He decided to make it look like she'd been mugged. He emptied the contents of her purse on the laneway, keeping the fifty-dollar note and a couple of credit cards so it looked like they'd been stolen.

But while he was at times a wily operator, he was not, in truth, very bright. Because when he bundled her unconscious body into the back seat, binding her hands and feet with cable ties, he slung her handbag into the boot. In the handbag was Kate Delaney's mobile phone.

And so, from Northcote to the Southern Highlands, until he heard it ringing and threw it into the bush, Kate Delaney's mobile phone and his mobile phone pinged on every single telecommunications tower along the way.

He hadn't given this inconvenient evidentiary fact a single thought.

This was an opportunistic crime, not a planned one. Kate Delaney had offended his dignity and he'd repaid her with brutal sexual assault. He'd been in prison before, not so long ago, and he didn't fancy going back. Rapists didn't have it easy inside.

He really didn't have it in him to kill her, in the moment. In his crim's hierarchy of felony, he didn't picture himself as the homicide guy. So, he panicked and clunked her over the head with the three-legged chair just hard enough to knock her out. He had to get rid of her, somehow, and so he'd set out on the Hume. It wasn't clear what he thought he was doing. But daylight was fast approaching. And daylight was not the friend of a rapist kidnapper with priors who had a redhead bound with cable ties on his back seat.

Before daybreak, he pulled over to the side of the freeway and started googling short-stay rental properties. He needed one where the key was left in a safety deposit box, accessible with a code. No human contact. Self-contained. Just somewhere to keep her for a few hours until night fell again. He found a granny flat located on its own lane at the far end of a bush block.

It had been built for an ageing mother who had come to live with her son and daughter-in-law, but who wanted to tell herself she had privacy and independence. It looked out onto a weir filled with yabbies.

The woman had passed away two Christmases ago and her cash-strapped son had finally steeled himself to clear out her stuff and list the granny flat online for the weary travellers who needed to, as the warning signs on the road said, STOP, REVIVE, SURVIVE, when they were driving between Melbourne and Sydney.

The Guy google-mapped the site.

'Perfect,' he muttered, noting the distance from the granny flat to the main house, the cluster of trees that surrounded it, the separate road in. He'd have to take the risk that the house owners weren't nearby when he arrived, but if they were, he'd just turn around and speed off.

Again, The Guy wasn't super smart. Something Kate had discovered from covering criminal trials for a few years was that crims generally don't get to be crims by being evil geniuses. It's not like those serial killer films with complicated plotlines where diabolical masterminds outwit world-weary cops. They're generally not Hannibal Lecter. They invariably make really dumb mistakes. Especially when they do things like rape a girl as a knuckleheaded payback, and in a blind panic knock her unconscious and take her up the Hume Highway to New South Wales.

They do things like booking a rental property with one of Kate's credit cards, because they don't want to have to shell out from their own pocket.

Welcome to Wombat Hollow! The automated email that landed in the inbox of his phone sang after the payment went through. *Your private, self-contained Home Away From Home. Sit back, make yourself a cuppa, watch lorikeets flying over our family weir, and relax.*

The Guy felt better. His stomach had been starting to writhe with acid. The stress of the past twenty-four hours and the long drive was making him feel gassy and bloated. He threw a couple of Quick Eze into his mouth, unbuttoned his Levi's, and vowed, as soon as he had got rid of the chick in the back, to get home and get back to the gym.

—

So now, as the morning sun glints through gums and his early 2000s Toyota Echo's wheels crunch over the gravel on Wombat Hollow's driveway, he resolves to stick Red in the back bedroom of the granny flat, make himself a cuppa, and take in the family weir. Just a few hours to wait until nightfall and he can dispose of this bloody problem.

The Guy is making it really easy for the cops to find him. The pinging mobile phone towers, using Kate's credit card. Unfortunately, the cops are still on a go-slow due to the matter of a statue of an infant Christ with a severed head.

8

ACCUSED

BY LATE AFTERNOON, Liam Carroll and Sylvia Estrellita are doom-scrolling on Facebook and Twitter, searching for any clues, when a text message flashes up on Liam's screen.

> Liam, oh my god, I am SO sorry. If there's anything, anything, I can do, just let me know. Suze ❤

Suze? *Suze?* Heart emoji?

'Suze' is Suzie Monroe, Liam Carroll's medical negligence defence lawyer nemesis. Her bobbed peroxide-blonde hair is ironed in neat waves and in the centre of her lips is a little dab of gloss. She wears billowy gossamer blouses that show the barest hint of cleavage. She's the human equivalent of a dessert so sickly-sweet, it makes your teeth hurt. Like meringue.

Suzie Monroe is beloved by dodgy doctors everywhere. She'll fire off letters accusing a string of mothers of stillborn babies delivered by a recalcitrant, elderly ob/gyn of not keeping up with their vitamins during pregnancy. When a social media influencer nearly dies of a fat embolism after a Brazilian Butt Lift performed by a fake cosmetic surgeon, she'll release photos of the young woman smoking and drinking on holiday. She'll tell journalists that patients given enough anti-psychotics to knock over a horse by a psychiatrist with a God complex were simply crazy.

'Look, I'm not going to criticise the mentally ill, because that's not what we do now,' Suzie would say, batting her eyelash extensions, fixing her alarmingly blue eyes and flicking her hair, 'but, off the record, crazy is as crazy does.'

A certain type of journalist loves her because she has no shame. She writes correspondence so unmatched in its tyrannical phraseology that while she causes him endless torment he'll never admit to, Liam has to doff his cap at her sheer pluck.

She calls to mind a combination of Nicole Kidman as the psychotically ambitious small-town weather presenter in *To Die For* and Reese Witherspoon as the maniacal high school girly swot in *Election*. She drives Liam Carroll to drink.

So, it goes without saying that to read a text message from Suzie Monroe in this moment, well-meaning as she would undoubtedly think it is, compounds Liam Carroll's trauma.

Don't think about her, Liam, Kate would whisper, biting on his ear. *She's a toxic drain of a human. And also, I'm pretty sure her dermal filler is uneven on one side. Congratulate her on how convincing her fake Birkin bag is. It isn't fake, so that will throw her off her game.*

He smiles at the memory of Kate. How she could be tender and wicked all at once. But wicked for a good cause. Then he feels the little pang that follows every time that happens. The *memory.* Don't be a memory, Kate Delaney.

It's been a few hours since John Dooley and Macey James left his apartment that morning and Liam has heard nothing from them since.

In the meantime, people have been posting endless theories on Facebook and Twitter about what has happened to Kate. Sylvia's posts have been victims of their own success. She and Kate's other close friends are scanning them and following up on anything that seems remotely legit. It's ninety-nine per cent nonsense. People have speculated about Liam, repeatedly, and he is just grateful at this point that no one knows about the stupid Child of Prague.

Starving, suffering cabin fever and needing to somehow fill the hours with something approaching normalcy, he made the mistake earlier of going out to get some food with Sylvia, who had one arm protectively around him, the other holding the leash of Boris, her toy Russian terrier. Liam was slightly annoyed she insisted on bringing the comically weird-looking puppy, which he thought looked like something you'd find in the woods behind Chernobyl. The stiffly coiffed TV reporter looked at them through narrowed eyes. The snappers and camera guys chased them down the street. 'Any updates, Liam?' *I wish.* 'How are you feeling?' *Well, utterly shit, obviously.* 'Tell us about Kate.' *Fuck off.*

Of course, he didn't give any of those answers. He tried to maintain the sad-neutral victim's loved one face he's always instructed clients to adopt when they are going into court. Don't smile, don't look angry, don't say anything, don't do anything. Don't create a picture, don't create a scene, don't give them a story.

He shudders now to think how hangdog he looks in their pictures. Unshaven, dark circles under eyes he's been rubbing furiously. *Clearly a criminal.*

—

The stiffly coiffed TV reporter, whose name is Keri Kane—an up-and-coming star at the network who is already reading the four-thirty bulletin and has her eyes on the weather presenter prize—heads back to the station and announces to everyone that she is *totally convinced it's the boyfriend.*

'Look, I can't say too much,' she tells a rapt group of colleagues who gather in a circle around her, 'but the cops are ready to pin it on him.'

'But Liam Carroll has always seemed like a sweet guy,' Marina Chang, a young producer, tries to protest. 'I have been sent to do pick-ups with him a few times and he seems really genuine and smart. And frankly, I'm really, really scared that she just went missing. I mean, Kate Delaney could be one of us.'

A couple of other women nod but Keri Kane rolls her eyes as if to say that Marina Chang knows nothing and is a naïve baby with shit cop contacts. Then she turns her back on Marina and keeps gossiping.

Marina slinks into an edit suite and slumps on a chair. In the suite, the editor, Sean, is giggling at his screen. She cranes her neck to see what he is up to. On the screen is an animated picture of Keri Kane's head. Periodically, Sean presses a key and the head explodes into hundreds of tiny pieces.

Marina clasps her mouth. 'Why are you doing that, Sean? You made that!'

Sean turns around on his swivel chair and puts his feet up on the console. 'I made it,' he deadpans. 'Yes, I made it. Can you think of anyone, *anyone* in this entire place whose head you'd rather explode?'

'*You're terrible, Muriel*,' Marina says, quoting her favourite film. 'But you know, in all seriousness, sir,' she whispers, *sotto voce*, 'you kind of have a point.'

'Shit, yeah,' Sean continues. 'I mean this is the same woman who, when the assistant chief of staff was crying in makeup because her kid had just been diagnosed with autism, asked said assistant chief of staff if she had vaccinated the kid and then declared vaccines were fucking poison because she had done some bullshit beat-up investigation. Shit human. *Shit* human and full of shit. Besides, my wife's a paralegal at Liam Carroll's firm, and she reckons he's the loveliest bloke ever. Everyone loves him there. And they all say he was mad about Kate. And you know what else? He doesn't need this.'

'Hard agree,' Marina says quietly. 'Hard agree.' They swivel their chairs towards the newsroom and look out the edit suite window to see Keri Kane across the floor, gesticulating wildly.

'Shit human,' Sean says again.

Out in the newsroom, Keri Kane can be heard, nodding sagely, telling the circle gathered around her that her sources are 'impeachable'.

Marina Chang quietly snorts.

—

As Kate Delaney's disappearance goes increasingly viral that evening, conversations like this are happening all over Melbourne. Thanks to her flattering photos and the fact that she is reasonably well-known (even the merest hint of celebrity is amplified markedly when it comes to victims of crime), Kate is the 'right' sort of victim. Middle-class, pretty, educated. Women like her just don't go missing in Northcote at night. Women who feel that they can relate to her feel chilled to the bone. Within a matter of hours, she had become the kind of story that would have had Kate herself madly hitting the phones.

Liam has reflected on this. That if she wasn't the one who had gone missing, if she was the journo chasing this yarn, she'd probably ring him. And then, when he didn't answer, she'd send him a text. He'd seen some of her texts to the partners and families of victims, which were always very sensitive, but nonetheless, persistent. Would he reply to the texts? Would he pick up? He is ignoring the other reporters. Would he make an exception for her? Would he find her as gorgeous if some other girlfriend of his had gone missing? Would he still want to lie down next to her and hold her? Would she say 'umm, sure' if she was on a story? Probably not, as he'd be cheating on his missing girlfriend. *Probably not, Liam. You'd have to keep it in your pants.* Okay, his mind is going in maddening, inappropriate loops. *Try to focus on something else, Liam. Kate is the girlfriend who is missing. There is no other Kate. There is no other Kate.*

He remembers how once, in the first throes of their infatuation, she had been stuck in an obscure country town on a story. She texted him and told him she wanted him to take off her clothes. He wanted to do that so badly, but his car was being serviced. So, he took an eight-hundred-dollar cab ride to her motel. It was so stupid and yet she thought it so sweet.

'You know what I like about you, Liam Carroll?' she asked, kissing him on his forehead as he lay back on the uncomfortable motel bed, gazing up at the pebble dash ceiling.

'You're hot and you're kind. There aren't that many people who are both hot and kind.'

'Right back at you, Kate Delaney,' he said, grinning.

'I love the way you smile at me like that,' she said. 'Like a kid who just found an unexpected fifty bucks under the sofa cushions.'

'Just think of yourself as the human equivalent of an unexpected fifty bucks under the sofa cushions, then,' he said, and kissed her nose. And he clasped her hand as she lay her head on his shoulder.

He thinks of that soliloquy from the character, Henry, in Tom Stoppard's *The Real Thing*, describing love. He remembers studying the play at school when he was hopelessly naïve, a virgin, with absolutely no prospect of anything approaching a girlfriend and only his wet dreams to keep him company at night. His Year Twelve English teacher, quite a progressive Catholic, had put Stoppard on the reading list. She'd been impressed when a shy young Liam, inspired by Stoppard, wrote a beautifully touching essay about a subject he didn't yet know: Love. He'd always remembered Henry's soliloquy, always imagined actually feeling this about a girl. He'd always wanted to experience it, up until that point. Knowing and being known.

He had it with Kate. Stoppard described how we share every other emotion with the rest of the world, even strangers—vivacity, sadness, sulking, joy.

But it didn't matter, Stoppard said, 'Let them eat cake', because knowledge, carnal knowledge, 'personal, final, uncompromised', was something else. What was it that he called it? The undealt card. 'And while it's held it makes you free-and-easy and nice to know, and when it's gone everything is pain.'

Everything is pain.

The phone rings. It's Dooley.

'G'day, Liam.'

'Um, hello, John.'

'I've got some news, Liam. A positive development.'

'You've found Kate? You know where she is?'

'Um, no, Liam. But we've found her purse.'

'Her purse? Jesus. Where?'

'Actually, not too far from your place. In a laneway. Contents spilled all over the place. Well, not all the contents. The, um, assailant, seems to have taken some credit cards.'

'Credit cards?'

'Credit cards.'

'Which laneway?'

'Blackstone Lane.'

'Blackstone Lane? I can see that from the back of my building!' As he's talking, Liam grabs his keys and runs out his front door, then bounds up the stairway to the rooftop garden of his building, which faces back towards the city. Panting, he tells the detective to hang on a minute. He looks down to the streets below—there, off a street in the next block, is Blackstone Lane. In the dying light, he can see flashing police lights and blue and white checked tape and an evidence van. There are some media crews milling about, too.

'I see, John, I see.'

'Yes, mate. I don't want to get ahead of myself,' the cop says, drily, 'but I think we can stand down the investigation into the headless statue.'

'No shit, Sherlock.'

'Now, now, mate. I'm sorry. We were just doing our jobs. Anyway, we've got some leads.'

'Leads?'

'Leads. I can't say too much, but let's just say that Kate's phone wasn't in Blackstone Lane. We've been able to start tracking it. Anyway, I'm hoping I'll be able to fill you in with more details very, very soon. What's important in the meantime is you get some rest.'

'But hang on, John, the leads—do these leads mean Kate's alive?'

'We don't know yet, Liam. We don't know. We're hopeful.'

'So, where do you think she is?'

'Well, Liam, we think she might be in New South Wales.'

'Wow, okay.'

'Yes. There's a bloke I've been talking to up there, because we're going to be doing a joint investigation with New South Wales Police. His name is Detective Senior Sergeant Peter D'Ambrosio. I'll text you his number. You can put it in your phone so if you get a call or text from him, you know it's legit. He seems like a good fella.'

Liam's heart is racing so fast he's finding it hard to digest the words. What is she doing in New South Wales? Who has taken her? Please, please, please, let her still be alive.

9
TRAUMA

PETER D'AMBROSIO IS standing on the side of the Hume Highway on the stretch south of the small township of Yanderra. He wipes his brow with one of the ironed brown checked handkerchiefs his mum insists on depositing over to his place twice a week. He puts his binoculars up to his eyes and looks out over the dense bushland lying between the Hume and the huge, snaking catchment that is Lake Nepean.

It's about here, somewhere, that the victim's mobile phone stopped ringing and went dead. It didn't ping on any mobile phone towers after that.

There are cumulus clouds on the horizon that look so heavy they could fall on out of the sky. From this distance, the search crews scraping the bushland are like little ants.

Up above, the sound of a chopper.

Helicopter noise always makes Peter D'Ambrosio feel a bit queasy. Like so many cops based in the area, he's often come out here to find the bodies of the jumpers.

Jumping does awful things to bodies. One memory that rattled around his brain for years was the time that he watched a crow circle the body of a woman found dashed on the rocks like a rag doll. The crow circled repeatedly, as if stalking her. Eventually, it swooped, plucked out one of her eyeballs and took off like a Concorde jet plane through a still morning sky. D'Ambrosio had been so shaken that he pulled out his pistol and discharged it at the bird. He missed. He watched the bird, its beak agape with the poor woman's eye, fly into the distance until it disappeared out of sight.

That had been D'Ambrosio's last day on the job for some time. He'd told the story to his trauma counsellor on many occasions.

'I know it's bullshit, but somehow I felt if I could kill that crow, I could somehow make it better for that woman's family,' he told her.

'You know you can't change it for them,' the counsellor would say.

'I know, but I kept thinking of whoever the poor bastard was who would have to ID her body. And how there would be an eye missing.'

'Even if you'd killed the crow, the eye would still be missing.'

'I know, I know. Of course I know that. Of course I know it's not rational or anything. I just wanted to kill that fucking crow.'

He'd jump with a start every time he heard the squawking of a crow after that. Then he'd feel the waves of nausea plough over him. A murder of crows. That's the collective noun. Peter D'Ambrosio has a thing for collective nouns. A charm of finches. A parliament of owls. A troop of ostriches. A flamboyance of flamingos. The English language is a beautiful thing, D'Ambrosio has always thought. But for crows, someone decided to choose a murder. A murder of crows.

D'Ambrosio is Scottish–Italian. His Italian paternal grandparents had owned an eponymous gelati parlour in a dreary seaside town on the west coast of Scotland. His maternal grandfather, Big Jim, was Scottish and, Peter always felt, much funnier than Billy Connolly.

Big Jim made 'Miss Piggy's Leg Soup' (pea and ham) and he used to sing a song about crows sitting on a wall in Scottish dialect that everyone in Scotland at that time knew.

Three craws

Sittin' on a wa'

Sittin' on a wa'

Sittin on a wa-aw-aw-aw-aw.

Three craws, sittin' on a wa'

On a cold and frosty mornin'.

The verses of Big Jim's song were hilarious—the first craw *couldnae craw at a'* (couldn't crow at all), the second craw *fell and broke his jaw* and the third craw *was greetin' for his maw* (crying for his mother).

Peter had remembered that as he watched that crow soar into the sky with that eyeball. His grandfather's song, which had always made him laugh out loud, had somehow begun to torment him as an inappropriate and omnipresent earworm, visiting him at the most inopportune moments. Now, whenever he thought of that day, he thought of the silly Scottish song, ruined forever by an unspeakable mental image.

He'd come back to work not because the PTSD had gone, but because the insurance company PIs were stalking him.

At first, he thought he was just being paranoid, but then he saw the PIs over and over. He eventually managed to get hold of their videos.

It was disconcerting to watch himself, with his short, neat, cropped hair and silverish goatee, walking in his slightly stained grey tracksuit pants (his standards had slipped terribly since he went off on sick leave) to the letterbox, like a crim.

To Peter D'Ambrosio, surveillance meant you were up to no good. He had had to run surveillance on people. But those people had committed actual serious crimes. He was just trying to recover from the dead people.

'The simplest way to explain it,' D'Ambrosio told his psych, once, 'is that I see dead people. And they won't leave. They won't go away. They just keep coming back.'

The grim roll call of dead people in D'Ambrosio's head features teenage car accident victims and thirty-something women on the wrong side of horrible DV incidents. Suicides he'd watched cut down from rafters. But mostly jumpers. Peter D'Ambrosio has been called to the bridges of the Southern Highlands too many times.

But the insurance company didn't see it that way. Its investigators were convinced he was a malingerer. PTSD was nothing more to those clowns than an acronym. He imagined those desk jockeys having a father die in their arms after he jumped but didn't kill himself immediately. And when they got to the bottom of the bridge, and they ran to him and scooped him up, he looked at them, wild-eyed and gulping, and said *sorry* over and over and over, because although he was dying, he was feeling guilty that someone had to witness it. Imagine those numbskulls dealing with something like that?

It got to the point where Peter D'Ambrosio was pasting tin foil on his windows to stop them from filming him inside his home. He was swallowing a cocktail of psych pills just to get to sleep. One morning he'd woken up with his head gashed open and he had no idea what happened. He'd wake up with the sheets soaking wet from fever dreams. All because the stupid company was paying him four hundred dollars a week to stay home and recover.

Before he was told he had to go off sick, as they called it, he'd had a meeting with a lady from HR who was all sympathetic coos. His boss sat in and told him that his wellbeing was their Highest Priority. But save for a sweet and scrawny kid, Mark Horvath, whom he'd mentored at the cop shop and who would check in every few weeks to make sure he was okay, he hadn't heard a single peep from anyone the whole time he was off. It was like his 'problem' was contagious. Best not speak to Pete D'Ambrosio, lest your own demons start to eat away at you, too. The secondary trauma load for every single officer was so unspeakably heavy, their cups so precariously full, that most of them just tried not to mention the war.

In the end, it all became too much. He hadn't had a girlfriend in years. In desperation, he'd even once visited a sex worker in a brothel on an industrial estate. She'd had dental braces and her blonde hair had black roots. She'd given him a lap dance and Tina Turner's 'Private Dancer' had played on the stereo. *Rock bottom, D'Ambrosio,* he had thought as she gyrated over him in cheap platform heels. *You have really hit rock fucking bottom.*

He was sitting alone, watching TV every night, often falling asleep on his sofa because it was easier. To his shame, he'd often buy a cheap bottle of wine at Aldi and finish it on his own as he watched reruns of *M*A*S*H*. He was starting to know Hot Lips Houlihan's sassy retorts off by heart.

Eventually, some force dragged him back into reality. Because otherwise, he figured, he might end up being another one of those jumpers. And then he'd be the source of some poor bastard cop's PTSD. He'd be the bloke that poor cop saw at the end of his bed every night, standing on the ledge of the bridge, before taking a step. That poor cop would see that scene over and over and over, and it would be his fault.

So, Peter D'Ambrosio went back to work.

And that's how he found himself looking for any signs of a vivacious redhead from Melbourne and wondering whether she might still be alive.

10

WOMBAT HOLLOW

SHE IS, THOUGH.

Kate Delaney is trying to think about Liam Carroll. She is trying to keep herself sane and alive by remembering his crazy stories. Liam is the sort of guy who always has mad stories. Crazy things just seem to happen to him as a matter of course.

There was that time he had stopped in Bali on the way back from a European trip. And not really being the type to go to Bali, he'd become bored after the requisite trips to the beach, the massages and shopping excursions. He'd asked a cab driver for suggestions about what to do and the cab driver had told him that the trial for Amrozi, one of terrorists behind the bombings of the Sari club in Kuta the previous year, was being heard at the Denpasar courthouse. Liam was a fairly recent law graduate and thought *why not?* But when the driver pulled up to the courthouse, they discovered court wasn't sitting that day.

'It doesn't matter, sir, I can take you to Kerobokan Prison instead, to visit Amrozi,' Liam told Kate he remembered the driver saying.

'So, please tell me, Liam Francis Carroll, you didn't then go to visit Amrozi in gaol?' Kate asked him, eyes widening.

'Well, I thought, "Why not? Could be an experience,"' Liam deadpanned as she nearly choked on her drink.

'Some people go to Bali to get pissed on the beach,' Kate said. 'You go to hang out with a criminal mastermind of a mass murder in a custodial setting.'

'To be fair, I didn't go to Bali for that purpose,' Liam said, 'But once that possibility presented itself, I thought it would be pretty fascinating. C'mon Kate, you would have done it, too!'

'Yes, but me meeting Amrozi would have been a Page One splash. You meeting Amrozi was future dinner party banter.'

'True that. But gripping banter, you must admit. Gripping banter. I could have dined out on that stuff for years.'

'You would have to choose your crowd,' Kate said. 'And ensure that they shared my black sense of humour.'

'Correct.'

He explained how the taxi driver had then had an animated conversation in Bahasa on his phone with someone connected to the prison, and said, 'Okay, sir, it's sorted—they let you in,' and then had taken him to the gaol. The driver had urged him just to go inside—they were expecting him. The driver would wait outside.

Liam told Kate how he then had to confect a convincing story to blag his way in about how the bombings had really affected him as an Australian and he wanted to confront the man who had caused this misery for his people.

'For *your people*?' Kate said, rolling her eyes.

'Well, yes. Which is not to say that the bombings didn't, you know, really affect me. That is, I was moved and saddened by the bombings,' he added quickly, knowing that Kate had been distressed to be asked to do 'death knocks' as a cadet journalist—contacting families who had lost their loved ones in the bombings to try to get interviews for the paper.

Bali had been one of her first big jobs, and after several days, she was one of many reporters who could be seen across the newsroom with their heads on their desks, weeping at the horror of what they were being forced to confront. The paper had called in a ditzy counsellor who told them they might want to do breathing exercises. They had chosen instead to go to the pub, where they got absolutely trolleyed and wept into their wine and talked about the ones who had lasted several days after the blast, but died of their burns.

'I mean, I'll never forget that day,' Liam continued. 'It was truly awful. And we had family friends in Sydney who lost someone over there. But I just had to think on my feet of a story that sounded convincing—you know, about why I might want to meet this guy. I mean, you have to admit, it would have been fascinating.'

Kate had had to admit that it would.

The official on duty at Kerobokan Prison had bought his explanation, ham-fisted as it was. This was some years before the gaol became notorious with the arrival of Australian inmates, including convicted drug smugglers Schapelle Corby and the so-called 'Bali Nine'. The official had ushered Liam through, and Liam was walking through the large prison yard when suddenly two Australian Federal Police officers came running from nowhere and yanked him into a little room.

'And the AFP guys were asking me why I wanted to see Amrozi and I said that the taxi driver had told me that I could go and see him, and I was a law graduate, and this was of interest to me, and, besides, I thought that it was something unremarkable in Indonesia—you know, when in Denpasar, et cetera,' Liam remembered. 'And they're looking at me, incredulous, like I was insane, saying, "What the fuck is wrong with you? He's not a fuckin' tourist attraction, mate. He's a fuckin' terrorist."'

'Well, they were right on that front,' Kate said, shaking her head at the absurdity of it. 'So, what happened then?'

'Well, I was worried they were going to keep me in overnight or something. Or have the Indonesian authorities arrest me. I mean, can you be arrested for visiting a terrorist in gaol in Indonesia? Clearly, I wasn't too familiar with the law in that jurisdiction. And what were AFP guys doing there anyway? They never told me that part. But they gave me a stern talking to, took a photocopy of my passport, and eventually sent me on my way.'

'And what did you do then?'

'Well, what else could I do? I got the taxi driver to take me back to the hotel. And I went to the swim-up pool bar, and I ordered a margarita.'

'Nothing else for it,' said Kate.

'Nothing at all,' Liam returned.

'I assume you have never attempted such a thing again.'

'Good lord, no. Although I can't say the opportunity to meet a terrorist mastermind has presented itself in any other context.'

—

Then there was the time Liam had gone to the Daintree National Forest for the first time (also his first time anywhere in Australia that was north of Brisbane) and decided to go on a crocodile tour and, boy-from-inner-Melbourne-who-hated-camping that he was, had asked the Steve Irwin-style croc-man tour guide if he could expect to see monkeys.

'Steve' had looked at Liam with great incredulity. 'You taking the piss, mate?'

Liam was not taking the piss. He actually did think there might be monkeys in the Daintree. He turned crimson and said nothing.

He was the butt of 'Steve's' jokes for the entire day after that.

'Should I feed "Monkey" over there to one of our apex predators?' he'd ask the other tourists on the boat, who would laugh nervously as Liam rolled his eyes. Two young Japanese students had given him sympathetic looks. A ten-year-old kid thought 'Steve' was hilarious.

'There are NO MONKEYS IN QUEENSLAND, DUMB-DUMB,' the kid had cackled at Liam all day.

From time to time when Liam was making fun of Kate for something like her pathological clumsiness, she'd look at him, cock her head to one side, and say, 'NO MONKEYS IN QUEENSLAND, DUMB-DUMB.' And Liam would say, 'You're absolutely right, madame. As you were.' And then they'd kiss. They never needed much of an excuse.

How she loved kissing his lips, which had a somehow pillowy quality to them. He was a lovely kisser. Kissing Liam Carroll brought her back to Year Ten, when kisses made her stomach spin in Catherine wheels. Holding Liam Carroll's hand, she could almost make out the thousands of tiny golden sparks flying between them like they were showering off a farrier's anvil. She hadn't expected she would feel like that again, but there it was.

She would try to tell him this sometimes. To find a way of putting it into words that didn't feel expected and saccharine. But he was, by his own admission, not terribly good at honest conversations about feelings. He'd change the subject or turn it into a self-deprecating joke. Kate wondered what had happened to him. She often thought that there was a little red flag in Liam that she couldn't quite work out. She would find this frustrating at times, and she'd tell him so. But she could never remain cross at him for too long, because he would do something altogether adorable, and she'd forgive him in a nanosecond. And she'd catch him in tiny little moments when he'd had a few drinks, or his guard was down, and he'd say the most beautiful things. And so, she would mentally cling on to those things, knowing how hard it was, ordinarily, for him to say them and hope that with time, he felt more at ease.

They were the sort of things that now, if he had her with him, he'd shout loudly at her over and over. And she knows that, and it is helping her not to feel so scared and hungry and sore and alone.

At Wombat Hollow, Kate is in the corner on the floor of the back bedroom, hands and feet still cable-tied. The plastic is starting to dig into her wrists. The scratchy carpet is burning her thighs.

She looks around the bedroom and wonders if there is any way of escaping. She's on one side of a queen-size four-poster bed adorned with a chintzy quilted duvet cover. The bed is way too big for the low ceilings, which are finished with narrow plaster cornices. Above the bed is an ornate faux Victorian plaster ceiling rose, which looks odd and out of place in this tiny, claustrophobic room. The walls feel thin and lacking in insulation. There is a faint smell of rising damp. She's already shivering with the cold, and it will be freezing in here as night falls.

On the other side of the bed is a narrow gap next to the window. The window has brown metal frames and appears to be locked. In the distance, through bushes and trees, she can make out the lights of the main house. But it's not close enough for anyone to see her.

She's wondering if she should start switching the light off and on in Morse code in the hope that the owners see it and come down to investigate.

That is, she reflects, exactly what the Famous Five would have done when they got into a Spot of Trouble on some sort of island after getting lost while on a picnic adventure. Anne would be so tired of adventures and would tell George she was a frightful tomboy. There would be something menacing about Germans. Looking down at her cable ties, Kate wishes she had paid more attention in Girl Guides. The Guides, like the Famous Five, would have a practical solution to her current fix. Kate was always in trouble at Guides. She didn't polish her shoes or badges and she never did learn how to tie a reef knot.

The thought of the Famous Five makes her start thinking about Enid Blyton foods and how it was another thing she and Liam had bonded over, as they had both devoured the now comically politically incorrect books as children. They both agreed that no one described food like Enid Blyton, from the mouth-watering to the comically retro. Baked potatoes simply dripping with butter. Cold tongue and tomato sandwiches. Potted meats. Blancmange. New scones. Strawberries and cream. Treacle. Her stomach starts rumbling again. She could murder a baked potato simply dripping with butter right now.

Focus on the Morse code, Kate, there aren't any baked potatoes or new scones.

Alas, being the sort of person who was hopeless at Guides, Kate doesn't know Morse code. Even if she did, it's still not quite dark, so the owners might not see it anyway. It's worth a shot in some form, though. Even a flicking *on-off, on-off, on-off* of the lights is sure to at least provoke their attention and perhaps send them down to investigate.

She starts manoeuvring herself to try to stand up in the cable ties. It hurts.

Just as she is almost on her feet, she hears him coming down the hall. She plonks back down on the carpet and hopes he hasn't noticed that she's trying to plot some kind of escape.

He hasn't noticed.

The door bursts open. The Guy, whom she observes is wearing latex gloves, tosses into her room a tube of Pringles chips and a plastic bottle of Fanta.

'Here you go, Blue,' he says. 'Get into it.'

Another reason to hate him, beyond the small matter of the rape and the kidnapping.

—

Kate is a terrible food snob. Maybe, in fairness, all things considered, if she is honest about herself, she is a bit of a snob, full-stop. She will tell the photographers when they are on the road on country jobs that you can always judge a café by its chairs and the font on its menu. She will drive for miles to try to avoid bad food, much to the chagrin of the weary snappers who are often quite happy to opt for Macca's.

'Shit chairs and shit font, you know you're going to get a shit meal,' she will declare. It's true. You know it as soon as you see those awful, moulded plastic seats, often in a garish shade of red, that seem to be beloved in certain regional locations. And as soon as you see Comic Sans font on a menu (or, indeed, a spelling mistake), you just know that you are going to get terrible food. Sundried tomatoes will undoubtedly feature. Salad will be bulked up with red onion, and saturated with gloopy dressing or a balsamic reduction sprayed across the plate like a Pro Hart painting in engine oil.

The pizza will invariably be a cross-cultural 'gourmet' horror show, involving ingredients like Tandoori chicken, or, in the worst example of the genre she has seen, bocconcini and bok choy. The milk in the coffee will be so badly burnt you scald your mouth when you drink it. The coffee will be served in those tall, slim, nineties glasses with the tiny, curved handle that is almost impossible to pick up and will, invariably, cause you to spill its contents right down your shirt. The soft drinks will always, always be in plastic bottles that make them taste soapy and go flat and warm within minutes.

It figures that The Guy is the sort of person who drinks fizzy orange empty calories (despite his gym habit) and eats the kind of chips that make you feel slightly sick after ingesting more than a couple.

But Kate is so hungry she is about to pass out. Sylvia has always teased her about how she becomes 'hangry' when she doesn't eat. It turns her completely bonkers, sapping her patience and draining her of a personality. Being hangry, she figures, isn't going to help her in this situation. She needs her wits about her.

So, she pours out the Pringles onto her lap with her cable-tied hands, noting that the smell of powdered sour cream dust all over her dress will drive her nuts for as long as she's still in these clothes. She then awkwardly shoves some Pringles into her mouth, washes them down with the Fanta, and wonders why the hell he is feeding her, anyway?

What does he want with her? Why is he keeping her alive? Where could this possibly end for her? And for him?

—

The Guy is thick, but not thick enough for it not to eventually dawn on him that paying for Wombat Hollow with Kate Delaney's credit card was a monumentally dumb move. He is dozing off, jeans unbuttoned, latex-gloved hand down his pants, in front of a re-run of *Everybody Loves Raymond*, when suddenly he sits bolt upright.

'The fucking card, fuck. FARK!'

He hastily buttons his pants and starts scarpering around the cottage, collecting his things and stuffing them into his bag, banging into a glass coffee table and smashing a mug and plate as he does. He is in such a state, when he goes to try to pick the pieces of smashed porcelain out of the carpet, he cuts his hand above the glove quite badly, and it then drips all over the carpet.

'FARK YOU!' he yells at the broken cup and kicks it across the room, smashing it into the door of the bedroom where Kate is cowering.

He runs into the kitchen and finds a Chux and some cream cleanser and begins to wildly rub into the fawn carpet, desperately trying to remove the bloodstains. The carpet is now covered with big, whiteish circles that won't come out and seem to be more or less bleached.

Sweat beads along The Guy's brow and collects under his arms. He can smell himself. He has struggled with perspiration since his teens—a fact which should dissuade him from buying tight shirts in man-made fibres, but doesn't.

Inside the bedroom, Kate hears the commotion and puts down her Fanta and falls back against the bed. What is he doing? What is wrong?

The door bursts open to reveal The Guy, wild-eyed with a serious gash on his right hand, blood soaking into a blue-checked tea towel he's hastily tied around it.

'We're out of here! Get up! Get the FARK up, you stupid bitch.'

God, he is vile, Kate thinks, stuffing a last Pringle into her mouth. How does someone become so vile? How can the genetic lottery, the education system, parents, have failed a child so miserably that he grows up to be this jerk? Although maybe that's all just a cop-out. Maybe he just has to take some personal responsibility for how awful he is.

He yanks her by the arm and pushes her out the door, shoving her again into the back of the Echo. Gravel flies up from wheels as he speeds out of there. As he does, he flings his own mobile phone into the weir.

Plop.

A small mob of swamp wallabies crouching at the water's edge cock their heads, their little black-tipped faces startled by the noise. They watch the phone floating for a few seconds on the muddy surface, then slowly disappearing into the water. The sun dips down behind the weir.

Inside Wombat Hollow, the unit looks like it has been trashed by rock stars. The floor is a galaxy of large, spherical bleach stains. Coffee runs in steady little rivers down the bedroom door. The jaunty piano music credits of *Everybody Loves Raymond* are still playing on the television. And on the arm of the sofa, under the coffee table, on the kitchen floor, are tiny puce-coloured blood stains.

On the back seat of the Echo, Kate Delaney presses her nose against the glass. She looks out the window at the landscape she has seen so many times before. And she begins to silently cry.

11
CRYSTAL

IN NORTHCOTE, SYLVIA Estrellita is packing her suitcase.

'I don't trust these cops to do their job,' Liam had told her.

'I trust whatever you trust, Chicken,' Sylvia had said, trying to sound reassuring, grinding her teeth.

'Okay, then, let's go to New South Wales and try to find her,' Liam had insisted.

'Sure, sure, sure, cool-cool,' Sylvia replied, loath to mouth the obvious fact that she was not at all certain what possible benefit a fashion journalist and a medical negligence solicitor could render to a large-scale police investigation.

So, now she's madly packing for a grim and, likely, pointless trip for two probably superfluous people to try to find their missing best friend and lover who has been, at very best, kidnapped. (Jesus Christ, how has Kate been kidnapped?)

She looks down at her cream hardside French suitcase with tan trim, thinking how Kate had shaken her head when she first saw it, in awe that Sylvia could keep such a thing clean.

'It means scrubbing it after every single trip,' Sylvia explained, nodding sagely at her friend, who had never bought luggage in anything but black or navy because Kate had a habit of trashing everything she owned. 'I use a toothbrush on the edges.'

What Sylvia does have in common with Kate is a tendency towards almost comical over-packing, and today she's rushing around her bedroom, tearing clothes off hangers and out of drawers, ignoring the constant stream of text messages from a frantic Liam, from sympathetic friends, from slightly annoying colleagues who seem to be enjoying the drama of what is fast becoming a Big Yarn (how can Kate be a Big Yarn?).

Into the hulking suitcase go seven pairs of shoes, a large cosmetic bag of over-priced skin solutions given to her by the beauty editor on the paper's lifestyle magazine lift-out, multipacks of tissues, a cosy cashmere wrap for Kate, for-when-we-find-her, because-we're-going-to-find-her (she'd want one after an ordeal like that), fourteen pairs of underwear (they might be gone a while), a needle and thread (you never know), a packet of condoms (bad idea? Again, you never know, best not to bring the vibrator, though), several jumpers (it will be cold), most of which retailed at a week's wage, a pair of jeans she can only wear on her thinnest days and thus almost never wears because they make her kidneys hurt, and a bunch of other random outfits she hasn't curated because she doesn't have time.

She hears the scraping sound of Boris's little paws padding across the floorboards. The Puppeteer, or the Fluffateer, as she likes to call him when he's being especially cute, looks up at her and cocks his head to one side.

'Come on, baby,' she says, scooping him up into her arms.

She bursts out her front door, dragging the suitcase behind her, to see Liam standing in front of his car, looking at his watch.

'You're late, Sylvia.'

'Well, technically, yes, but late for what . . . ?' she says, with the end of the sentence trailing because she sees the look in his eyes. 'Oh sweetheart, it's going to be okay.'

Liam pauses for a second and then reaches over to grab her suitcase. 'Holy shit, Sylvia, this weighs as much as your average Year Four kid.'

'In Guides we learned "Be Prepared",' Sylvia shoots back, trying to help him fumble the case into the boot of his car.

'Yep, prepared for a drive to find my missing girlfriend, not for London Fashion Week.'

She ignores him and they clamber into his car and Liam starts the engine.

In Sylvia's handbag, he hears a muffled little bark.

'Boris!' she mutters. 'I told you to be quiet, baby.'

'No, Sylvia, just no,' Liam says. 'Boris is a *no*.'

Sylvia looks at the sweat collecting on Liam's brow, the slightly wild quality that's developing in his eyes. He seems to have given up on brushing his hair. His hands are shaking quite a bit and his nails are bitten right back. She thinks he could really do with a manicure. She senses now is not the time to mention that, nor to push it with the dog.

She tells Liam to drive across town to her mum Gloria's place. Boris barks most of the way, and Liam turns up the radio and tries not to lose his shit altogether.

—

They finally pull up to the little blonde-brick eighties unit where Sylvia grew up. The doormat says HOME SWEET HOME in folksy font. In the corner of the verandah is a gold hanging basket of maidenhair fern. Liam can see, through the windowpanes, fussy lace curtains and a cream and gold faux neoclassical sofa that looks like it came from Franco Cozzo, the gaudy Italo-Australian furniture retailer.

Sylvia catches him sizing it all up.

'Mum's philosophy has always been "more is more",' she whispers, giggling. 'I'm notionally kinda with her on that, although we part company on the taste front.'

She presses the doorbell, which sounds out the theme tune from *Love Story*. From down the hallway sounds the clack-clack of stilettoes on tiles. A tiny woman in a sparkly silver top, frosted pale pink lipstick and fluffy magenta kitten heels opens the door.

'Crystal! To what do I owe this pleasure?' Gloria Estrellita says, barely looking at her only child and winking at Liam.

'*Nanay!*' Sylvia says, kissing Gloria on either cheek. 'I told you not to call me Crystal anymore. It's Sylvia. It's been Sylvia for a good ten years.'

'Why on earth you would choose to change your name from a beautiful name like Crystal completely escapes me, daughter!' Gloria says, for the eleventh-billionth time. 'I named her after Crystal Carrington in *Dynasty*!' she tells Liam. 'She was so glamorous.'

Liam smirks as Sylvia, on cue, mouths her mother's well-worn script.

'So glamorous, Nanay,' Sylvia returns. 'I know, like, what's wrong with me? Who wouldn't want to be named after Crystal Carrington?' Sylvia throws her hands up in the air theatrically and rolls her eyes at Liam.

Liam daren't tell Gloria that the only other person he's ever known with this name was a mate at uni who would moonlight in a drag show under the moniker Krystal Karrington, wearing exaggerated, contoured makeup, enormous shoulder pads, lace tights and earrings that resembled chandeliers. He makes a mental note to tell Sylvia later, though, as he expects she'd love it.

'Anyway, Nanay, as we have gone through countless times, you are not exactly averse to changing a name yourself,' Sylvia says.

When she left the Philippines for her new life in Australia, Gloria decided to drop her actual surname, Andrada, and just go by her middle name, Estrellita. She'd been named Estrellita after her maternal grandmother, a lovely woman who was called Lita for short. As a child, Gloria had always wondered why her grandmother had shortened her beautiful name, which meant 'star'. She figured that in her new country, no one needed to know that she was an Andrada. Gloria Estrellita could be, at least in name, a star.

—

Gloria Estrellita has always been a devoted fan of the eighties power soapies. She knows every episode of *Dynasty* off by heart. It took her years to come to terms with the fact that it was Kristin who shot JR in *Dallas*. Sylvia has always joked that as godawful as her birth name is, there had been a real and appreciable danger that she would be christened Sue Ellen, so she ought to count her blessings.

While the Aussie kids were running through lawn sprinklers and grazing their bellies on Slip 'N Slides, Sylvia Estrellita spent her summers reading books and vintage copies of *Vogue* she found at op shops while listening to the hum of her mother's sewing machine. This scene was always set to the dreary opening credits of *Days of Our Lives.*

'*Like sands through the hourglass,*' Sylvia would whisper in Kate's ear while Kate sat in their newspaper room pod years later, hurling 'fuckety-fucks' at her computer screen because she was stressed out filing a story.

'Yeah, yeah, Sylvia,' Kate would say. '*So are the days of our lives.*' Then Sylvia would whistle the theme tune and dance around the pod in the fluttering style of Kate Bush in 'Wuthering Heights'. Kate would cackle, despite herself, and blow Sylvia a kiss.

Sylvia Estrellita always had a way of making sure that Kate Delaney didn't take herself too seriously. They'd met in shorthand training when they started off as cadets on the paper. Kate had been briefly infatuated with a roguishly handsome and altogether unsuitable fellow cadet named James, who was also learning shorthand. When she was bored, she would sit in class and imagine James pushing her up against a wall and ravishing her. She would absent-mindedly write his name over and over on her notepad. Sylvia was sitting next to her one day as Kate repeatedly scrawled the shorthand for 'James'—which resembled a forward slash on top of a little hill, with a tiny circle at the bottom of the hill for 's'.

Sylvia leaned over and wrote on Kate's notepad in perfectly executed Pitmans.

'It's okay, I won't tell him. Your secret is safe with me.'

Sylvia then pressed her lips together, suppressing a giggle. Kate went crimson. But she snorted and wrote the shortforms for 'Thanks, lovely!' on Sylvia's pad.

James noticed none of this. He was bone-lazy and failed shorthand three times. Sylvia and Kate passed with flying colours and became thick as thieves.

—

Thinking of Kate now jolts Sylvia back into the task at hand.

'We've got a teensy-weensy favour to ask, Nanay,' she says to Gloria, in her best-behaviour voice.

She thrusts the toy Russian terrier into her mother's arms. Boris starts scratching at the sequins.

Gloria Estrellita is not a dog person. She is not amused.

'No! No! That dog is *nakakabwisit*!' Gloria says, handling him like he's a pet tarantula. She always uses Tagalog—in this case saying 'so annoying'—when she's grumpy.

'He pees on my sofa, Sylvia! I hate that stupid scrawny little thing! Why do you insist on having such a stupid dog? He's a stupid dog, no?' she says, looking at Liam, who wholeheartedly agrees, but now is not the time. He needs Gloria Estrellita to take the dog.

'He has his, ahem, charms,' Liam begins.

Sylvia pinches him on the leg, and he stifles a yelp.

'Please, Ms Estrellita,' he says, giving Gloria a plaintive look. 'We don't know what to do. We've heard Kate is up in New South Wales. I can't stay home. I can't. How can I sit here and wait for these people to do their job? Do they expect me to do nothing? But I can't bring Boris in the car. His barking . . . my, my mental health.' Liam raises his eyebrows meaningfully at her and motions to Sylvia. 'I promise I'll find a way to make it up to you.'

Gloria reaches up and tousles Liam's hair. 'Oh darling, call me Gloria,' she says. 'You look pale. Why don't you two come in and I'll fix you something to eat? You look skinny, Sylvia—all that hanging around with those fashion types. You're not eating enough.'

'We can't, Nanay,' Sylvia says firmly. 'Liam is keen to get on the road. He's really so worried. We both are. And the police aren't doing a very good job. We don't trust them.'

'I'm so sorry about your girlfriend,' Gloria says to Liam. 'Kate is a beautiful girl, but more than that, she's strong and very, very smart. They'll find her.'

'It's not Kate's brains I'm worried about, Ms—Gloria,' Liam says. 'It's the stupid cops.'

Gloria sighs, hastily wiping a tear from a mascara-laden eye. 'I'll pray for her. I'll go especially into the city to St Patrick's Cathedral and light all the candles,' she says. 'I'll get the Sisters of Mercy onto it, too. They could power a whole suburb with the force of their prayers, those sisters.'

Gloria volunteers for the nuns, no-nonsense feminist warriors who help rescue sex trafficking victims, many of whom are Filipinas lured to Australia on false promises of jobs as domestic helpers. She brings meals around to the young women, runs them up outfits on her Janome and helps them to find work in the garment trade the way she did when she and baby Crystal arrived in Melbourne all those years ago.

Gloria was from a poor but charming neighbourhood of Manila that was well-known because the houses, while very small and modest, were painted in an array of vivid pastel colours. It bordered a very well-to-do district, with high walls and cleaners and closed-circuit television cameras. Gloria's daughter's paternity had always been a taboo subject—she refused to discuss it in any way. But Sylvia noticed, when they returned on a family holiday to Manila, the way her mother bristled when they drove through the neighbourhood with the big fancy homes. She guessed that her father might have something to do with those places.

Gloria had faced ignominy as an unmarried mother in a deeply Catholic family, and there was considerable pressure for her to give little Crystal to the nuns for overseas adoption by some childless Western family who, the sisters assured her, could give the child a better life. But when Gloria looked at her little Button, as she called her, in her arms, she just couldn't contemplate it.

The squirming baby with the comically generous head of black hair had a fizzy personality right from the beginning. She cooed and she smiled, and it wasn't just wind. Gloria swore this child had lived before.

So, Gloria Estrellita joined the endless wave of Filipinas leaving their homeland to find work. She knew another seamstress who had ended up in Melbourne, and her friend wrote back and said there were plenty of jobs for outworkers. It meant you could watch your baby at home while you worked, sewing each garment by the piece. The more clothes you made, the more money you earned. The money wasn't great, but it was far better than Gloria could ever have expected to take home in Manila. And she was fast. She would build a better future for herself and her little Button.

And she had. Gloria was proud of the bright, sparky daughter she'd raised. Even if she now insisted on calling herself Sylvia instead of Crystal.

Gloria knows resisting her daughter in this moment is futile, and, in truth, probably unfair. She can see that while Sylvia is pretending to be her usual bubbly self, she looks wan. Her eyes keep darting over to Liam, who looks terrible, too.

'Okay, come on, little Boris. But if you pee inside, Grandma will not be happy! You spend the night *outside* on the concrete with no dinner!'

'Thanks, Nanay,' Sylvia chimes. 'You're tops.'

'Yeah, yeah,' Gloria mutters. 'Tops. Now you two be careful on the road. No speeding! No texting when driving! If you're tired, pull over!'

Boris patters down Gloria's hallway as the door clicks behind her.

Sylvia and Liam get in the car and head for the Hume.

—

As they make their way up the freeway, Sylvia is grinding her teeth, gold cowboy boot on the accelerator, shakily singing ABBA songs to try to keep things normal. Warbling the lyrics quietly, pronouncing the 'D' as a 'T' in a mock-Swedish accent.

Liam Carroll is slumped in the passenger seat, biting off the quicks of his thumbnails.

'You know what, Sylvia?'

'Mmm, Chicken?'

'We're not Steve Coogan and Rob Brydon in *The Trip*. Like, we're not about to go and eat some fabulous lobster bisque washed down with a cheeky Chablis in the Lake District. We're not playing for laughs at who can do the most convincing Agnetha Fältskog impression. We're aimlessly driving in the general direction that someone appears to have taken after abducting my girlfriend, because the cops are fucking hopeless.'

'I know. I'm just thinking that Kate would sing along in this situation. She totally would. Also, Kate loved *The Trip*.

'Loves,' she adds, quickly correcting the tense. 'Loves.'

Liam looks out the window. 'Also, I know "Chicken" is a term of endearment, and that is very nice of you, Sylvia, but I don't feel like being called Chicken right now.'

'What do you want me to call you?'

'Well, Liam would do fine.'

'How do you feel about "Li"?' she ventures.

'I do not feel good about "Li".'

He thinks of how Kate used to hate the way that Australians always shortened names. How she'd told him her mother, Mary, had considered it virtually a war crime when they had moved to Melbourne from Ireland and people had shortened her two syllables to one. *Mares.*

'But you call me Kate instead of Katherine, isn't that a bit hypocritical?' Kate would tease her mum.

'That is completely different. Kate is a completely acceptable and lovely name,' her mother would say. 'Mares are female horses.'

12

GHOSTING

LIAM HAS CALLED John Dooley several times, but the detective hasn't picked up. He's tried that D'Ambrosio bloke in New South Wales, but he isn't answering either.

He texts Dooley.

Hi John, it's Liam Carroll.

Dooley knows full well who it is.

I'm just wondering if you have any more news on Kate?

Every five minutes, he checks his phone again. Nothing.

John Dooley is seeing Liam Carroll's messages, but he's ignoring them. He doesn't think there is anything to be gained from constantly updating this guy. In truth, he resents having a know-it-all lawyer as the next of kin of one of his victims. He still doesn't like the cut of Liam Carroll's jib. He accepts that the mobile phone pinging on towers far away from the boyfriend has probably ruled him out, but he just doesn't particularly rate this guy. He doesn't like Liam's hangdog expression. He finds the way Liam runs his hands through his messy hair foppishly irritating. He looks like the sort of person who doesn't polish his shoes regularly enough and probably doesn't keep up with his flossing. Dooley knows none of these things are an excuse not to communicate with a missing person's next of kin. But nonetheless, he ignores Liam's messages and, knowing but ignoring how deeply passive-aggressive he's being, lets him stew.

In the car, on the Hume, Liam is mainlining antacids and trying not to take it personally that the investigating officer is ghosting him like there's no tomorrow. Sylvia is still singing in a tiny voice.

For fuck's sake. She is singing 'The Winner Takes It All'.

'Sylvia!'

'Sorr-ee,' she says, blinking out at the road. 'You know, "The Winner Takes It All" is universally recognised as one of the best break-up songs of all time . . .'

'Yes, Sylvia. It is. And no one is breaking up here.'

He knows she's just trying to bring levity to a horrible situation. He knows that underneath it all, she's as stressed and frightened as he is. He notices her hands on the steering wheel.

The whites of her knuckles are showing. And sometimes, when he closes his eyes for a while, they are jolted open when she strays on to the white rumble strips on the sides of the road. She can't focus but she insists on driving because she wants to be useful.

They get out of Melbourne and up the Hume and the landscape in northern Victoria becomes so monotonous. Kilometre after kilometre of flat, dusty bushland, gum trees. Unlovely country. He always has the feeling of holding his breath until he gets to the border, when the Hume becomes pretty again.

He knows that out to the sides of this road are beautiful places—smooth-pebbled riverbeds filled with cool, clear water, wineries and artisan cheese rooms, places to go for long, lovely bike rides. When all this is over, he thinks to himself, he'll have to bring Kate up for a weekend in a pretty B&B.

And then he catches himself. When all what is over? What is this? How will it end? Where does it go?

He feels nauseous.

'Let's get up there as quickly as we can,' he says to Sylvia, dreading the seven-odd hours of monotonous driving that is ahead of them. Dreading what's at the end of it. Dreading the sense of uselessness his rational brain knows he will be left with when they get there.

'Of course,' she says, biting her lip.

13

ACACIA HILLS

MUCH FURTHER UP the Hume, Kate knows the landscape, because she has driven on the freeway so many times before, with her former boyfriend, Michael King. Michael died four years ago in a car accident.

Michael was originally from Sydney or, more particularly, from Acacia Hills. Making their biannual pilgrimage north, they would take the Hume to past Campbelltown, and head up the freeway to Acacia Hills—bypassing the shimmering loveliness of Sydney's harbour for its sprawling, humid west. It was a place of McMansions, shopping malls, ballet concerts full of children fattened on cola, macarons pronounced 'macaroons' and, to Kate Delaney's abiding horror, funnel web spiders.

Acacia Hills was also in the Emerald City's Bible Belt, home to JoyChurch—the blockbuster evangelical Christian movement founded by Jamie Van der Linden and his wife Shayna. Kate had always been fascinated by JoyChurch, which touted the message—a message completely at odds with her own more ascetic Catholic childhood—that above all, Jesus loved success.

Shayna was a tanned, bouncy and ageless woman with enhanced cleavage, a vacant Botox stare and a penchant for hot yoga. Her husband Jamie answered the phone 'Y'ello!' and used phrases like 'of a night'. *Of a night, we like to sit by the fire and thank our Lord Jesus Christ for his mercies.* Jamie was fond of giving spontaneous stress massages to the younger male members of his flock. Shayna pretended not to notice.

Kate had become acquainted with JoyChurch through Michael's family. The Kings were among JoyChurch's first converts. Michael's mother, Judy King, was a nail art aficionado who clack-clacked her bedazzled cerise talons on the kitchen counter as she sat on the phone. She was a netball umpire with eyes like sequins who often kept her whistle around her neck. The wrinkles on her face formed lines consistent with years of narrowed eyes and pursed lips. Years of waiting for people to reveal that yes, in fact, they had tickets on themselves.

'Tickets,' she would say, clacking her tongue as she filed her nails. 'That woman has tickets.'

For Judy King, having tickets on oneself was effectively a mortal sin. It seemed at odds with her infatuation with Shayna Van der Linden, because Shayna had more tickets than a train station. But they were somehow the right kind of tickets. And what Judy King's arguments lacked in consistency, they made up for in venom.

Kate Delaney knew that Judy had always lain in wait, like a crocodile, waiting to snap, waiting for Kate to misstep and prove that she was, as Judy suspected, 'up herself'.

Visits to the Hills were always exhausting, with Kate straining so hard to be humble and sweet and not to reveal her inner tickets that it almost hurt.

A mostly functioning alcoholic whose favourite tipple was New Zealand sauvignon blanc, 'for its pineapple and passionfruit tones', Judy would occasionally lapse into wine-fuelled furies and the target of her rages were invariably women.

Kate had always known that her time would come. One day, her mask would slip, and she would no doubt reveal some conclusive evidence of tickets.

The family's most loyal JoyChurch convert was Michael's sister Mandy. Mandy King lived in a large home that had been built on the back of the huge, subdivided King block. A single mother, she was the sort of woman who made Kate feel guilty. Guilty because Mandy was kind of heart, but irked Kate Delaney so much she made her want to scream.

Mandy had large, bovine eyes that always seemed slightly startled, a lank helmet of naturally white-blonde hair and a habit of pushing her food nervously around on her plate. A former chronic dope smoker who also dabbled in ice with her deadbeat, now ex-husband, she had *found Jesus* through JoyChurch. Although, it seemed to Kate that Mandy King worshipped not so much Jesus, per se, as Jamie and Shayna and the certainty they brought to life.

Mandy had eschewed her formerly seedy lifestyle for what Kate saw as little more than 1950s housewifedom. But instead of the glamorous *Mad Men* frocks, Mandy had cargo pants and Pandora charm bracelets. Her domestic docility knew no bounds. A fact, Kate thought, that was all too often exploited by Judy King.

Judy treated Mandy as a favourite indentured slave—the plantation mistress's pet. *Milly Mandy Moo, you are your Mumma's best girl*, Judy would croon, before sending her daughter out to buy smokes, or beseeching her to *be a love and clean the pool.*

Kate Delaney had always felt sorry for Mandy King, who was raising three bratty tweens she had birthed in quick succession during a furious attachment-parenting phase. But quite apart from the children who had suckled quite unsuccessfully at her breast until their preschool years (attachment parenting and illicit drug use seemed never to be at odds with one another in Mandy's young eyes), the real parasite was her mother.

Mandy was prisoner of Judy's chronic selfishness. But to her guilt and shame, Kate did not feel sorry enough for Mandy to stop herself from mentally eye-rolling at her ninety per cent of the time she spent at Acacia Hills.

No, she didn't watch *The Biggest Loser*, Kate would say, smiling through gritted teeth, as Mandy assured her that she was 'missing out'. No, she hadn't read *Fifty Shades of Grey*, she would gulp, trying to blot out the mental image of Mandy reading soft porn she had picked up in a towering bargain bin at Costco. No, there was really no need to schedule her Tupperware party around their next visit, but *what a lovely offer.*

As the air-conditioned days wore on, staring out to the yard at the Kings' bull mastiffs Axel and Rose as they licked the sliding door in long, greasy stripes, Kate would feel her stomach cramping and her mind wondering how on earth her beautiful, sensitive, erudite political lobbyist, Michael King, shared these people's DNA—and why she had always been so preternaturally disposed to choosing boyfriends with awful families.

'They're not so bad, Kitten,' Michael would say, his smile stiffening. 'They mean well, and they think the world of you.'

Allowing him this fiction, she'd go to bed early with her 'tummy issues' and Mandy would sympathetically tut-tut and offer some herbal remedy or another while, lying on the sofa sipping sauvignon blanc, Judy's sequin eyes would narrow. *Tickets.*

—

Michael had died suddenly in one of those accidents the commercial news reporters described in breathy live crosses as a *Horror Smash*. It had happened on his way back from doing pro bono work at an Aboriginal community centre in Geelong. On hearing the news, Judy King's brittle veneer melted like a glacier in a sudden and unforeseen heat wave. She was a screaming mess and, when she came down to Victoria on news of his death, she couldn't bear to see her boy's lifeless body. Kate had been dispatched to identify him.

Darling Sylvia went with Kate, terrified but stoic.

'I love you like a tiger,' Sylvia whispered, clasping her hand, Kate nodding mechanically.

As they entered the dull, soulless antechamber of the morgue—minty walls, scratchy home brand tissues on Laminex coffee table—Kate peered around the doorway, too afraid to actually walk into the room where Michael's body lay.

The first things she saw were his unmistakably stubby fingers. Curled. In what she knew to be rigor mortis.

That's what fingers did, when someone was dead. She'd learned that in a rather gruesome legal studies class where homicide detectives had passed around forensic photos back in the day before something like that risked parental litigation. And that was the only way that Kate Delaney could compute that this was real. For despite the accident, apart from a bump on his head (how could that sweet little bump knock the life out of him?), he just looked like he was asleep.

He'd been dead for hours, but his olive skin kept him as handsome as ever—just the way she would find him dozing in the morning. His thick lashes resting against his face.

She ran howling from the room. Sylvia held back her hair as she bent over, snot streaming into her mouth.

'It's going to be okay, Tiger. It'll just take time,' said Sylvia, barely convincing herself, clutching at straws.

'No, it's not. It's not ever going to be okay.'

—

Kate told her counsellor, when Michael died, that it was like some dreadful gargoyle beast had got its claws into her and they couldn't be removed without ripping through flesh. And so, she just had to let it dig itself deeper until it decided, of its own accord, to safely slide them out. It had taken the better part of two years. She cried every day for at least one of them.

She walked around as if encased in Perspex, unable to read books or watch movies beyond comedies and satires for fear that someone might die, and she might be plunged without warning into that awful place. She must have watched *This Is Spinal Tap* forty times. And that Metallica documentary, which wasn't meant to be like *Spinal Tap*, but was.

Lots of people were sympathetic and lovely, and lots of people just had no idea what to say.

She remembered going back to work after a couple of weeks and the paper, in a moment of typical insensitivity, had sent her to do an infrastructure announcement with the Roads Minister, not far from where Michael had died.

The Roads Minister was tall and thin and cocky and single. He fancied himself a great deal. He fancied Kate a bit, too. He'd been told of her bereavement. Before the press conference started, he'd sidled over to her and put his hand on her shoulder, patting it in a way that felt like he'd learned it in those empathy training classes the politicians were forced to do these days.

'Kate, I am very, very sorry for your loss,' the Roads Minister said.

Kate nodded and forced a 'thank you'.

'I've had lots of girlfriends in the past, and I would have been devastated if one of them had been killed in a car accident.'

What did you even say to something like that? Politicians really could be the worst humans.

Friends tired of her, thinking she was slightly mad. She was. Grief was a form of mental illness and the only way she thought she had any hope of recovering was to ride it until she could ride no more.

Since then, she had never managed to drive or fly to Sydney, nor even contemplate the thought of doing so.

—

Judy King had written her off—dazed by her own maternal grief and glad she no longer had to pretend that she liked this accomplished young woman with tickets on herself.

But Mandy had missed Kate. She had watched her successes from afar, proud of her. She'd sometimes click onto the newspaper website just so she could see Kate's photo by-line, because seeing Kate's face reminded her of her brother. A tear would plop down her cheek.

On the whole though, Mandy King has never been much of a consumer of 'the news'. She finds it depressing.

Which is why, up until this point, she has completely missed the fact that her deceased brother's pretty girlfriend has gone missing.

14

BLOOD

PETER D'AMBROSIO AND his crew turn up to Wombat Hollow after sundown.

The owners hadn't heard the commotion owing to the distance of the cottage from the main house. The son is horrified.

'You can't get carpet-layers for quids around here these days,' the son tells Peter D'Ambrosio.

'What am I going to do in the meantime? How am I going to rent this place out?'

D'Ambrosio feels the familiar bristle of his PTSD flair up. His face feels hot and his stomach churns. How could someone think about carpet when a young woman is missing and has been held captive on their property? What is wrong with people . . . ?

'Well, sir, I don't think carpet is the priority right now, do you? Do you know what's taken place here?'

The son colours and shrugs. 'I wish I bloody knew what had taken place here,' he says. 'Look at it.'

D'Ambrosio walks around the room. What the hell happened to the carpet, anyway? He puts on a glove and runs his forefinger through one of the circles, lifting it to his nose. There is a mintiness to it. Jif?

As he is doing that, he looks at the sofa. On the pale lime jacquard fabric are little spots of what appear to be blood. He calls the forensics blokes over. Under the coffee table is another spray. What has the bloke done to her?

He takes his phone out of his pocket and rings the Victorian detective.

'G'day John. Not great news. Yep. Yep. We've tracked down that Wombat Hollow place. Yep. But the kidnapper's gone. Yep. Yep. She's not here. No. No body or anything like that. No prints. Must've had gloves or something. But there's a fair bit of blood. It's kind of in, you know, drops on the sofa and under the coffee table. And he seems to have tried to clean up some more of it with Jif. Yeah. Big stupid swirls all over the carpet. Yep. Doesn't seem like an Einstein. Nup. He's made a mess of the place. I don't know what he's done to her—we'll get forensics onto it. Kinda looks like drops rather than a spray. All a bit random. Yep. Smashed coffee cup against the bedroom door. Yep. I'll keep you posted with anything further. Aw-kay. Later.'

D'Ambrosio prises open the bedroom door. On the corner of the floor is an empty bottle of Fanta. Outside the window, there is movement on a eucalypt trunk, shining silvery in the moonlight. D'Ambrosio eases over to the window, his heart starting to pump with a little flutter of anxiety. He starts to feel the tingling in his fingertips. He turns over his hands and looks at his palms and his wrists. The red starts to track up his arms. When his PTSD starts to flare up, D'Ambrosio breaks out in hives. Not the small itchy bumps that you normally see, but big, angry welts.

'Giant urticaria,' the specialist with the rounded English vowels told him. 'Ruddy nuisance of a thing. You have it, Peter, from stress. Is there any way that we can reduce your stress load at work?' D'Ambrosio had scoffed and said, 'In a word, doc, nope.' Since then, he has worn his pain on his skin. It feels like a swarm of wasps is nesting under the epidermis.

He reaches into his wallet and pulls out a blister pack of antihistamines (useless, but he keeps trying) and a blister pack of steroids (more effective, but they make his face all puffy). And he sighs as the burning sensation snakes up his arm.

A tawny frogmouth sits on a branch, staring at him through the grass. He stares back at the owl, which has a small lizard in its beak. Something about the frogmouth's bouffant plume of feathers, the pointed faces, had always reminded him of the former prime minister, Bob Hawke. There was one who often perched on the peak at the top of D'Ambrosio's garage and when he watched it on those long nights when he was off on stress leave, he half expected it to carp, *Any boss who sacks someone for not turning up today is a bum.* It had made him laugh, despite himself. He'd christened it Bob. This one stares at D'Ambrosio, looks both ways, then opens its wings and takes to the night sky with its lizard supper.

—

D'Ambrosio texts John Dooley. And Dooley fires off a text to Liam Carroll.

> hi liam
> we've found a property where we believe her abductor has taken her
> nsw police didn't make it on time, unfortunately
> No one there. I do want to prepare u that things arent looking good, mate
> There were items of significance found on the premises. But their are so many people working on this. We're really trying and we try to stay hopeful
> promise ill keep u up to date if anything more comes to light
> JD

Liam wonders what makes a person think it is okay to abbreviate 'you' to 'u', or to dispense with capital letters and punctuation, in a circumstance in which they are discussing the other person's abducted girlfriend and a property they suspect she's recently been taken to. Would this guy mix up his 'there' and 'their' when he was telling someone their loved one was dead? Would he drop his apostrophes? This message would shit Kate to tears. She'd be taking her mental red pen to it.

He realises that he is doing that thing he does when he is faced with trauma. Dissociating. In this case by focusing on punctuation and spelling and grammar.

'What's wrong, Chic— Li— Liam?' Sylvia says, noticing his knee is shaking and his foot is tapping the floor.

'They found a property where they think she's been. "Items of significance" found there,' Liam says, staring out at the red brake lights of the truck in front of them. '"Items of significance." God, I hate cop-speak. What does "items of significance" even mean?'

'Oh.' Sylvia puts her foot down on the accelerator and overtakes the truck. In that moment, it seems the only thing she can do.

—

While police knew that Kate Delaney's mobile phone had pinged on towers up to the point where The Guy had thrown it in the bush, they did not know the identity of the perp. To do that, they'd need to have his number, too. While the telecommunications company could confirm that a certain phone number provided by police had registered on individual towers, they couldn't pull every single number that had hit every single mobile phone tower that night out of their system.

It was something that Peter D'Ambrosio had often thought of as a major flaw that should be fixed. You needed to have a suspect, first, and to know their number. Then you could match it up with the victim's phone. It seemed crazy. And crucially, it wasted time. He had done too many of these jobs to realise that time was not his friend. Crims who have done something really bad don't want to risk leaving a witness to tell her tale. It was only a matter of time before this guy cracked.

Dooley and his Victorian team were working on trying to narrow down suspects so they could run some mobile numbers through the system. The depressing reality of criminality is that the perpetrator is often recidivist, so the first point of call for detectives was always to scour the area around the crime scene to see what known sex offenders they could find.

Dooley had knocked on doors of several locals who were on the sex offender register. Most had decent alibis. One had been on holiday in Thailand for two weeks (*Of course he had*, thought Dooley). Another was working night shifts in a factory. A third had been admitted to hospital. And none of them really fit the profile, anyway. Thailand bloke liked them younger. Factory worker was more of a groomer. And the guy who was in hospital was far more partial to trans sex workers. None of them had been the type, up until now, who would just pluck someone off the street.

As it happened, The Guy didn't live anywhere near Northcote. He had just come in that night to try his luck at the bars. His handful of tradie mates, who lived near him in the suburbs and had no idea about his sustained flirtation with criminality, were married forty-somethings who spent their days wrangling primary school runs and invoices, and their nights lying bone-tired on the couch. He'd driven the Echo a good thirty-five kilometres from his place, leaving it in the driveway of a divorced friend who had moved to Heidelberg West. Then they'd cabbed it in to High Street.

The Guy himself had no idea about how any of this policing would work—his crime wasn't planned, and was, the more he thought about it (he was trying not to think about it), spectacularly stupid. But he knew he had to be careful now that he'd been dumb enough to use Kate's card at Wombat Hollow. That put him in the Southern Highlands region, and he had to get away as quickly as possible, but not speed too fast lest he got pulled over by a diligent traffic cop who spotted Blue in the back.

15

MODS

THE GUY IS really sweating now. He looks in the rear-view mirror at Blue, who seems to be dozing off. He reaches into the glove compartment and fishes out a box of Valium he keeps stuffed in there. But the blister pack is empty. Fark. As he feels around for another packet, he notices a rolled-up bag of weed. While dope makes some people paranoid and skittish, he has always been a bit naturally hyper, and it usually manages to calm him down.

The bong is still rattling around the floor in the back.

He looks up at the road and sighs. He has no idea what to do with this woman. A cone would really help right now. The Guy is convinced that he is a clearer thinker and a better driver when he is stoned.

So, he waits to find a turn-off to a country lane, drives up the little road and swings into a paddock. He throws on his puffer, locks the sleeping Kate in the Echo and sits on a log and pulls a few cones. He lies back and gazes at the blanket of stars bedazzling the night sky. As the mull kicks in, he feels that familiar rush of warmth. The stars seem to somehow join up. He is floating above his body. He pulls what is left of a chocolate bar out of his pocket and feels, for the first time in a few days, absurdly happy.

In the car, Kate is, as it happens, not asleep at all. She is very gingerly watching this idiot and very quietly trying the locks on the doors. None of them work. She looks around at the vast field of yellow grass shining under the stars, a dark line of Monterrey pines along a boundary in the distance. No sign of buildings anywhere close by. No point in making a noise—it will only wake him up. No phone. The car keys are on the grass outside next to him.

It hurts so much to sit down. All she wants, the only thing, is to lie in a big bath and wash him off her and cry. She has spent enough time around courts, interviewed enough victims of sex offences, to know should she make it out of this alive that would not be an immediate option. There would be rape kits, internal examinations, lying back under fluorescent lights while some well-meaning, apologetic doctor tried to ask her about her favourite football team to distract from the hideous thing that was happening.

How will she feel about sex from this time on? Kate has always loved sex. Has thrown herself into it with gusto. Has had such a great time with Liam. The thought of his mouth on her body, his face between her breasts, his hands around her waist, makes her sigh for a tiny second, despite herself. He makes her feel so good. Would the crime play out in her mind? She tells herself off for analysing everything too much, all the time. Here she is, imagining her potentially compromised sexual future, post-rape, when she is still mid-abduction.

—

A huntsman spider is crawling slowly across the windscreen—the hairs on its fat body and long legs lit up by the moon. This is the sort of thing that would usually prompt the pathologically arachnophobic Kate to call for the car to be burned to the ground. Instead, she freezes as it makes its way across the car and crawls down the side and out of sight. She hopes that it will crawl onto The Guy, that he, too, is arachnophobic, and that it will scare the shit out of him. He deserves to be scared. Actually, the way she feels now, as she shifts uncomfortably on the seat, in acute pain, is that he deserves to die.

It makes her think of her old friend Danny Rubensztein, who was on her university debating team, and is now a merchant banker who can talk under wet cement. On a weekend away with all of the debating friends a few years ago, she'd been talking about her Nana, and telling Danny how she was the firstborn and favourite grandchild.

'We all are!' Danny had laughed. 'Have a look around,' he said, pointing to the wildly gesticulating friends sitting in the minibus they were taking to a winery tour. 'Firstborn-Favourite-Grandchildren-who-went-on-to-study-law-and-fought-over-who-got-to-be-Third-Speaker-in-debates. We're all practically the same person.'

He was laughing, but she could see that his eyes were shining a bit. Danny was an endearingly emotional guy at the best of times, but he always got misty-eyed when he thought about his beloved grandmother. She had escaped the Holocaust and every single one of her extended family had been murdered by the Nazis. Mrs Rubensztein adored Danny with a fierce passion. She was a diminutive but incredibly tough old lady, then ninety-eight, and Danny had always joked that she'd make the most perfect assassin because she was so loveable, but such a hard-arse.

Danny's grandmother had inspired his evil genius plan for a hit squad of ninety-eight-year-old grandmothers who went about and quietly took out bad people.

'Geriatric Assassins, I call them,' Danny explained. 'So, they just turn up, on their walking frames or whatever, and blow people's heads off. It's perfect, because no one will suspect them. They only target really very horrible humans who need to go—you know, paedophiles who got off on a legal technicality, conmen who've ripped off pensioners, that kind of creep. Even on the unlikely chance that the grannies get caught, well, they're ninety-eight! Will they ever make it to court? Unlikely. Will they get a custodial sentence? Not a chance. It's perfect.'

Danny thought they could also perhaps do a secondary line in arson: burning down problematic buildings in the dead of night when they were empty. His first target, he said, was the casino, for all the misery it caused.

'Absolutely fucking genius, Danny Rubensztein,' Kate had said.

Kate Delaney pictures one of Danny Rubensztein's ninety-eight-year-old hit squad grannies ambling along on a walking frame and taking out The Guy as he pulls cones under the Southern Highlands stars.

Pop!

Hasta la vista, Loser.

—

Gallows humour has always been Kate's stock in trade as a reporter covering misery. Gallows humour is how they all get by. Gallows humour is helping her, even now.

She'll never forget the first time she got her non-journo friends and her journo friends together for a small housewarming party at her first share house when she started her cadetship at the paper. One of her colleagues, Candy Murphy, was running late. Candy was a brash, big-drinking, hard-nosed brunette with skin sallowed by years of chain smoking and a mouth that was an angry red line, permanently poised for argument. Her nickname was 'Sugar'—an obvious play on Candy, but also because it was so hilariously untrue. Unless she was sweet-talking cops at a crime scene (which, granted, she could do with a performative skill that would put Meryl Streep to shame), saccharine sweetness was a foreign concept to Candy.

Anyway, on this particular night, at nine thirty pm, Candy Murphy finally burst into the party.

'Hey, Sugar,' Kate had said. 'How goes it?'

And Candy had turned to Kate Delaney and said, right there in front of Kate's friends, that she was royally pissed off that she'd had to stay back late to cover a train crash *and not a single fucker died. Not even an injury. I think they're burying it on Page Nine.*

It has always been a grim and inescapable truth of newspapers that *if it bleeds, it leads.*

A journo or two at the back of the room smothered a laugh but Kate was mortified. She could only see it through the eyes of her non-journo friends, who were gasping.

'Isn't that a good thing, that no one died?' Kate's old school friend Patricia, a particularly soft-natured fashion buyer, said, with a note of genuine alarm. 'Why would you want anyone to die?'

Candy just gave Patricia a fixed smile like she was a simpleton and wandered into the kitchen saying, 'Someone get me a drink!'

Kate understands that the gallows humour is completely inappropriate if witnessed by the uninitiated. But it's a coping strategy for tragedy. For being forced to do 'death knocks', for seeing way too many forensic photos of mangled bodies and gaping mouths and rolled-back eyes in court, for standing at the edge of police tape on roadways taking notes as emergency service workers remove bodies from a twisted wreck.

Kate is known for her empathy and sensitivity—as a journalist and as a human. But even for her, speaking about terrible things in a humorous way has sometimes been the only way not to go mad.

Gallows humour will be Kate Delaney's friend throughout this terrible journey. Kate Delaney will not go mad.

So, imagining her rapist thrown off his game by a large hairy spider, or popped off by a comically maniacal murderous granny, seems perfectly normal to her.

So, speaking about her kidnapper like he's just a dickhead (which he is) instead of focusing on the fact that he is someone capable of genuinely terrible things (also true) is just a way to get by.

Had Candy 'Sugar' Murphy's heart not suddenly given up after years of wrecking her body and rendered her dead at forty-two, she would be proud.

—

Down the hill, on the freeway, Kate sees two police cars whiz by, and hopes that something might make them turn around and come up the road. But it doesn't. They become tiny little flashing specks in the distance, cresting a hill and disappearing.

The Guy is still lying back on his fallen tree beneath the stars, his addled head lolling to the side, pale eyelashes framing heavy lids. He is considering whether to pull out his phone and jerk off to some girl-on-girl porn when he opens his eyes, and another thought occurs to him.

Pheasants Nest.

—

The Guy now lives in Melbourne, but he didn't grow up there. If he had, he would have been, in his teens, what was unkindly referred to in the circles Kate Delaney moved in as a 'bogan'. Bogans wore tight acid wash jeans, sported mullet hairstyles (before mullets were embraced as an ironic fashion statement many years later) and had musical tastes tending to soft metal.

In Sydney, where The Guy spent his formative years, bogans were called westies. The bogan's or westie's nemesis, in those years, was known as the mod—later to be eclipsed by goths, then alternatives, then emos. Mods listened to alternative music, had retro black clothes, wore cherry red Doc Martens eight-ups, sat in the corner of Blue Light discos mournfully reading books from the literary canon and looked down their noses at bogans and westies. Kate was, or would have been, The Guy figured from first glance, a dead-set mod.

When The Guy was growing up in the outer suburbs, he'd get his own back at the stuck-up mods by hurling unsolicited abuse at them at the local shopping centre. 'Stupid fuckin' mod!' he would yell out as they walked by, resenting them just for existing.

'Well, let's face it, friend, it's better than being a stupid fucking westie,' he remembered one girl saying in slightly affected rounded vowels and deliberately sharp consonants, dripping with contempt. He could still picture her so vividly: tartan miniskirt, white makeup, exaggerated winged eyes, dark red lipstick on a cupid's bow mouth and a black, messy beehive. She had *The Importance of Being Earnest* stuffed conspicuously into the front pocket of her hessian backpack, which had peace signs and *The Cure* written on it in black Texta. Her get-up was, in his view, faintly ridiculous, but she was gorgeous nonetheless. On the one hand, he wondered who the fuck she thought she was, dressing and acting like that in the outer-western suburbs. On the other, he remembered the humiliation of feeling that she was right. It *was* better than being a stupid fucking westie. He remembered wanting, in that moment, both to fuck her and to hurt her.

In the highly stratified late-eighties suburban ecosystem, The Guy lusted above his station. And knew it. And resented it. And never stopped resenting it.

That night in the bar with Kate, in her sixties minidress with her sixties hair, he had lusted after her in the same way he always had after the mods, who never wanted anything to do with him. He could never quite understand why. He was fit. He was okay-looking. He could crack jokes and had some mean card tricks. He looked a bit like a guy in a beer commercial. *You can get it walkin'. You can get it talkin'. You can get it workin' a plough. Matter of fact I got it now.* Or a one-day cricketer. *C'mon, Aussie, c'mon.* They got hot women. Why not him?

So, when Kate circled back behind him and made fun of his arse, something cracked inside of him.

For one thing, his arse was a sore point. His personal trainer had done so much glute work with him, but it was still flat as a pancake. The PT would try to make encouraging comments, but The Guy knew he was humouring him.

But secondly, he was catapulted back into that moment with that chick with the black beehive and the tartan miniskirt. And so many other moments. So many other disappointments and humiliations and times when he hadn't remembered his station.

—

For Kate, who was a fair bit younger than The Guy, being a bookish teen who moped in the corner of discos reading books was not something she did because, as he thought, she was stuck up.

It was because she had been a migrant kid who was teased within an inch of her life at her primary school full of xenophobic fair-haired kids who looked a bit like The Guy. It was her reaction to and rejection of those kids—finally finding her tribe.

While Australia was enjoying a huge wave of multiculturalism, it had not yet reached Our Lady of Perpetual Hope—a 1970s-era A-frame church with a school made up almost entirely of demountables (the perpetually sozzled parish priest was a terrible financial manager and the school's building fund had mysteriously disappeared as the parish grew and grew).

Our Lady's, as it was known, was in a bland suburb of Melbourne's outer east. When Kate's parents Mary and Billy had moved from Dublin, they had been tossing up between Port Melbourne, which in some ways resembled the southside docks where Mary had grown up—and the suburb they ended up in—an area once entirely covered in apple orchards but now with brick veneer homes as far as the eye could see. You could get a quarter-acre block, a built-in garage and a rumpus room for the same price as a small 'old' house in the inner suburbs. Why would the Delaneys pass that up? Kate had cursed her parents for this decision as soon as she grew old enough to realise how desperately she wanted to get out of the place.

They had arrived in Melbourne in September, meaning that Kate, who was already being marked out as academically bright, had finished the school year the rest of the class was partway through. She was well ahead of the other children. It was another reason for them to loathe her. When Mrs Hunter-Patterson asked a question of the class, Kate's white, skinny, freckled arm was always first to shoot up. Mrs Hunter-Patterson would sigh, and scan the room for someone, anyone, to answer the question instead of Kate. When silence ensued, Kate would duly respond. '*Perestroika* is the word you were looking for, Mrs Hunter-Patterson,' Kate would say. 'It means "openness".'

Kate was already developing her lifelong news junkie habit. Mary Delaney plonked her only child in front of the ABC news religiously every night. She couldn't stand children who weren't well-informed about the world. Hand-wringing mothers who worried about news being depressing or causing anxiety in their darlings irritated Mary no end. Children needed to know about the world they inhabited, good and bad. The day would start with the radio snapping on to 3LO and the broadsheet newspapers being spread out across the kitchen table like Mary was a general preparing maps for war.

Kate, at the very tail end of the generation of children who grew up with the Cold War, was plagued with nightmares and couldn't even look at a picture of a nuclear power station. But that was life, Mary Delaney figured. The child needed to know.

At the back of the class, as Kate answered all the questions their teacher asked, Narelle Stevenson would roll her eyes and nudge her best friend, Kirsty Smith. Narelle Stevenson, like most of them, was blonde and sporty. In summer, she would wear terry-towelling playsuits and go brown as a berry. She'd peel off the first layer of sunburn in long stripes, and then wait to tan up underneath. A petite kid, she played centre in netball and her mother, who had teased-up, lacquered hair, a belt hanging with gold seashells and too-tight high-waisted jeans, was coach.

For reasons best known to Narelle, she had made it her life's mission to make Kate Delaney's life a living hell.

—

One occasion in Year Six was forever burned into Kate's mind. She had been minding her own business with her friend Sarah, sitting on top of the monkey bars at the far end of the playground. Pausing in their chatter from time to time to hang upside down from their perpetually bruised limbs, they had been discussing the *Narnia* books when Narelle Stevenson and Kirsty Smith arrived.

'Those are MY monkey bars. Get down!' Narelle barked.

'No, they are not yours, and no, I'm not getting down,' Kate had answered.

Sarah sat tight-lipped, afraid of the blonde pocket rocket.

Narelle kept at it, needling Kate and Sarah, calling them nerds, saying it was her turn, she owned the monkey bars and they had better do what she told them.

After about twenty minutes, Kate and Sarah tired of it and decided to leave and find something better to do.

'Okay, I'll get off the monkey bars,' Kate said, glaring at Narelle. 'But you know what? I hope that when you get up here, you fall right down and break both your arms.'

Narelle and Kirsty stuck their tongues below their lower lips in what back then was politically incorrectly called the 'retard' face and leapt up on to the monkey bars.

As Kate and Sarah turned and walked away across the oval, they heard a scream.

Something darkly miraculous had happened.

Narelle Stevenson had fallen off those monkey bars and broken both of her arms.

Kate turned to Sarah, their mouths agape and the hairs on the backs of their tween necks standing up on end.

They walked slowly over to see Narelle Stevenson lying in the scrubby grass, screaming like a banshee. Poking through the skin of her right arm was what appeared to be her ulna. Her left arm was on a strange angle.

A crowd of kids gathered around Kate and Sarah.

Kirsty Smith looked up at them. 'You did this, Kate Delaney!' she yelled.

'Kate Delaney made Narelle break both of her arms! Kate Delaney is the devil!'

'You're a *terrible* person, Kate Delaney,' said Jacinta Moore, sucking air through her teeth.

'How could you make Narelle break both of her arms? What kind of a crazy psycho are you?' said Matty Dwyer, shoving Kate. 'What's *wrong* with you, Kate Delaney?'

Kate just stood there, open-mouthed and unable to speak or to fully comprehend her clearly witchy ways.

Sarah quietly squeezed Kate's hand and cupped her hand over her ear. 'Narelle Stevenson has had it coming for years,' Sarah whispered. 'It's the universe showing her what's what.'

Narelle required surgery and some weeks off school. When she returned, she never looked at, nor bothered Kate Delaney again. They finished primary school some months later, and Narelle went off to another high school and Kate never saw her again.

But she had heard that Narelle Stevenson had, in the parlance of the time, 'gotten herself pregnant' at sixteen.

In secondary school, Kate Delaney found her tribe—the people The Guy would have called 'stupid fucking stuck-up mods'. No one teased her anymore. She grew into her gangly looks, took pride in her white skin and had a boyfriend who had his hair cut into a quiff like Morrissey. They lay in a field behind the local shopping centre together, with a Discman, holding hands, one earpiece in each of their ears, listening to Joy Division. She wasn't stuck-up. She just didn't have to care what people like The Guy, or Narelle Stevenson, or Kirsty Smith thought of her anymore.

Kirsty Smith had, as it happens, eventually come good, and by the end of Year Twelve, she and Kate reached something approaching a détente in their relationship. Not exactly friends, but not enemies either. Mutually respectful. Kate was by that time the school's star pupil. In the days before final exams, Kirsty dropped a letter into Kate's locker.

I'm so sorry for what I did to you, Kate. I think you're very impressive. I know you're going to grow up to be the most amazing person. I hope you can forgive me.

—

The Guy had not grown up to be an amazing person. He had become more and more resentful of life, and women, as he got older.

Rebuffed at all turns by the stuck-up types who were the objects of his futile affections, in order to satisfy his sexual needs, he had turned to lower hanging fruit.

And that's how, some years ago, he had come to meet Mandy King at Mount Johnson RSL.

16

MANDY

MOUNT JOHNSON RSL was a western Sydney megaclub lovingly referred to by its members and patrons as 'Mo-Joe's'.

A brutalist monolith of a building, it had a huge fountain in the entrance laced with giant fibreglass dugongs and, inside the venue, the flashing, coloured lights and monotonous trills of hundreds of poker machines. The carpet was luridly patterned in cobalt blue and aquamarine. There was a vaguely nautical theme, although the club was nowhere near the sea. It was, famously, the place where a failed political aspirant had given the most ungracious concession speech in living memory, keeping the party faithful waiting for hours as their fried morsels went cold and their beer went warm.

It was also the place that Mandy King liked to go out with The Girls when she needed a break from her kids and overbearing mother, Judy, at Acacia Hills. Mandy was quite partial to the pokies and on a Thursday night, she and her friends would go and pump some hard-earned cash into the machines and wait for the Over-28s disco to start. Then they'd dance around their handbags to 'Groove is in the Heart' and as the night wore on, get sexy to Prince's 'Cream'.

Mandy was somewhat awkwardly gyrating with her friend, faux-lesbian style, wearing a bandage dress and platformed heels, Midori Illusion shot glass in hand, when she caught The Guy's eye.

Mandy King was not the type of woman The Guy would have naturally gravitated towards. But gravitating towards the wrong women had always ended badly for him. He looked at the short girl with the lank white hair and little upturned nose, throwing back emerald-green shots, her docile brown eyes shining with intoxication, and thought that she might do.

When he sauntered over to the bored and exhausted single mum, Mandy King thought he looked pleasant enough.

'G'day, Blondie,' he said. 'Your hair is beau-ti-ful, tonight. Get it?'

Mandy blushed. 'Oh, *stop it.*'

But she liked Blondie's 'Atomic'. And she liked the way his eyes crinkled up at the sides when he laughed. She thought his nails looked well-manicured and he seemed to take pride in his appearance. He was clearly pretty cut. Mandy had replaced her dope habit with the gym, following a twelve-step program by a celebrity fitness instructor that had seen her drop a good two dress sizes. So, she appreciated that he looked after himself. He seemed friendly and he was interested. Mandy King was in.

Their union started unceremoniously, in a disabled toilet at the Mount Johnson RSL. Mandy recalled him pressing her up against some rather cold tiles. Bobbing up and down against the porcelain as he had his way with her, she silently stared at the grubby baby change table in the corner of the cubicle. She remembered being stuck at this very place years ago with her own screaming toddlers, whose toilet-training regime could have been best described as recalcitrant. It was fair to say that the image and the thought killed whatever buzz hadn't been done over by the spectacularly unromantic circumstances of their liaison. But Mandy King leaned back, tried to block out the smell of soiled nappy emanating from the large bin and thought of . . . loneliness.

It was over quite quickly, and it was not an experience Mandy could properly describe as pleasurable, and yet, nonetheless, she gave him her phone number. It was slim pickings for a single mother of three children on the other side of forty and as Judy King always said, *any port in a storm*. Mandy blamed the sexual mediocrity on the alcohol and his over-hasty desire for her. Which wasn't a bad thing, right?

—

Their meetings after that—always when Mandy's kids weren't around; she never brought men to the house—were at first pleasant enough. They went to a multiplex to see the latest action flick and shared an enormous bucket of popcorn that meant Mandy wasn't allowed any carbs the following day. They went for dinner at a local Thai and had a green curry. She went back to his place and, while far from mind-blowing, the sex was at first passable enough.

But little by little, his peccadillos became painfully apparent.

There was the time she met his 'buddies' at a bowling alley. Mandy was the only woman there and she felt conspicuous as 'the boys' threw back Coronas and needled her about her new relationship. The boys were the sort of men who didn't respect the intimacy of their friends' bedrooms and, from what she could glean, The Guy was the type to deliver his buddies the graphic detail of his conquests.

'You two doing it up the arse?' one of them asked Mandy. Mandy was shocked—she didn't think anyone had ever discussed such a thing in her presence before. And it was certainly something she would never talk about with anyone.

'No!' She blushed crimson.

The boys laughed maniacally as if she was a deluded fool, like it was the funniest thing they had ever heard.

'What, he hasn't even given it a nudge?' another said.

'No,' Mandy lied.

'Well, that is a surprise to me because Big Boy over here is what's known as a *real anal sex bandit*,' one of the buddies said, laughing uncontrollably.

The Guy rolled his eyes good-naturedly, like they were saying he was overly fond of motor sports, or pizza, or re-runs of *Hogan's Heroes*.

A real anal sex bandit. The thought made Mandy feel queasy.

Mandy had low self-esteem, but she soon tired of The Guy and his rougher predilections.

The painful accuracy of The Guy's friends' assessment of his sexual preferences had finally fully dawned on Mandy King when he took her to Pheasants Nest.

—

The Guy had started working as a roads inspector a couple of summers earlier. He was required to go to the Pheasants Nest Bridge and others in the area to ensure that maintenance was up to scratch.

The Pheasants Nest Bridge was actually two box girder bridges, constructed side by side in 1980 across the rocky Nepean River. As you crossed the bridge, it seemed like a fairly simple roadway. But underneath it was actually a three-hundred-metre stretch of tunnel. Before the two boys had, in 1990, climbed into and walked along the tunnel and fallen to their deaths inside the concrete pylons, the entrance to the tunnel had been open. But now, to prevent another tragedy like that, the entrance had been caged in.

The Guy had all the codes to the cage and also knew how the security system worked. But he sometimes just liked to go and hang out under the Pheasants Nest Bridge and pull cones. He said he found it relaxing.

Mandy thought this a bit odd when he brought her there, because the sound of the traffic thundering across the bridge above brought to mind an aircraft terminal. Maybe he had been one of those babies who was soothed to sleep, like her second youngest, by white noise.

She was actually a little annoyed when he said they were going to a place that was special to him and then pulled up at a bridge in the middle of nowhere and walked her underneath. She thought he might be bringing her to a fancy restaurant, or a picturesque lookout. The landscape here was scrubby and rocky. The bridge was stained and graffitied. It was freezing cold even though it was the middle of summer. It was, frankly, creepy. And even if it hadn't been, it was the sort of place you would hang out when you were a teenager. Mandy King was a (now) responsible mother of three kids. She didn't want to loiter under bridges and smoke bongs.

Her girl hackles had been starting to rise for some time now about The Guy and this was the tipping point. But she continued to go along with things she didn't quite feel comfortable with, as women often do with insistent, pushy men like him. She didn't immediately tell him to rack off, as she wanted to, when they pulled up in the long grass on the side of the road by the bridge. She didn't tell him to grow up when he suggested pulling a few cones, even. She actually did pull one cone and it had been so long that she coughed and spluttered like an amateur (Mandy had once been the sort of girl who could manage a bucket bong with some aplomb). She felt nauseous and giddy all at once as the THC flooded into her bloodstream and up to her cerebral cortex.

'I think it's about time we did what I know you want, Mandy babe,' The Guy said to her.

He then pushed her, a bit too roughly, face down on to the ground and started doing things to her she didn't like. *A real anal sex bandit*, Mandy King thought, as he began to hurt her.

'It's alright, Mandy babe, it's alright. Don't tense up.'

In that moment, Mandy pulled all of her strength together, bit his pinkie hard, threw him off her and said in a very loud voice, 'No. No. No. No. No. Don't call me babe. Bloody *no*!'

Mandy was quietly proud of herself. It was the most assertive she had been in years. She wished she had the same courage with her demanding mother.

The Guy looked at her in alarm. 'What the fuck's wrong with you?'

'I don't want to do that,' Mandy said. 'I don't want to do that. Not with you and especially not here. I'm too old to be treated like shit anymore. Take me home, please. I don't want to be treated like shit, by anyone, anymore.'

'I was just trying to give you a good time, babe,' he sulked.

'No, you weren't. You were just doing what *you* want. *I* don't want it. I could be *anyone*. I'm walking to the car now. And you're taking me home. And if you don't, I'll hitchhike. Or, better still, I'll— I'll call the cops. And you're never taking me here again. I deserve to go to a bloody nice restaurant in the city. I'm not doing anal under a bloody bridge!'

'Fuck's sake,' The Guy muttered under his breath. 'Alright then, let's get you home, little lady.'

She got into the passenger seat and ignored him as he silently pressed his lips together in a white angry line all the way to Acacia Hills.

Mandy looked out the window and quietly sang JoyChurch's latest Christian pop hit, 'Sweet Jesus, I Thank Thee'. The Guy rolled his eyes and pressed his lips even harder together.

Happy clapper. Shouldn't have gone there in the first place, he thought, chewing his gum vigorously. *They're all mad.*

'When everything else in my world is pain,' Mandy trilled in the saccharine, faux-American accent the JoyChurch band's singers adopted for all their vocals. 'When you come, oh Lord, to save me again, Sweet Jesus, I thank thee.'

She stared defiantly out the window at the bushland.

—

The Guy stopped calling Mandy King after that day at Pheasants Nest. And Mandy King figured that she'd had a lucky break. She threw herself into JoyChurch, hoped she'd meet someone through service and tried to forget she'd ever had anything to do with The Guy.

Mandy's rejection had hit The Guy hard. Not because he was that into her, per se, but, in truth, because he wasn't. Even someone like her—a forgettable churchy type from Acacia Hills—didn't want him. Or at least, wouldn't acquiesce to his desires. It made him angry. The anger percolated. He viciously raped a stripper who was giving him a private lap dance, whose bolshiness, like Mandy's, he sorely underestimated. She went to the cops. And that's how he lost his job as a roads inspector and wound up in gaol. He hasn't been to Pheasants Nest since.

17

THE CODES

AS THE BUZZ begins to wear off and he rolls off his log under the stars, The Guy's agitation returns.

He just doesn't want to actively kill the redhead. He can't bring himself to take the physical action of ending a life. He couldn't draw a pistol, or plunge a knife into a chest, or place a pillow over a head. He couldn't watch a life ebb away from someone in front of him. The thought of that happening by his hand makes him feel nauseous.

But if he just leaves her somewhere, and she dies as a consequence, that, he supposes, is another matter. Somehow, he thinks, that makes him feel less culpable. Less seen.

In his moral hierarchy, this is a more palatable solution. Her gradual, unseen expiration wouldn't cause him great anguish. Out of sight, out of mind, he supposes. And, in the unlikely event that someone eventually finds her, well, good for her, then. He'll be well out of the picture. He isn't given to over-analysis of life's ethical questions, nor indeed of the realities of the criminal justice system and his rather jaw-dropping evidence trail. He is much more worried about being caught right now.

That's why he needs to get his wits about him and act quickly.

Pheasants Nest.

The Guy knows from his time as a roads inspector that while the cage sitting at the entrance to the tunnel under the bridge's roadway looks high-security, it's more for show.

Yes, the entire area is caged in, with a locked gate. Yes, the cage is topped with nasty metal spikes that prevent anyone crawling over. Yes, there are signs everywhere warning that the area is under twenty-four-hour surveillance. And yes, you need to know the codes to enter into the keypad at the gate to get in.

But if you do know the codes, and you aren't identifiable, the area is not genuinely under surveillance.

Or at least, it wasn't when he worked there. That is, no one was watching the cameras. The CCTV monitors were in a large room and were rarely actually physically supervised. They were basically there in case there was an 'incident', so Roads could go back and investigate what had taken place. But there had never been an 'incident' since the cages had been installed. In normal circumstances, the vision cards were erased at the end of every fortnight, without a soul having looked at a single frame of the CCTV.

The Guy still has the numerical code—knows there are many others who will have it, too—and he is willing to bet good money that the pen-pushers at Roads haven't changed it since he left five years ago. He was there long enough to observe that the wheels of change turn achingly slowly in bureaucracy, with an attitude of if-it-ain't-broke-don't-fix-it.

The Guy is a simple man, but he is wily.

He just has to find a way to disguise himself and he should be good.

He walks over to the Echo and ponders for a moment. He can't risk, at this late stage, going to a service station or convenience store that will likely have video surveillance to buy a beanie that can be made into a balaclava. He can't turn up to a friend's place with her in the back of the car. She's spirited.

'Okay, Blue, stockings off,' he barks at a startled Kate.

'Why stockings off?' she says. 'It's bloody freezing. Come on, mate, please don't make me take them off.'

'Sorry, love, but there's nothing else for it. They need to come off. Chop-chop. If you don't do it, I will. And I don't think you'll like that, from our previous experience.'

He grins sunnily like he's some sort of amiable jokester. The grin fixes on her, in that way he has, for a few beats too long and a wave of panic comes over Kate as she contemplates another act of violence, maybe the last act of violence. Maybe the end of her.

Meanwhile, she tries to keep some semblance of cool. She mutters under her breath and slowly peels the black opaques off her legs. The nylon catches on the dried blood and Kate winces as it rips off part of a scab. She looks down at her legs, starting to get fuzzy and unshaven. She feels so, so humiliated and so cold. Her teeth feel furry from not being brushed. Her hair is tangled and matted. She glances at her face in the rear-view mirror and sees that what is left of her mascara has smudged terribly under her lower lashes. She's so pale and looks a bit like a panda.

She watches as The Guy pulls out a pair of nail scissors and starts hacking into the tights. He gets frustrated with the latex gloves he's been wearing since they got to Wombat Hollow and throws them on the ground. What's he doing?

'Ta-da!' he says, beaming.

She looks up and he's got her stockings over his head, with two holes cut out for eyes, and a slit for his mouth, like he's in some sort of stick-em-up flick from the 1970s.

'Whaddya think, Blue?'

She groans.

What, so you're planning on robbing a bank now after raping me? Cool, cool, you do you, she says, all sassy retort in her mind. If she was being played in the movie of her life, the role would go to some sort of tough broad like Lauren Bacall or Katharine Hepburn. Of course, in the real world, in the Southern Highlands, in this stupid car with this stupid man, she doesn't say any of that. She doesn't say any of it, because she's really, really scared.

—

She thinks again about all the criminal court cases she's sat through. Many of the crims were just as thick as The Guy. Being stupid wasn't any sort of guarantee that someone was harmless. Quite the opposite. Kate Delaney is still psychologically scarred from covering the crimes that stupid people who had seemed relatively benign had committed. Like John Dooley, she has always scoffed when someone is written off as 'just a nutter'. A lot of people—let's face it, a lot of women and children—have lost their lives in gruesome ways because of stupid, mad men.

In her mind is a roll call of all the dead people she's heard evidence about, all the crime-scene photos she's peered at over the shoulder of a Crown prosecutor in court, all the unspeakable, unspeakable things that guys like The Guy have done. Run-over women, babies drowned in baths, toddlers attacked with staple guns for sick kicks. Black eyes, purple abdomens, brains spattered on pavements, knives plunged into chests, bodies found in attics, bodies thrown under trains. Life carelessly ended for no good reason. *Dumb Ways to Die,* went the oddly cheerful rail safety ad jingle. It resonates with Kate Delaney. *So many dumb ways to die.* So many dumb guys.

The Guy has already done something to her that she fears she will never shake off. She doesn't want a dumb way to die. She wants to kiss Liam. She wants to hug Sylvia. Hell, she wants to do more amazing stories and win more awards and buy more frocks and drink more champagne and swim in the ocean and laugh at films and cry at films and make eyes at Liam Carroll in the Reading Room of the State Library and live her messy, funny, full life.

So, she doesn't sass or retort like Katharine Hepburn or Lauren Bacall. She smiles weakly and hopes that this moron won't kill her. And she feels afraid. Kate Delaney feels very, very afraid.

'We're going to one of my favourite places,' The Guy says suddenly, his voice muffled by the stockings. 'You're gonna love it.'

18

TEXTS

LIAM CARROLL AND Sylvia Estrellita have been on the road for several hours and are on their way to meet Peter D'Ambrosio. Sylvia is still driving because, frankly, she wouldn't trust Liam at the wheel at this point.

Liam has stopped talking. His head is pressed against the window, looking up at the telegraph wires. He remembers that as a little kid he would count the beats between the poles. Thirteen beats, pole to pole. *One, two, three, four, five, six, seven, eight, nine, ten, eleven, twelve, thirteen*. And again.

They're finally over the border and the landscape opens up like a promise. He loves this stretch of road between Albury and Gundagai. Undulating hills carpeted with what looks like gold velveteen, studded with granite and thistles. Glossy, jet-black cows, grey sheep, so still they look like they're made of stone and the hills are a cemetery.

The Paterson's curse has come out early, and there are large sections of almost startling purple. He knows it's a noxious weed but gosh, en masse, it's pretty.

After they drive for another hour or so, Sylvia sees Liam's spirits seem to have lifted. She's lonely and bored and stressed and desperate for conversation.

'What's your favourite funny place name on the Hume?' she says.

'Hmm,' he ponders. 'I guess it's a toss-up between Dookie and Wee Jasper.'

'Wee Jasper is definitely a winner,' Sylvia says. 'I'm also a big fan of Yass.'

'Yass? Why Yass?'

'Well, every time I see it, I just think, *Yaassss, Kween*,' she says, snickering. 'And then of course there was that time when they put up that billboard that said, "My Yass".' She turns to him and mouths, 'MY ASS.'

'I will never think of Yass in the same way again,' he agrees, laughing despite himself.

When they finally do get to Yass (Kween), they need to fill up the tank and get some snacks. The filling station looks out across the valley. The light is beginning to fade. On the horizon is a strip of light and, above that, the darkest grey clouds. The golden sepia light has gone, and the entire landscape has taken on the moody tones of a dusky Turner painting. It's freezing cold.

As they stand in the carpark, mechanically eating boxed sandwiches, which taste like the cardboard they're packaged in, a woman in a sundress with a huge armful of fried chicken packages bumps into Sylvia and swears at her. 'Outta my way, stupid gook,' the woman says, looking at Sylvia like she's a foreigner. Sylvia knows what's going on.

'Planning on eating all of that yourself?' Sylvia says, in her broadest Australian accent. 'Maybe it's just me, but it gives me horrible indigestion. Also, it's freezing, love. You may want to consider throwing a cardi over that frock. They do hide a multitude of sins.'

The woman colours and walks off, muttering to herself.

'Sorry you have to put up with that shit, Sylvia,' Liam says. 'Also, the Academy Award for unscripted sass in a filling station carpark goes to . . . Sylvia Estrellita.' He feigns the sound of crowds cheering in the distance.

'You can't help stupid.' Sylvia shrugs.

In the distance, over the hills, thunder sounds. All the colour has leached out of the landscape, and it seems like it's painted in black and white.

They both go silent for a while.

'I don't feel very positive, Chicken,' Sylvia says.

'Me neither, Sylvia. And by the way, it's Liam. But me neither.'

They get back in the car.

—

After a time, the scenery changes again. The road feels almost claustrophobic, hugged by an endless green canopy that stretches out on either side. Liam wonders what colour Kate would call it. Kate is obsessed with correctly naming colours. It's never dark grey—it's battleship. Not aqua, but duck egg blue. Not dark pink, but fuchsia. Is this forest green or hunter green or moss? She'd know.

His mouth is agape and his mind wanders. He suspects he is drooling a bit and is almost past caring. He wonders what is happening in the bushland below. And why, every time a sign says wombats for the next ten kilometres ('Kids! Keep your eyes peeled for wombats!' his mum would always say), he never sees a goddammed wombat, no matter how peeled his eyes are. Instead, the only wombats he ever sees on the Hume are mangled on the side of the road. Wombats collected by B-doubles and buffeted to their untimely deaths, along with the kangaroos, the possums, the echidnas and the odd fox. *Wombat Stew*, he thinks to himself, darkly, remembering the much-loved children's book he'd always (controversially) found boring.

He's never had the misfortune of hitting a wombat or a roo. He can't imagine the damage a fat wombat would do to his small European car. Wombats look heavy. Dense. Safe to say that Liam Carroll has never had cause for a protective roo bar on his car. He's the opposite of a roo bar kind of guy.

Is Kate somewhere out there? Is she in the bush? Kate would hate that. The snakes. Even the very thought of the potential for snakes has always been enough to keep Kate Delaney largely away from places like this. Along with the cold. Her hatred of polar fleece and hiking boots and trail mix and what she calls 'geography-teacher clothing'. Her inappropriate footwear.

He tries to remember exactly what she was wearing when she disappeared, but can't. He knows she wasn't dressed for traipsing through dense forest like this, though. She was definitely wearing high-heeled boots. The thought of her in those knee-high boots stirs a brief moment of sexual longing in him. He puts his jacket over his lap just in case, mentally dying at the thought of Sylvia noticing his inappropriate arousal.

Kate got those knee-high boots after inquiring if he had a thing for them. Yes, he quickly confirmed. He had a thing.

'Pegged you as the type,' she replied, with a sweet little coquettish smile. They were in a tiny, expensive-looking shop in Flinders

Lane, where the items for sale were placed sparingly, on plinths, like sculptures. The sales assistant confirmed that it was only right and proper that the boots be hers. Liam quickly dug out his wallet and forked out what seemed, to a bloke, an eye-watering amount of money for a pair of footwear. But they were worth it. She once danced for him in only the knee-high boots and her underwear. It nearly blew his mind.

He had been depressed, that day, and she'd been struggling with the dark story she was covering at the time. It had been early in their courtship.

'I hope you don't think I just see you as sexual Valium,' she had said as they lay in bed together, propping her head up on her elbow and turning to kiss him.

He had laughed. 'No, I don't think that,' he said, kissing her back. 'But I'd be fine with it even if you did.'

Sylvia has no idea that Liam is fantasising about his missing girlfriend's long legs in her knee-high boots. She is trying to cheerfully ignore the fact that he appears to be intermittently losing his mind.

She has been screening calls.

As they pull over for a toilet break, Sylvia looks at her phone to see that Gloria has texted twenty-seven times, asking if they've found Kate yet, and telling Sylvia not to forget to eat, failing to see the irony of instructing her not to look at her phone while she's driving.

Sylvia and Kate's editor at the newspaper, Cameron Patrick, has texted well-wishes and awkwardly executed hug emojis. But Sylvia just knows he wants her to file a moving first-person piece on what it's like for your best friend to go missing.

Cameron texts.

Hey Sylvia, just checking in.
This must be such a terrible time for you. I don't want to be gauche, but make sure you're writing everything down.

Cameron. This is not the time. She's my best friend. We're beside ourselves. And anyway, I write about fashion.

Sorry, Sylvia. But you have a beautiful turn of phrase. We're all struggling. Give my best to Liam.

Cameron Patrick is what is euphemistically known as an ebullient character, and more honestly referred to as a pants man. He has made his way through half of the women in the newsroom. The notable exceptions are Sylvia, Kate and anyone else aged over thirty-five. He is diminutive and swarthy, and has black, thick, angular designer eyeglasses in the style favoured by arts administrators. He has a classic short man complex.

Kate is about a head taller than him and didn't take kindly to it when, at her first Walkley Awards night when she was very young, he spontaneously approached her on the dancefloor, put his hands around her waist and held her aloft above his head. When she landed back down, Kate, who was wearing towering silver wedges that night, stood as close as she could to Cameron Patrick, and peered down her nose at him. 'Don't ever fucking do that again,' she said. He didn't.

As for Sylvia, she figures she's probably too quirky for his tastes. Cameron wouldn't dig tan boiler suits or gold cowboy boots.

Despite his expensive tastes, Cameron likes to sell himself to the world as a man of the people. He's a broadsheet editor, but he has driven the paper in a direction that is far more racy and tabloid—much to the chagrin of some of its more rusted-on AB-demographic subscribers who buy it for the ballet write-ups and quality coverage of Indigenous affairs.

He publicly pretends he's an anti-intellectual, a man of the people, but he privately has a penchant for pretentious literature and films. His calling card with his often much younger conquests has always been getting them to watch Woody Allen's *Manhattan* in bed. Between the sheets, he is famous for reciting Italian love poetry in a terribly affected accent.

Sophie Jeffreys mimicked it for Sylvia and Kate once, her head in her hands, it was so embarrassingly awful.

Con la tua viva fiamma, con le tue bracce rossi,

Fuoco della mia casa,

Tanto tanto mi piace.

'Christ on a bike,' Kate whistled. 'You took one for the team going there.'

'Never, ever again,' Sophie said. 'I cannot tell you how much of a dud root Camo is.'

'La, la, la, la, la,' said Sylvia covering her ears. 'I do not want to hear the words "Camo" and "root" in the same sentence. In fact, I do not want to hear the word "root" in any context, ever again. This isn't *Puberty Blues*, Sophie. We have standards around here.'

'Well, the record would show, dear Sylvia,' Kate chimed in, 'that young Sophie here does not, in fact, have standards, or she would not have been reciting an Italian poem about a fire, first conveyed to her by a swarthy editor of short stature with a penchant for female cadets.'

It has always amazed Kate how men who are clearly so sexually inept could still manage to make their way through a relatively small pool of women without word getting around that going there was a waste of time. Time that could be better spent at home painting one's toenails, applying face masks and watching bad reality television.

Cameron Patrick pretends to be splashy and confident but is actually deeply insecure and has a drinking problem that is notorious across the Melbourne media. At one Christmas party at the publisher's swanky apartment, he spent the latter part of the night snoring and paralytic under a glass coffee table covered with empty champagne bottles and ashtrays.

'Camo's a monster,' everyone sighed, stepping over his splayed legs to get another drink. 'Can't be helped.'

Kate once told Sylvia of another night at the local pub where Cameron brought one of their young colleagues into the toilet. He could be heard having his way with her from halfway to the bar.

When he emerged a few paces behind the young woman, her fixing her skirt, him wiping his brow, Kate and her friends rolled their eyes and said, 'You're incorrigible, Camo.'

Camo just smirked and said, 'What?'

Most of this took place years before #MeToo, and that was probably lucky for Cameron Patrick, as his standards in relation to workplace power dynamics and sex were antiquated at absolute best. Which is not to say that anyone had ever accused him of anything rabidly non-consensual. But a workplace investigator would, in more enlightened times, have had a field day with him.

There is still, in fact, something of a mutually assured destruction on that front between his newspaper and the city's tabloid, which has a disgustingly avuncular sex pest on staff who has terrorised women in the industry for years.

The broadsheet spiked a story about the tabloid sex pest when the tabloid's editor had had a quiet word to Camo about a story they were considering on his own exploits. The sex pest was left free to potentially pester some more. Thankfully, the very real risk that another media outlet with no concerns about mutually assured destruction might someday run the story put the fear of God into him. From that time on, he has reluctantly played nice.

—

Cameron Patrick, who prides himself on having the mobile phone number of every single person of any note in Melbourne, is also texting Liam.

> Anything, anything we can do for you mate,
> you just sing out.

'You know, your industry makes me kind of sick,' Liam says to Sylvia, when they get back into the car. His first complete sentence to her in a couple of hours.

She's relieved to hear him mouth actual words.

'We're not all bad, kiddo. What about me? Your knowledge of *farshun* would be horribly lacking without my insights.'

'Yes,' says Liam, looking down at his crumpled shirt and his ratty jeans. 'It's clearly having an effect.'

'I could do wonders with you,' Sylvia says. 'Those *Queer Eye for the Straight Guy* dudes ain't got nothin' on Sylvia Estrellita. But it would take work. And investment. Farshun don't come cheap. Anyway, what about Kate? Earnest, Walkley-Award-winning, credit to her profession, super gorgeous Kate?'

She starts choking as she says it. And Liam starts choking. Then both of them start crying.

'I think we're here at the cop shop,' Sylvia says, spittle flying on the windscreen. 'Peter D'Ambrosio, that's the bloke's name, right? Come on, Chicken, let's get our shit together. It's going to be alright.' She blows her red nose messily into a tissue. 'Let's go.'

Not noticing that she has again called him Chicken, Liam is now in that crying space where you can't make your way out. Like when you are a little kid, and you fall over and hurt your knee quite badly, and as you pick the asphalt out of your graze and head to your mother for some Mercurochrome, it's an excuse to let it all out and cry about every single sadness or misfortune that has ever befallen your young life. Your fights with your brother, your bad grades, seeing pictures of skinny kids your age dying in the famine in Africa, reading *The Diary of Anne Frank*. Liam cries for every single thing in a way that he hasn't cried in years. He has so much to cry for, so much he hasn't let out. But most of all he cries for Kate.

He thumbs a text to Cameron Patrick.

There is nothing you can do for me, thanks, all the same, Cameron. Unless you know where Kate is.

Cameron Patrick sends him a sad face emoji and Liam Carroll wipes his eyes, snaps the cover of his phone shut and puts it in his pocket.

'Let's go and meet this D'Ambrosio fellow,' he says to Sylvia.

'Deal,' says Sylvia, trying to pump his fist, but missing and clocking him on the jaw.

19

LUCKY

THE POLICE STATION is a low building the colour of clay. It's surrounded by what Kate calls 'service-station plants'—agapanthus and wild iris and boring native grasses. The barred windows are tinted so you can't see inside. Not that there's much to see. The light is that sort of awful fluorescent that makes even the most attractive person look like a ghoul. On a corkboard are pamphlets for language translators and missing persons lists.

Missing persons lists, Liam thinks, remembering those American kids on milk cartons in the eighties that had so disturbed him as a kid on a family holiday to Honolulu. *How the fuck is Kate on someone's missing persons list?*

Puffy-eyed and red-nosed, Liam is embarrassed as he enters the police station because, as much as the moment technically calls for high emotion, he is a man, after all. And as he once sang into his teenage mirror, in his most self-flagellating and tortured private moments, 'Boys Don't Cry'.

Kate sang that song beautifully. Sometimes he would quietly listen to her as they were driving along in the car. He would always tell her she had a lovely voice. Although Liam thought she could do almost anything. That made her laugh and call him a complete dag. She would remind him of all the things she did terribly. Like maths and camping and cross-country running and chess and reporting on finance.

He never told Kate that the song reminded him of his mum and that he had been crying into his teenage mirror for Pauline Carroll after she'd died young, of a sudden heart attack when Liam was seventeen. Like Kate, Pauline had red hair, although she cut it short like Lady Di. The night she died, they'd all gone to bed and Liam's Dad, Johnny, had been out with his mates and had had a few. At seven am, the phone had started ringing; this was back in the days when the phone was on a curling cord in a hallway.

'Ah, for God's sake, Pauline, would you not get that phone?' Johnny had mumbled, nudging her.

But Pauline hadn't answered and hadn't moved.

'Pauline!' Johnny had said again. But again, no answer. Johnny took the pillow off his head and turned around in the bed to see his wife staring motionless and open-mouthed at the ceiling.

Seconds later, Liam and his brother and sister heard a blood-curdling scream from their father, a sound they had never heard before nor since. The three kids came running into their parents' bedroom to find Johnny crouched over Pauline, trying to give her mouth to mouth and in between breaths yelling to Liam, the eldest, to call an ambulance.

But the ambulance was too late. Everything was too late. Pauline had been dead for hours. An autopsy later showed that she'd had undiagnosed heart disease for some time. She was forty-three.

'Teddy times.' They were the last words she'd said to Liam the night before, still using the phrase she'd used to indicate bedtime since he was tiny. 'Come on, Liam, you've got school in the morning. Teddy times.'

'Mum, you really have to stop calling it "teddy times",' Liam had said, good-naturedly scolding her. 'I'm seventeen, you know. I'm not a baby.' And before she could say anything else, he'd said, 'Yes, I know, seventeen, *but still your first baby.*'

'Night, Mum.'

He'd kissed her on the forehead, and she'd squeezed his hand and winked at him. And she'd never done it again.

Everything is pain.

He hadn't told Kate that he had promised himself never to be hurt again, and to keep his emotions in an orderly, colour-coded drawer in his head. From time to time, they had spilled over into the anxiety Kate had witnessed, but didn't yet quite comprehend, and that she had messily mopped up with kisses and sex.

He never told her that he had thrown away his school essay about Tom Stoppard, abandoned any idea of *knowing and being known*, and promised his adolescent self not to love, because to love might mean having to lose. So, for all his adult life, he had pulled away from deeper emotional connections, fleeing from relationships, blanching at commitment and baffling the perfectly suitable women who should have made him happy, making them think that there must be something wrong with them. *He's just not that into you,* their self-help books and girlfriends told them. *He's not worth it.* But it wasn't them, as the cliché went, it was him. *It's not you, it's me.* He couldn't even allow himself to open the door that might allow him to be into them. That might risk pain.

That is why this nice guy, this handsome lawyer with the shock of almost black hair who is outwardly two parts sweet-bashful and one part smart-steely, this man who is loveably flawed in a way that would tick a lot of women's boxes, has found himself single long after he should have settled down.

That was until he met Kate Delaney and couldn't keep it all locked away anymore. Kate Delaney taught him to feel again. And to perhaps start allowing himself not to worry about feeling again.

And that is why, now, he can't stop weeping, like a little boy in one of those old-fashioned chocolate box illustrations with curled eyelashes and a rosebud mouth.

As the silver creeps into his temple and his stubble, and the unavoidable thickening and slowing down of approaching middle age has its way with him, Liam Carroll has opened his heart to love for the first time since he was seventeen. He has allowed himself not to be scared. He knows he loves her. He knows she loves him. They just haven't said it yet.

And now someone has taken her away from him.

He realises when he claps eyes on Peter D'Ambrosio that he needn't have worried on the crying front.

D'Ambrosio has doleful blue eyes that seem permanently on the verge of tears. He blinks an awful lot. And then he stares a bit. Then he starts blinking again. Liam momentarily wonders what it's about, but on reflection, he's seen it before, in clients who have been put through the mill and have complex post-traumatic stress disorder. This guy's a cop and he must have seen some truly awful things.

'Nice to meet you,' Liam says, as they walk into a small room with concrete yellow walls and horrible downlights. 'Sorry, I just had a moment out there.'

'Totally understandable, my friend,' Peter says, resting his hand on Liam's shoulder. 'Totally understandable.'

D'Ambrosio doesn't speak like the cops that Liam has known. Cops don't call you 'my friend' in that gentle way this man has. He has a much softer voice than Dooley and speaks at times in a halting manner, his voice catching before he gets the end of the sentence out. He gives the immediate impression of being a very nice man.

'You didn't need to come up here, you know,' D'Ambrosio says to him. 'You're going to need to reserve your energy and you might have been better staying home where you can get a decent night's sleep.'

Liam lets out a bitter little cough of a laugh. 'Sleep? I don't think so,' he says. 'How am I supposed to sleep?'

D'Ambrosio nods sympathetically, gesturing to him to continue.

'I just couldn't bear to be in Melbourne when she's somewhere up here. I needed to be closer to her. I need to be close to her. I need to be with her. I need her.'

Sylvia starts crying again. 'I need her, too,' she says. 'Not in the biblical sense, but I need her.'

Liam shoots her a look.

'It's okay, guys,' D'Ambrosio says, 'We're doing absolutely everything we can to find her. I'm sure she needs you, too.'

He pushes some tissues across the Laminex table.

And then he pulls on a pair of gloves and slides across a plastic evidence bag. In it is a familiarly tacky mobile phone cover studded with faux diamonds and rubies that Kate picked up at a shopping mall in a moment of high irony.

'Tiger!' gasps Sylvia.

'Well, her phone—if by Tiger you mean Kate,' D'Ambrosio says. 'Now I caution you, don't touch it, because it's evidence.

'I know we haven't found your girlfriend yet, my friend,' he continues, turning to Liam, 'but I wanted to show you this to perhaps give you some confidence in New South Wales Police.'

Liam is one part grateful that D'Ambrosio has shown him the phone and one part curious about whether it is entirely professional of him to have done so. He also wonders, for a moment, whether D'Ambrosio is testing him in some way. He knows the cops can't have fully ruled out the possibility that he knows something about Kate's disappearance, even though he doesn't. And that there could still be an operational shadow of suspicion over him. He tries to maintain his neutral court face, even though he feels absolutely wretched.

'That thing might be glitzy, and to be honest, it was a bonus that it is,' D'Ambrosio continues, 'because something like that is a needle in a haystack in thick state forest like we've got all around here. I want you to see this as a symbol of our commitment to finding your girl. That was some pretty forensic policing, finding that phone.'

—

As it happens, it had been more good fortune than forensic policing. In the dying hours of the previous day, the faux ruby and diamond case had caught the sun's rays at the right angle and, as the police chopper flew over the bush, it kept catching the reddish and silver flare from below.

'What's that?' one of the Air Wing cops had said. 'Down there, what's that glowing thing?'

The chopper flew back and forth over the spot with the flare-like object flashing every time the sun glanced on it.

'I'm going down,' the cop said.

The helicopter slowly made its way down towards the valley below and the Air Wing guy winched himself onto the ground. As he scrambled onto the forest floor, there it was. Glinting in the afternoon sun was the phone cover with its diamante background, and spelled out in imitation ruby capital letters, the word LUCKY.

'I had bad feelings earlier today, but for some reason that's changed, my friend,' D'Ambrosio says to Liam. 'Now I think she's lucky.'

Liam glances up at D'Ambrosio to see that the detective looks ever so misty-eyed again. This cop really does seem to have PTSD.

'Kate's always been lucky—she wins the Melbourne Cup sweep almost every year,' Liam says, trying not to lose his composure again.

He sits for a moment, gazing at the glittering phone in the evidence bag, and then snaps out of the reverie and into plaintiff-lawyer-who-occasionally-likes-to-scare-the-shit-out-of-junior-opponent mode.

He's been seduced by D'Ambrosio's sad eyes.

'Detective Sergeant D'Ambrosio, that's clearly some really first-rate policing that you've found Kate's phone in thick forest like that,' Liam begins, 'And please do pass on to your Air Wing colleagues my huge praise and gratitude.

'But you see, the phone is not the girl. The phone is not Kate. What's happening on the Kate front?'

'Well, many, many lines of inquiry, Liam,' D'Ambrosio says. 'But . . . and I'm going to be honest with you here because I know you're a smart guy . . . unfortunately, they're moving a little bit slower than Operation Finding The Phone.

'For instance, we've dusted the phone for fingerprints, but because of the matter of the, erm, diamantes on the case, it's very hard to catch anything. The rough surface, you know. We did check on the inside, but only Kate's fingerprints were on it.'

Kate had been arrested once at a student protest when she was at university, and some over-enthusiastic constable had taken her prints to put the fear of God into her. In a shocking development, Kate had given the young officer a piece of her mind and he had rewarded her by keeping her in the lockup overnight.

Still, her hot-headed university days had now provided a blessing in the form of fingerprints that they could rule in or out as hers on any surface that may have been touched. Unfortunately, on the glass screen, only Kate's had been found.

The phone's tracking device only told them what they already knew: that she had been out bar-hopping with her friends in Northcote, that she had wound up in a laneway, that she had been driven up the Hume Highway, and that her phone had been tossed out the window in the Southern Highlands.

'What about the Airbnb?' Liam asks. 'Were there any prints there? Do you have any more information about that?'

'Well, no to the prints—we've determined that the kidnapper must have been wearing gloves because there isn't a single print on objects they've obviously touched, but yes to more information, as a matter of fact.'

Liam gulps. His mouth feels so dry. He pours himself a glass of water.

'Because we don't think it's Kate's blood that we found there,' D'Ambrosio continues.

'What do you mean?' Liam asks. 'I didn't know you found blood! All you spoke about were "items of significance".'

'Well, yes, we don't like to give away too much, but Kate's hospital records show that her blood type is O positive. The initial testing on the blood at the scene does not appear to show that it's O positive. So, what we're trying to do now, is get a DNA match on the blood that was there. It's tricky because it's a fine spray, on furniture.

'But we're wondering now if maybe the kidnapper injured themselves at the scene in some way, and if that's how the blood got everywhere. Or maybe Kate did something to them, trying to get away. Who knows? It was a bit of a mess at the scene.'

'Not Kate's blood,' Liam says, pressing his lips together.

'Most likely not Kate's blood,' D'Ambrosio nods.

Liam wonders, again, if the detective is testing him, to see his reaction to the blood. He catches D'Ambrosio looking at his hands and his arms. He looks at them, too. No scratches, no cuts. They catch each other's eyes. Liam looks straight into D'Ambrosio's and the detective looks away.

'Anyway, what we'll need to do is cut out those sections of the sofa that the kidnapper bled on and run some tests. They will take some time to come back.'

'How much time? Surely this is crucial!' Liam says.

'Anything up to about forty-eight hours, depending on how easy it is to extract the sample,' D'Ambrosio says.

'And what happens to Kate in the meantime?'

'Well, that we don't know. I'm sorry, Liam, we're all working as fast as we can.'

He then snaps shut the folder he's had open on the desk and explains that he doesn't have a lot more to tell them at this stage, but he will fill him in as information comes to hand. He suggests that Liam and Sylvia try to get some accommodation in the area, have something to eat and get some rest.

'Just before you go, could I grab your number, too, Sylvia?' D'Ambrosio asks, looking up at her. 'Probably for the best in case I can't get on to Liam.'

'Sure,' says Sylvia, and writes it down on the block of yellow sticky notes he throws across the table.

'Great. Here's mine. If you think of anything, anything at all, don't hesitate to call. I always tell the young constables here that in policing, there's no such thing as a stupid question, and there's no such thing as too much information.' He smiles at her in a way that is somehow simultaneously calm, kind and utterly exhausted. He gives her a little pat on the hand.

'They used to tell us that in journalism school, too, Sergeant D'Ambrosio,' Sylvia replies.

'Please, call me Pete.'

'Pete. Okay,' Sylvia Estrellita says, blushing slightly. 'Pete.'

Sitting in the car outside the police station with Liam, Sylvia finds a crappy motel on a last-minute booking site that's a few minutes up the road and she calls ahead to reserve two rooms.

As she hangs up her phone, a text message flashes up from the number she's saved for the detective. *Pete.*

Are you on your own, Sylvia?

I can be. Give me five.

She tells Liam she needs to go to a chemist and pick up some secret women's business—the phrase she and Kate stole from their Indigenous friend Laura, who says it when she's talking about tampons.

She walks up the street and calls D'Ambrosio.

'Is everything okay, Sergeant . . . Pete?' she says, still feeling awkward with the first name basis.

'Sylvia, I just wanted to say if there was ever anything, anything at all that you needed to call me about, or speak to me about, you know, *on your own*, well, you know that you can call me any time of the day or night.'

She likes this guy, a bit too much for her own good given he's a cop working in the sort of place that she and Kate, who would never dream of living in the country, would have joked about as the ideal location to drown yourself in the bath. But she's also worried he has got the entirely wrong end of the stick about Liam.

'That's really sweet, um, Pete, but I just want you to know that Liam and I are in this together. He's rock-solid. Twenty-four carat. I promise you. He's a keeper. I would have found cruel and unusual ways of scaring away any boyfriend of Tiger's who wasn't. Kate's been through enough.'

'Oh, for sure, yeah,' D'Ambrosio says, 'I warm to him, too. I just wanted to give you an avenue for anything that troubles you, or worries you, or, you know, anything at all you think I need to know. You just give me a call.'

'No worries, Pete,' Sylvia says.

'No worries, Sylvia.'

—

Not too far up the Hume, one of D'Ambrosio's New South Wales Police colleagues, who is exhausted by the search, has pulled off the freeway to go in the bushes.

As the senior constable relieves himself next to a large log, his partner, who has got out of the car for some air, starts shouting.

'Jack, Jack, look!' she says.

The senior constable glances down at the ground and there in the long grass are two latex gloves.

He picks up his phone and calls Peter D'Ambrosio.

Liam Carroll and Sylvia Estrellita drive to the crappy motel, where they check in, peel into their respective rooms, and bite their nails to the quick.

20

FAMILY

MANDY KING IS sitting at home with her mother Judy, watching a rerun of *The Real Housewives of LA* on pay TV, slowly and deliberately eating a salted caramel protein ball that will tide her over till dinner time so she can skip lunch.

Ever since Michael died, Judy has not been the woman she once was. Her acrylic nails are long gone, and her real nails are cracked and stained yellow. She's letting her natural grey hair grow out and it's the colour of dirty sleet, halfway between that and the harsh dye she had before. She has quit umpiring netball and the whistle lies in the same place on the speckled kitchen bench where she put it down more than a year ago. She spends her days gazing at Mandy's television, not quite listening to the dialogue. She doesn't really care about who has 'tickets' anymore.

She doesn't like being in her house alone, so she mostly only goes in there to sleep. Mandy has had to organise a cleaner because 'Mum's just not able anymore'.

As they are sitting there, Judy slowly says to Mandy, 'Kate. Kate Delaney. I heard something about her on the wireless.'

'Mum, if you are going to be nasty about Kate, I'm not listening. What is it? She got a big story again?'

'I'm not being nasty, Mandy. I heard something about Kate on the wireless.'

'What did you hear?'

'She's missing.'

'Mum, what? Why didn't you tell me about this? Poor Kate!'

'I thought you knew, love. I thought you knew. I think it's a big story. The choppers have been up. Apparently, she was taken from Melbourne and somehow ended up coming up towards this way.'

'My godfather, Mum, I did not know! I would have talked to you about it. That is so awful. I'm turning it over to the news.'

Mandy grabs the remote and switches the television to a commercial channel. The afternoon bulletin is just about due to come on. After a couple of items, a reporter appears for a live cross, standing on the side of the Hume Highway.

'We have another development in the terrifying disappearance of high-profile Melbourne journalist Kate Delaney,' the reporter says breathlessly.

Mandy gasps. How did she not know about this? She feels like a complete idiot, and guilty, too. Since joining JoyChurch, Mandy has avoided watching the news. She tells people she likes to focus on the positives. She gets most of her news from uplifting Facebook posts and lives her life in a contented bubble. But now her contented bubble has burst, spectacularly. Kate has been missing for some days now, and she hadn't known. And despite not having seen her for a couple of years and only receiving the odd text, she loves Kate. She does.

The coiffed woman with the steely eyes on screen continues: 'After the shocking discovery in the bushland off the Hume Highway of Kate Delaney's mobile phone, police have now revealed that they have found a pair of latex gloves at a north-bound turn-off. Police say they do believe these gloves are linked to Kate's disappearance. You can see the vision here of the scene. Police have been scouring the area for more clues, but they're optimistic they may be able to extract some DNA from these gloves that they hope will assist them with their inquiries. Back to you.'

Mandy feels like she's been punched in the stomach. She starts to weep.

'Oh Mum, poor Kate,' she says.

'Poor Kate,' Judy says. 'I always liked that girl.'

Mandy raises her eyebrow. 'Mum! You said she had tickets on herself and thought she was too good for us.'

'That's right, love. I did.' Judy stares at the television and sips her instant mochaccino. 'But people change. I've changed. I was wrong. Or maybe I was partially right but judged her a bit too harsh. Life is short and precious, Mandy. Short and precious.' Judy sniffs and leans over to pick up a framed picture of Michael from the credenza.

—

Mandy is not utterly convinced that Judy has changed that much, despite grief and trauma softening her edges considerably. Knowing her mother as she does, she wagers that there is a fair measure of tragedy porn in all of this for Judy.

Before Michael's death, Judy had never loved anything more than a good drama. As soon as someone died, they were elevated to saint status. When Mrs Kitson who lived down the road used to come knocking, ostensibly seeking a cup of flour but actually seeking gossip, Judy would sniff that she was a terrible busybody. But when Mrs Kitson had a sudden heart attack in her sleep and died, Judy King got up at her wake and made an impromptu speech about how Mrs Kitson had been one of God's true angels on earth. Several sauvignon blancs later, Judy had, much to Mandy's mortification, insisted on singing a warbling rendition of Bette Midler's 'The Wind Beneath My Wings'.

But Mandy is truly horrified. What has happened to Kate? Why has this happened? She starts reading everything that she can find online, and keeps the television on all the time, waiting for the next update.

She feels sad that she can't even call Kate's mum, to pass on her love and find out more.

One night when Kate was staying at Acacia Hills, she and Mandy had had a rare bonding moment and Kate had told Mandy the whole story of her parents.

Kate was an only child, and her father Billy had died a few years before. Billy was an alcoholic. The sort of alcoholic who showed very little emotion and had very little to say when he was sober at home, but, as people always insisted on telling Kate, you got to know her daddy at the pub. 'I don't want to get to know my daddy at the pub,' Kate would say. 'I want him to be himself when he's not drunk.'

At the pub, Billy Delaney was the life and soul of the party. He was full of all the best stories. He was hilarious and gregarious and charming and fun. He was not trained as a singer, but he had a good set of pipes and at the end of the night he would often treat the gathered patrons to 'Danny Boy' or 'Dirty Old Town'.

But then Billy Delaney would inevitably have one pint too many. And when that happened, he would become angry and sarcastic and mean. He'd come home to Mary, who rarely went to the pub these days, and he'd berate her. He would slam doors and break glasses, and when Mary would try to convince him to go to bed, he'd shout about 'that stupid bleedin' woman and her airs and graces'. It was generally Mary, rather than Kate, on the receiving end of his bile, but it had scared Kate all of her young life.

Mary Delaney was streets ahead of her husband, intellectually speaking, but like so many women of her generation, had never met her promise. A librarian by training, she had taken time out of the workforce to try to get pregnant but had had a series of miscarriages. By the time Kate was born, she was emotionally and physically spent.

When Billy died of pancreatic cancer, Mary was too proud to admit that he hadn't been a good husband. She'd focus on the positive things—that he was a good provider (he was), that he adored his only daughter (in his own way, he had), that he was a very generous man (to a fault). But he had sucked the life out of her. Having always been what is referred to as a 'handsome' woman—stylishly dressed in what the fashion magazines described as 'investment pieces' in cashmere and tweed—she was thin and pale and old before her time. Her cheeks were gaunt. Her famously well-turned ankles looked like they might break in two.

Not long after Billy died, Mary Delaney was diagnosed with an aggressive form of breast cancer.

Mary told her daughter that when she died, she wanted to be cremated, but that she wanted her ashes stored in an urn and put in Billy's grave. Billy had insisted that he be buried.

But Kate Delaney did not want her mother's remains, for what they were, confined to that stupid grave for the rest of eternity with her insufferable bully of a father.

And so Kate ignored her mother's wishes.

When she received the ashes after Mary's funeral, Kate Delaney drove down the Great Ocean Road, which Mary had loved because that coast with its dry-stone walls and its emerald grasses and its angry clouds and its gunmetal sea had always reminded her of Ireland.

She stopped at Port Fairy and walked out to the Griffiths Island coastal reserve—right out to the lighthouse at the tip of the island—and she threw Mary Delaney's ashes into the sea.

'Bye-bye, Mammy. I love you,' Kate said, tears running down her face in messy little rivers.

Mary Delaney's soul would swim with the seals, not be buried with an angry alcoholic in a manky old grave at a Melbourne cemetery.

Kate walked back to Sylvia, who had been waiting, as instructed, on the walkway that led to the island.

'Mammy's free,' Kate told Sylvia. 'Mammy's free.'

They drove to a friend's winery at Killarney, poured a glass of sparkling, ordered a cheeseboard, and toasted a good woman whose life could have been so much more.

Mandy King had sat silently on her recliner as Kate recounted the story. Her brown eyes had filled, but Mandy didn't have the words to say. She loved Kate, but she found her intimidating. She sensed that her conversation often disappointed her brother's girlfriend. She just reached over and held Kate's hand and said, 'I'm sorry.'

Kate wiped away her own tears and said, somewhat brusquely, 'It's okay, it's okay. It's all in the past, isn't it? All in the fucking past, hey, Mandy?'

—

How awful it would have been, Mandy King thinks, for a mother to go through her daughter disappearing in these horrendous circumstances. Maybe it's for the best.

Mandy hops in her car and heads over to JoyChurch. She pulls up at the big warehouse-style building that houses the congregation. ('My gosh, it's a bit of a barn, isn't it?' she remembers Kate saying when she had brought her there to show it off. 'Well, yes,' Mandy had replied. 'That's because JoyChurch is so popular. I'm pretty sure seating capacity is ten thousand.' She remembers Kate's eyes narrowing ever so slightly, in the way they did when Judy and Mandy insisted on doing the Nutbush City Limits dance on the lounge-room tiles when they were several glasses of vino down.)

Mandy presses the doorbell that's there for when church is not open for normal service. After a couple of minutes, Shayna Van der Linden comes bouncing down to the door, wearing fluoro active wear. Her cheeks are flushed, her pupils are dilated beneath her false eyelashes, and her hair is all mussed up. Mandy recalls that Jamie Van der Linden is away on a JoyChurch Mission for Jesus at a school for underprivileged kids in Thailand.

'Oh, Mandy, dear girl, what's up?' Shayna says. Shayna has always been good with names, despite the fact that there are now thousands of believers turning up to the megachurch each weekend. Shayna Van der Linden is the sort of woman who prides herself on never, ever, on pain of death, forgetting a name.

'My sister-in-law, well, my former sister-in-law, although actually they weren't married because she didn't believe in it—well, she's missing. She's that girl. Who is missing. From Melbourne. You know? On the news?' Shayna's eyes widen with recognition, and she nods. 'And I just need . . . I don't know what I need, but I need to be here,' Mandy says, her voice breaking and her words tumbling into one another like she's a verbal washing machine.

'Oh my goodness,' Shayna says, her jaw clenching ever so slightly. She strokes Mandy's hair and thinks how Mandy could do with some volumising shampoo.

Shayna's teeth, Mandy notices, again, are the whitest teeth she ever seen. In fact, they're almost blue. 'Oh my goodness,' Shayna repeats. 'That's so awful. I had no idea that's who it was, Mandy. No idea. Come in, Sweetness.'

Shayna ushers Mandy into the huge auditorium where JoyChurch gathers each weekend. 'Just give me a minute, Sweets, and we'll pray together for her. I can see that you need prayer.'

'I think I do,' Mandy says, nodding dolefully.

Mandy sits at the end of a pew for a while and Shayna disappears. As she sits under the downlights, staring at the highly polished wooden floor, she remembers how just before Michael's death, when Judy King's superlative talent for accumulating gossip hadn't yet been deadened by grief, Judy had discovered that Shayna's real name was Rhonda.

Shayna had changed her name when, as middle age approached, she began to sting with the realisation that almost no Australian child had been christened Rhonda since circa 1970 at absolute best. The Beach Boys' 'Help Me Rhonda' had been released in 1965 and a bevy of little Rhondas had been welcomed into their mothers' arms around the country. But the age of the Rhondas was short-lived. Young people were not called Rhonda. Rhonda just would not do.

Mandy thinks it's a shame. Shayna is one of those stupid made-up names. And she never met a Rhonda she didn't like. In Mandy's experience, Rhondas are usually no-nonsense and sensible. Rhondas can whip up enough casserole to feed a footy team. They can steer a committee. They can balance their books. Mandy once had a drug counsellor called Rhonda and that

Rhonda had a rare and magical ability to call out bullshit and to soothe Mandy King in her darkest, most self-loathing moments.

That said, Mandy can see through the Shayna exterior to the inner Rhonda. And while her mother, who went off JoyChurch when Michael died, now sees the fake name as a sign of 'tickets' and inauthenticity, Mandy just sees it as a faint twinkle of insecurity and vulnerability. And as a person who has struggled with confidence all her life, Mandy gets it. In her eyes, it makes this glamorous, wealthy pastor's wife much more approachable.

After a few minutes, she hears footsteps padding softly down the stairs at the back of the hall and turns to see Shayna hastily ushering a tall blond man in white tennis shorts out of the building. Mandy clocks with a little start that it's Ken Matthews, the 2IC at JoyChurch.

Shayna breezes back in and Mandy notices, and ignores, a waft of aftershave that's mixed in with Shayna's characteristically heady perfume.

'Poor Ken,' Shayna says, nodding far too much. 'He's really been struggling lately. He needs to find his way back to the Lord. I'm showing him the path. Sometimes the way back to the Lord is long and lonely, Mandy. Long and lonely.' She nods, raising a tattooed eyebrow as much as the Botox will permit, biting her lip and giving Mandy a fixed stare. Mandy notices a trickle of sweat running from Shayna's Tiffany necklace, down through the crepey crease of her surgically enhanced cleavage.

Mandy colours and she nods, too. 'That's good of you, Shayna.' Then she starts to cry, and buries her head on Shayna's shoulder, trying to ignore the smell of aftershave and sex.

'Okay,' Shayna says, straightening. 'You and me, we need some Jesus time.'

The two women get on their knees and close their eyes, and Shayna leads Mandy through prayer.

And you know, it makes Mandy King feel better. It always does. They pray for Kate Delaney to be alive. They pray for the police officers who are tasked with finding her. They pray that the sinner who has taken Kate will see the error of his ways (let's face it, they agree, no woman would ever do this, it's got to be a man) and let her go, they pray for everyone who loves Kate and wants to see her survive, and they pray for Kate herself. And they pray for all women. Because, they agree, women get a raw deal in this world. You don't see nice men disappearing off the streets after a night out with their friends.

They pray demonstratively, and loudly, and in a way that Kate herself would describe as absolutely fucking excruciating.

But Mandy feels heard, by her Lord. And loved by Shayna.

Shayna sees Mandy out of the complex and shuts the door behind her and leans back on it and sighs. Then she puts her phone into her sports bra and clicks a photo of her breasts and sends it to Ken Matthews. Ken sends a googly eye emoji.

—

As Mandy drives home, the Jesus love bomb wears off unusually rapidly. Who would kidnap Kate? she wonders. She assumes Kate has upset some sort of crime family she had been reporting on. She doesn't know how Kate can be so forthright and so brave.

She doesn't for a moment think of The Guy.

He disappeared out of her life without a trace and his conviction for raping the stripper was never publicised, because a pole dancer at a seamy nightclub is not someone like Kate Delaney. The tabloids can't put a picture of a stripper in an oval.

And anyway, those cases are a dime a dozen in the District Court. It's *expected.* When court reporters are busily scanning through the lists in the morning, there are enough celebrity defamation cases, gripping murders, spectacular business fallouts and worthy class actions to keep them occupied. A random guy no one has ever heard of raping a woman who takes her clothes off for a living, and who, in any event, enjoys anonymity at law because she is a victim of a sexual crime, is hardly going to whet their editors' appetites.

So, The Guy got his conviction, did his time and moved to Melbourne. And Mandy King moved on.

Tonight, she goes to bed early and lies there, shaking and thinking of poor Kate. Poor Kate.

21

STALL HIM

LIAM CARROLL IS back at the police station the colour of clay, pacing up and down in the foyer.

A very skinny, very young junior constable is behind the window, sighing. The junior constable has a thin nose and pimples dotted across his forehead like a galaxy and the collar of his blue police uniform shirt is rather too big for his neck, giving him the appearance of a popsicle. Sylvia Estrellita is mentally giving him a makeover to try to kill stress and time. She thinks she'd go all out and shave his head. Use a bit of concealer and powder on the zits. A sharp double-breasted suit with a stovepipe pant cut off at the ankle. A silk handkerchief in his pocket for a pop of colour. A touch of androgyny. A chunky patent leather brogue.

'Mr Carroll, I'm really sorry that I can't let you in at the moment. Sergeant D'Ambrosio will be with you as soon as he possibly can.'

'Okay, look, please call me Liam—we're long past formalities. But I wanted to point out that we've read on News Online that you found gloves,' Liam says, trying not to get too frustrated. 'You blokes must have been up and down past this spot a thousand times in recent days and I'm really, really wondering how it can have taken so long to find those gloves. Weren't you scouring the whole area?'

The young constable sighs. 'Of course we were, Liam. Scouring. Look, it's a really positive development that those gloves have been found.'

Liam ignores him. 'And I've seen on News Online that people are reporting you're hoping to get a DNA match. I need to know who this guy is and what you're doing. I need to talk to Sergeant D'Ambrosio about what the f— well, what the hell is going on. And how long they think those gloves were there. And whether they think Kate's alive. Kate doesn't have any living family to keep informed about all of this. I'm all she's got. I'm the only one to look out for her.'

'Mr . . . Liam,' the young constable stammers, 'you know, I'm not making the decisions around here. It's way above my pay grade. I know you're frustrated. I'm really sorry—I can't imagine what this is like for you. And yes, I know, I would say that. Words are not adequate in this situation. To be honest they aren't really adequate in most of the situations we deal with around here. Someone will be with you soon. I'm just wondering if you have maybe a mental health practitioner that you can speak with in the meantime?'

'A mental health practitioner!' Liam laughs. 'A mental health practitioner? Listen, Constable—' he looks at the badge '—Horvath, I am not crazy, okay? I'm worried. I'm worried about the length of time it takes to do anything around here. And not just around here. We had a long delay at the start of this because the geniuses at Vic Pol found a broken religious statue in my apartment and assumed I had used it to harm Kate. Thank Christ they came to their senses before that went on too long, but I just don't get the delays. Or at least, maybe someone can talk to me and explain the delays. Maybe they're normal. Maybe this is routine. I don't know, because no one will tell me.'

Constable Horvath nods nervously. He's sick of being the fall guy. He wasn't even meant to be working tonight. He's come in to cover another colleague who is off sick. And to be honest, he's beginning to evaluate his life choices. He's already been called out to his first jumper off one of the bridges on the Hume. This job is not really what he thought it might be when he signed up. He cranes his neck around the partition that leads into the police station behind the glass vestibule Liam and Sylvia are waiting in. He catches D'Ambrosio's eye and motions to him as if to say *well?*

D'Ambrosio, who, while clearly a bit messed up by the job, is a pretty cool guy in Horvath's estimation, puts his head against a wall and motions as if he's banging it, repeatedly.

'Stall him,' D'Ambrosio mouths.

Horvath gives him a thumbs up. 'Roger that,' he mouths.

'It really won't be much longer, I'm sure,' he says, wheeling his swivel chair back to the front desk and turning towards Liam. 'I'm told that Sergeant D'Ambrosio informed you that it could be up to forty-eight hours before we have an update.'

—

In truth, D'Ambrosio has made absolutely no progress whatsoever. He can feel the familiar tingle in his hands and down his throat. He's about to break out in hives again. The heat radiating in his extremities. The welts burning and sort of pulsing, like they have little lives of their own. Will it get really bad this time? Will his eyes almost close over? Will he have difficulty breathing? Will his lips swell up like one of those girls on social media who go to dodgy nurses for bad filler jobs?

In the back office, listening to Liam rant at Horvath, he washes down a couple of antacid tablets and an antihistamine and steroid with a mouthful of cola. He knows that this is not a healthy life choice. He is nothing if not inconsistent. But he needs a sugary caffeine hit to keep him on his game.

Whatever his game is. There is no game. There are no new leads. John Dooley, perhaps plagued by guilt of his own because he wasted time thinking Liam was the perp, has been ringing him up non-stop. But D'Ambrosio, while using nonchalant bloke phrases like *Nah mate, she's all good, we'll get there*, has nothing new to report to his Victorian colleague.

Both of them are starting to feel overcome with dread. Dooley is eating too many sweet biscuits a day. He's avoiding his colleagues' eyes when he walks through the office. *Still no news of Kate? No news of Kate. We'll get there.*

D'Ambrosio is watching the welts crawl up his arms.

'You're shit at your job, Pete D'Ambrosio,' he says, looking in the mirror. 'You're a complete fucking failure.' He slaps his face and tells himself to snap out of it. He lies on the couch for a moment and tries to practise those breathing techniques that the psych always tells him with such confidence work a treat and that he, to date, has found nigh-on completely useless.

'Tense all of your muscles on the inhale, then relax them on the exhale,' D'Ambrosio says to himself as he stares at the ceiling. He does it several times. Nope. Nothing. Still fucking stressed.

Horvath spies all this out of the corner of his eye as he looks into the back office and hopes Sarge isn't going to lose it again. He's heard from the boys about the last time Sarge lost it. The main reason he doesn't want Sarge to lose it is, he admits to himself, a selfish one. D'Ambrosio is nicer to him than anyone else around here. Doesn't talk down to him like he's the new kid. Has a kind way of explaining things that doesn't make him feel like an idiot. Horvath doesn't want D'Ambrosio to go off on sick leave again. So, he tries to help by attempting to talk Liam Carroll off a ledge.

'In the meantime,' Horvath continues, 'if you don't want to speak to a mental health practitioner, how about you go and grab a bite to eat? Because I don't want to be promising things I can't deliver, here. I don't want to say you'll be waiting X amount of time when in fact it will be Y. I don't want you to feel any more frustrated than you already are.'

A bite to eat. The thought of finding anything even halfway decent for dinner exhausts Liam. He smiles, despite himself, thinking again of Kate's chair/font rule. He suspects she would disapprove of most of the chairs and fonts in these parts, ergo most of the food. If he has to eat another dry chicken parmigiana or overcooked pasta with dried herbs or steak with pepper sauce and chips and salad with too-large, roughly cut red onion, drenched in gelatinous, too-sweet mustard-dotted vinaigrette, he will . . . well, he won't do anything, because he's too polite. He'll sulkily eat it and then go home and pinch his gut, then suck it in and think about how he's going to make it up to his body when this bloody nightmare is over. Emphasis on the *when*. This nightmare will be over. It really will.

Liam Carroll has no idea that Kate has been surviving on very little food at all. She is delirious with hunger.

22

THE CAGE

NEPEAN RIVER, SAYS the sign written in black letters against a white backdrop, glowing in the headlights. PHEASANTS NEST BRIDGE.

The Guy drives back and forth over the bridge a few times, waiting for a genuine lull in traffic.

Then he pulls off the freeway on the northbound side of the bridge and waits until there are no cars around to get Kate out from the back seat.

'Okay, Blue, we've arrived. Make a single noise and I throw you, no questions asked, into that ravine.'

As she hobbles alongside him, hands and feet roughly bound, she notices three small posies of faded imitation carnations tied to the side of the bridge.

She wonders who they were for, and how the person or people died. A car crash? Does each posy represent a person? A jumper? Three jumpers?

To her right, alongside one of the stained concrete roadblocks, there is some graffiti of a person's name and, in cursive, *RIP*.

To her left, a fairly elaborate memorial set up in one of those corrugated iron raised garden beds, with a photo of a young man who seemed to be into motorcar racing. Another, more austere, has a simple stone cross and a heartbreaking photo of an even younger man. In the poured concrete base of the cross, someone has scored in the word MUM.

Will this fate befall her, too? Will there be faded carnations for her at the side of the Pheasants Nest Bridge? She hopes at least for peonies.

Vale Kate Delaney. Who if nothing else, in the end, had taste.

Will Cameron Patrick lobby the media barons who own the newspaper to erect some sort of monument there in her name? Will he run a campaign for 'Kate's Law' to correct some egregious loophole in the criminal justice system that is somehow relevant to her case?

Will they announce a scholarship at her university? A prize in her honour for the dux of her fair-to-middling school?

A special commemorative Walkley Award? *The Kate Delaney Walkley Award for Social Affairs Reporting.* Will they remember her when they are sitting in whatever plaza ballroom they're holding the awards in, waiting for their names to be read out, and then bitching because they don't win?

Will Liam and Sylvia get up and make a speech while everyone is eating their prawn entrée and throwing back glass after glass of Australian sparkling? Will Liam or Sylvia have to say, *Excuse me, shhhhhh*, while they valiantly try to be heard above the din of media gossip, try to wax lyrical about what a bright talent Kate Delaney had been until her life was cruelly cut short?

Long dried grass shines silver under the full moon. She looks up at the night sky. No sight or sound of the police chopper now.

Twigs scrape against Kate's freezing bare legs as The Guy yanks her away from the still-empty roadway. Scattered on the scrubby ground are various items of detritus. One of those old-school Neapolitan ice-cream containers that everyone scraped the chocolate out of first, then the strawberry, leaving a lonely vanilla mountain in the middle. It's half full of muddy water. A soiled disposable nappy in a plastic bag. A rather nasty-looking black dildo. Some bubble wrap. A brown banana skin. Some broken glass.

'I love this place,' says her abductor.

Kate turns and looks at him, narrowing her eyes. *You really are a dickhead*, she says, in her mind.

He certainly looks like one, she thinks, with her stockings fashioned over his head, distorting his facial features, smudging his nose to the side like a figure in a cubist painting.

He leads her along the trail that snakes down towards the undercarriage of the bridge. To her left, she glances down and sees the deep ravine. At its base is the Nepean River. It is a long way down. Water gleams in the moonlight and she can see the outline of sharp rocks. Best be silent for now. To her right, in the far corner of the underside of the bridge, is a metal cage.

—

Kate notices immediately the signs saying the area is under twenty-four-hour surveillance and the cameras dotted around the back of the cage's anteroom. Why would he bring her to a place that is so high security?

'This is going to be home for you for a while, Blue,' he says.

She watches as he stands before the metal door.

'Here goes,' he says. 'Let's see if the pen-pushers are still as hopeless as they've always been.'

He punches an eight-digit code into the keypad and the door immediately springs open.

'Nice one, suckers!' he says, fist-pumping the air.

And he pushes Kate Delaney into the anteroom, onto the three little wooden steps that lead up to the passage underneath the bridge.

'I'm gonna leave you here, little lady,' he says, brightly, pulling some packets out of his backpack. 'I've got some food for you, and I hope for your sake that they find you before all this runs out.'

He pulls out a large bottle of water, a half-eaten packet of Iced Vo-Vo biscuits, a bag of Burger Rings chips and an apple. Kate, who has always suffered terrible indigestion from highly processed foods, groans. Then he gives her a dirty polar-fleece blanket that has been on the back seat of the car.

'Now, up above you there is the tunnel. That goes all the way along the underside of the bridge. You can go up there if you like—might be a bit less cold away from the wind—but it's pretty fuckin' creepy, I can tell you from previous experience. If I was you, I'd stay here. And wait till someone comes. At least they'll see you straight away.'

'What about you, are you coming back? Will you bring me more food or water?' Kate asks. 'Please, please get me some more food and water. You know I can't survive for long on this. Please. I've been patient with you.'

'Patient!' he says, with a scoff. 'What else were you going to be, Blue? Odds weren't exactly stacked in your favour.'

Kate reins in her fury and tries to give him an appealingly beseeching look, aware that she looks like utter shit and it's highly unlikely that feminine wiles are going to get her through this one. Her coquettish powers are sorely diminished, and he seems to take perverse pleasure in that.

'Please, if you are going to leave me here, just give me enough food so there's more time to find me,' she begs.

She's wailing now. She's lost her cool. He enjoys that. A smile sweeps across his thin mouth, and he clenches his arse cheeks as he remembers her burning him back in that bar in Melbourne. The flick of her hair and the clack of her boots as she turned on her heel. The giggles of her girlfriends. Now look at her. Just look at her.

'Not on your Nelly,' he quips. 'Not on your Nelly. Bit too late for you to be all nice to me now. You've got enough food and drink for a bit. I coulda left you with nothing. So, let's hope for your sake your luck's in, hey? Because I'm getting out of dodge. Anyway, see ya, Blue. It's been real.'

And with that, The Guy beams at her like he's a *Playschool* presenter, turns around and clambers out through the steel gate, clattering it behind him.

She watches his feet move steadily out of sight through the night, then hears the Echo's engine start. Then he hoons away like he is driving some sort of hot rod.

—

Kate hobbles across the cage to the gate in the anteroom. On this side, as with the outside, there is a keypad. It hadn't occurred to her to look at the number he entered when he opened it because she hadn't thought there would be a keypad on this side, too. She hadn't really known what he was doing at that stage. All she remembers, when she recalls the motion of his hand, 1-2-3-4-5-6-7-8, is that it was eight digits. She wonders whether if she started punching random combinations in, and it repeatedly failed, it might alert some sort of alarm system. Would someone come?

She tries several different combinations, but no alarm system seems to be triggered. It just keeps allowing her to punch the numbers into the keypad, over and over again. Her maths skills are terrible, and she wonders how many combinations there could be, and how long it would take her to exhaust them all, and whether anyone would notice that she was here before she did.

She looks up at the top of the cage. There is a gap between it and the concrete ceiling, but it's topped off with nasty-looking forked metal spikes. Even if she could find a way to hoist her way up to the top, and she doesn't know how she could, as there are no bars or spaces in the cage big enough to find a footing, those things would slice her open.

She takes some heart in the security cameras. But she figures that The Guy wouldn't have risked putting her here if he thought they were particularly well-monitored. He obviously has some working knowledge of the place, given that he knew the security code, and given his comment about the pen-pushers. But nonetheless, surely someone will notice, eventually?

And how long can one last on half a packet of Iced Vo-Vos, some Burger Rings and an apple? Would one die of indigestion before anything else? She will also have to be cautious in rationing herself sips of water. It's a decent sized bottle, but she could be here for a while. Would she die of hypothermia first? Would a ratty old polar-fleece blanket be enough to stop that from happening?

She starts banging on the metal as loudly as possible, making a terrible din. But she knows, when she thinks about it, that it would require someone to be on foot rather than passing by overhead in a car for them to hear. She's probably wasting her energy in the middle of the night. She wonders how many cars actually stop here—particularly at night. It wasn't that easy, she observed, to stop. This isn't like one of those roadside rest areas with the picnic tables and toilet blocks. She figures people would only stop here if they were really desperate—the kid's dirty nappy odour had become too overpowering, they were busting to wee, or they really had to dispose of a giant black dildo, pronto, before they trucked back home.

Ugh. It doesn't look good. She has to hope that someone at Roads wanders into wherever it is that these security cameras are playing, if in fact there is such a place. And sees her moving in there. And comes to get Kate Delaney out of here.

—

She sits back down. She looks outside through the little narrow slits in the cage. The closest trees are drooping she-oaks. She-oaks have always reminded her of primary school because they were mass-planted in the tan bark along the perimeter of the playground at Our Lady of Perpetual Hope. She remembers how she would take the long, pointed scales that were the leaves of the she-oak and fold them at the little branchlets that featured every two centimetres. She'd sit alone, a pale Irish kid with opinions, trying to avoid the likes of Narelle Stevenson, and anxiously fold the scales in her hands. *One. Two. Three. Four. Five.* They reminded her of great long green spider legs. Sometimes she'd be startled by fluffy spitfire caterpillars, which the naughty boys threatened to throw at the younger kids if they told on them.

Since then, she has always found she-oaks depressing. She-oaks signify loneliness and spitfires and a kid in dusty, drab suburbia who does not belong.

On the sharp stones on the ground outside the cage are more faux carnations, once red, now a dirty pink, that must have fallen from a memorial up on the bridge. A scrunched McDonald's bag has been tossed from an overhead car, along with another banana skin, petrified mission brown.

And then, Jesus God, a screwdriver and a long, rusty knife with a wooden handle. Why are they here? Who put those here?

A chill goes through her body. Kate Delaney is so, so scared. The thoughts wash around in her mind. She really knows nothing about The Guy. Is he part of some wider rape syndicate who'll come back and assault her again? Do other scary people know about this place? Do they also have the combination to the cage? He seems too stupid to be able to coordinate anything, but maybe he's lower down the food chain. Will he think better of leaving her here because he doesn't want a live witness to his crime? Will he come back and just kill her? How will he kill her? *So many dumb ways to die.* Or will she just slowly run out of food and water and waste away? What does that slow death look like? Christ, now she's thinking of those two boys in the pylons. Did they fall, unconscious, and not know that they were fading away to their deaths? Or did they scream? Did they hope to be rescued? She feels them. She feels death. Death is around her.

She wipes away a tear and tries to take her mind off the terror by taking a bite of an Iced Vo-Vo. She remembers that at high school, the kids had made up a song to the tune of Vanilla Ice's 'Ice Ice Baby' called 'Iced Iced Vo-Vo'. She whispers it in the dark, *Iced Iced Vo-Vo, da-na-na-na-na-nana.*

Look, she likes the biscuit for its retro appeal. It has a funny name. But as she bites into the coconut-covered strawberry marshmallow, on a bed of sticky strawberry jam, topping a fairly miserable, flavourless biscuit, she remembers how deeply over-rated they are. That they are the sort of things Australians like simply because they are theirs.

They are a bit, Kate figures, like Vegemite, which all the mothers at Our Lady of Perpetual Hope had told her new migrant mother their children adored.

Mary Delaney had taken the mothers' word for it and spread the Vegemite as liberally on Kate's sandwich as one might spread Nutella. Except she hadn't told Kate about the new spread she was using. Little Kate chomped merrily into her sandwich thinking Mary had treated her (Mary always insisted she have healthy lunches, so this really was a treat) and, expecting hazelnut chocolate flavour, got a solid mouthful of acrid yeast. She spat it out, horrified, and had never let Vegemite pass her lips since. Even the smell of it still makes her want to vomit.

While Kate is much more of a savoury foods girl, Iced Vo-Vos are significantly less unpleasant to her than Vegemite, and in her present situation, needs must.

She finishes the biscuit and gingerly sips the water, conscious she has to make it last. Then she tightens the polar-fleece blanket around her legs, lies back on the little wooden stoop, and tries to go to sleep.

23

FORENSICS

THE FOLLOWING MORNING, Peter D'Ambrosio wakes, having slept on the couch in the station overnight. Although calling it that required a pretty loose definition of 'slept'. The couch is a cobalt faux-suede atrocity and has hard, poorly padded arms with a grimy sheen, and a weird uncomfortable bar in the middle that only becomes apparent when you've been on it for a few hours.

D'Ambrosio has done a few all-nighters on the couch, and every time he decides to do it again, he forgets just how uncomfortable that bloody thing is.

'Nah, she'll be right,' he said, when his colleague, Michelle Wang, looked at him doubtfully the night before and indicated that it was not a great idea for him to be sleeping there.

'I'm one of those crazy humans who can sleep anywhere,' he lied. 'Promise. Could practically sleep standing up.'

Michelle Wang shrugged. She can tell that Peter D'Ambrosio never gets much sleep at all from his grey pallor, permanently defeated expression and addiction to caffeine, but it's his life. One which, from what Michelle Wang can determine, is not altogether fun.

He rolls off the couch and falls on the floor at six am. Christ. One of the younger constables has a habit of eating dry two-minute noodles on night shifts and when D'Ambrosio wakes up and walks into the bathroom, stuck to his face are little pieces of stale noodle that have fallen down the sides of the sofa cushions.

'Livin' the dream, Pete,' he says to himself as he picks them off and splashes his face with cold water. 'Livin' the dream.'

He wanders into the kitchenette to find that they only have that eye-bleedingly bad powdered instant coffee. The Italian in him won't have it. He walks back to the bathroom, runs his face under cold water again, brushes his teeth with the spare toothbrush he keeps in the office, and sprays some deodorant under his arms. Hopefully he doesn't stink too much. He'll head back home for a shower later on. But he's got work to do. He jumps in his car and heads down to the fast-food joint on the freeway for what is, let's face it, a pretty terrible caffé latte. But he needs to wake up and he doesn't have time to be fussy. Or at least, he's kidding himself that he doesn't have time. Because no one is getting back to him, and until they do, he has all the time in the world.

—

He's not letting on to Liam Carroll, but Peter D'Ambrosio is starting to get pretty bloody cranky with the crew down at forensics. They cut out those bits of sofa fabric three days ago now and have had the gloves for a good twenty-four hours. They know that this is one of those cases you can't stuff up. Although, perhaps, in their minds, they have already succumbed to the belief that she is gone forever.

You can't make mistakes on any high-profile case in which the media are following your every move but the scrutiny is magnified a hundred thousand when you're talking about one of their own. It's every cop's nightmare to have a journo victim—particularly a pretty one. Particularly when you don't know if she's alive or dead and so every second counts.

The press is so desperate for information, you have to feed them something. The guys over at police media are banging down your door asking for something they can give to show that you're all doing your jobs. Hence dropping the news about the phone and the gloves. But then that means they are now saying, 'Why haven't you got the DNA back yet?'

The Chief Commissioner is on the blower for him.

'Hello, Detective Sergeant D'Ambrosio, I'm pleased to see someone of your talent and ability has been assigned to this job,' Kel Greene says.

'Please, Chief, call me Pete.'

'Goodo, Pete. I trust that everything is going well with you? That you're looking after yourself? One of the really important things in this job is self-care. I've always said that. We can't be too careful.'

You gaslighting arsehole, D'Ambrosio thinks. The Commissioner is clearly referring to his PTSD. Why is it that when you have complex PTSD caused by your cup being too full, on account of repeated exposure to secondary trauma, that everyone in your workplace simultaneously keeps saying *you* need to look after *yourself*, while continuing to do things to retrigger your trauma, or at best not address it?

I hope you're looking after yourself, Peter.

Look after yourself, mate.

Make sure you look after yourself.

If Peter D'Ambrosio had a dollar for every time someone had said that to him, he could buy himself a few slabs of fairly fancy craft beer. D'Ambrosio is fine at looking after himself. What he has needed all along is for the force to better look after him. For the insurance company to look after him. He didn't get that, but he didn't like who he became when he was off sick, so he came back. And now he just hopes that people like Liam Carroll don't clock that he's struggling not to bawl when they're talking about their loved ones.

He doesn't want to take the Chief's bait. And he's really invested in this case now, and wants to get a result. That Kate Delaney looks and sounds like a nice girl. She doesn't deserve this shit.

'Oh, absolutely, Chief. It's so important. And we are pulling out all the stops, as you say, Chief, all the stops.'

'I should hope so, Detective Sergeant. You just give me a call if you need anything.'

D'Ambrosio expects that the Chief has had a call from the editor or proprietor of Kate's paper. And/or the Police Minister; the Premier; hell, even the PM. If this sort of case is a nightmare for him, it's hell for an ambitious Chief Commissioner, whose biggest task in life is, let's face it, to kiss arse.

He's always been a bit suspicious of Kel Greene, too, for no other reason than that he's very matey with that JoyChurch bloke, Jamie Van der Linden, and has been worshipping at the church for a few years. D'Ambrosio thinks JoyChurch is basically a glorified multi-level marketing scheme. But more than that, New South Wales Police has had some intelligence that Van der Linden is not the upstanding citizen he paints himself to be. And he wonders how the Chief couldn't know about this—it's pretty common knowledge that the blokes over at the sexual offences unit have been looking into his activities for a few years now. Why a Chief Commissioner would go anywhere near something like that stumps D'Ambrosio. But JoyChurch has its tentacles into all sorts of places, not least several ministers' portfolios in the current state government.

Jamie Van der Linden has just returned from some dodgy junket to a school for needy kids in Thailand. D'Ambrosio knows for a fact Interpol has had eyes on that, because there were reports to police of what he gets up to with young house boys when he has his men-only JoyChurch 'Pray-Ins' in his Bali villa, leaving Shayna in Sydney to hold down the fort.

D'Ambrosio would rather eat glass than attend a male-only Pray-In, even leaving out the seedy liaisons with house boys. And it shits D'Ambrosio to tears that Jamie and Shayna have in recent days been out at Acacia Hills, leading their congregation in prayer for Kate—something he sees as pure marketing and which, from his conversations with Liam Carroll, he knows would drive Kate Delaney mental.

'Bloody Ponzi scheme,' he mutters to himself about JoyChurch, remembering how that bastard Van der Linden put out a press release advertising the fact that they were the first Australian church to introduce EFTPOS swipe machines to make 'offerings' more convenient, rather than simply passing around the collection plate for cash. Jamie had seen it at a brother church in Oklahoma City. The machines were set in little cradles that were bolted onto every fourth or fifth pew. A press release! *Here's another way we can suck money out of you*, D'Ambrosio remembers thinking when he heard about it from a journo mate. Of course, press release aside, Jamie Van der Linden, like any business owner, much preferred cash. So, he'd also installed ATMs at the entry.

'Jamie just thinks of everything,' Shayna once said in one of their promotional videos. 'He's a real details man.'

—

D'Ambrosio tries not to think about the dodgy pentecostalists and rings forensics again.

'G'day, Faheer. Any word yet on those sofa blood samples from that Airbnb or the gloves they found out near Yanderra?' he says, trying to sound ever-so-friendly and nonchalant, rather than how he really feels, which is like he wants to scream.

'Nope, Sarge, we're still waiting. I don't want to hurry them up because they're as stressed out of their minds as you are. The Chief's office has been on to us, too.'

'Sorry, mate. I know it's difficult. I don't want to tell you how to suck eggs, but this one's important.'

'Yep, well and truly aware of that. Could not be more aware. I'll give you a bell the second we hear a thing.'

'Thanks, Faheer. You're a legend, mate.'

'Takes one to know one.'

The switchboard keeps getting calls from crazy people claiming to know Kate's whereabouts. They've blamed everyone from bikies, to a crim the caller has forgotten is in gaol or dead, to someone's dodgy neighbour, to the Illuminati, to abducting aliens. The patient operators take down their details and thank them ever so much for their Very Important Information.

D'Ambrosio sits clicking one of those retractable four-colour ballpoint pens. *Blue. Black. Red. Green. Blue. Black. Red. Green. Click, click, click, clack.* He googles things he already knows the answer to. And opens the file and reads through it, twice over, hoping something will jump out at him. The words start to swim on the page. *Snap out of it, D'Ambrosio. Don't have a panic attack now.*

His eyes are closing over when suddenly the phone rings.

'Faheer! Shit. What've you got?'

'Yeah, we've got a match, Pete.'

24

GHOSTS

KATE DELANEY WAKES up that same day to find it's still not a nightmare. It's a sunny but blowy day and the wind is whistling in through the cage. She looks at her fingers and sees they have a blueish tinge. She can feel her hip bones, which haven't protruded since her teens. She remembers the boy next door, Mario Giordano, teasing her about them. They were standing in front of a mirror in her bedroom, and she was looking at her skinny legs and her protruding bones.

'You really are disgusting, Kate Delaney,' Mario said, shaking his head at her hip bones, which jutted out at right angles.

Kate could not disagree. 'You're absolutely right, Mario,' she said.

Mario's family were like brothers and sisters to the lonely-only Kate. She had made up a song about them to the tune of 'Hava Nagila' (a Hebrew song from Eastern Europe, but details, details).

Ma-rio, Mario Giordano, Mario Giordano, Mario Giorda-a-a-a-no, she used to sing at him, to tease him.

The Giordanos were from Reggio Calabria, on the tip of the toe of the boot that was the map of Italy. They grew and bottled their own tomatoes and slaughtered their own goats. Mr Giordano even made his own, fairly terrible, wine, crushing the red grapes in a big barrel with his feet. Kate always remembered wondering why anyone would want to drink something that had been created by Mr Giordano's stomping bare feet.

Mario's mum's tomato passata was a revelation to Kate. To this day, she has never tasted anything quite like it. When she asked Mrs Giordano for her recipe, Mrs Giordano would just smile coyly and say, 'It's all in the simplicity—tomatoes, garlic, olive oil, oregano and basil—and the secret ingredient—a little bitta sugar.' But try as she might, no matter how spectacular the heirloom tomatoes she could source, no matter how pricey the olive oil, nothing came close to Mrs Giordano's recipe. It had a stickiness and an incredible umami flavour. It tasted of sunshine.

Kate Delaney would kill for some of that tomato passata right now—just that, on some really good quality al dente pasta, some Reggiano shaved over the top and maybe a touch of chilli oil.

She is so hungry, it hurts. While she has a reasonably slim build, she has never been able to skip meals. She has never been able to understand women who have eating disorders. The willpower it would take not to eat mystifies her.

She's not a fan of eating fruit first thing in the morning—too acidic. So, she looks at her other options: Iced Vo-Vos or Burger Rings. That fucking, fucking stupid arsehole. She picks up the packet of Burger Rings and eats three. Maybe she'll eat the apple after them as it won't be so harsh after some carbs.

—

Her whole body hurts. She would kill for a Chinese massage now. It was one of the things she and Liam had bonded over. They both loved Chinese massages so vigorous that the masseur was almost beating them up. While she could just surrender to it, Liam told her he would feel a rising sense of anxiety almost halfway through.

'Why's that?' she had wondered.

'Because I know the end is nigh,' he had explained. 'It troubles me greatly to think that it's about to finish. I can't book a half-hour massage because from the minute it starts, I'm worried it's about to end.'

'What if you can only get half an hour?' she had countered.

'I'd rather go without. The stress is too much.'

'I'd take the risk of stress,' Kate laughed, 'for the half-hour of pleasure. But that's just me. You do you.'

She smiles a little as she remembers them lying like spoons, her breasts on his back, the way she would massage his head when he was stressed from work. And then feeling his body relax, and seeing him turn around to say, 'Okay then,' and the way he would look into her eyes and put his hands on her body and kiss her and tell her she was magnificent.

—

She can see out the side of the cage into the bush. A flock of red-crested gang gang cockatoos is perched on a tree, feeding on something or other. It gives the tree the appearance of a magnolia—each bird a flower. She remembers from primary school that the collective noun for cockatoos is a chattering. A chattering of cockatoos. Why did she never get that question at a trivia night?

The gang gangs make a call that sounds like a squeaky gate. They're pretty, with their white-tipped charcoal plume and cerise heads. She always loved the name 'gang gang' and resolved that if she were ever to become a grandmother, she would insist on being called Gang Gang.

Why is this place, she wonders, called Pheasants Nest? Are there pheasants in the area? Do they nest near here?

She remembers a story Liam once told her about how he was in a pub somewhere in the sticks, having a pint on his own, and he noticed that all over the walls were different pictures of pheasants.

'There were like, I kid you not, ninety-three pheasants on those bloody walls,' he said as they lay in bed.

'What's with the pheasants, mate?' Liam told her he had asked the barman, whom he correctly guessed was the proprietor.

'I just like me pheasants, nothing of it,' the proprietor had answered, somewhat defensive. 'Have a look around—I think you'll find they're a quite splendid creature.'

So, Liam walked around the pub looking at all the pheasant pictures. He didn't much get it, until he came to a picture of a particularly magnificent bird. Its breast was the brightest vermillion, its neck banded with cobalt and orange. Its crest was a quiff of brightest gold; its eyes, its beak, its feet and its upper feathers also gleamed golden.

'Bet you'll never guess what that one's called?' the publican said to Liam. 'Free drinks on me for the rest of the night if you can. No one has ever got it, in thirty years.'

It sounded like a fair plan to Liam.

As the publican poured a Guinness and waited for it to settle, Liam gazed at the bird for about thirty seconds.

'I'm, uh, going to say, I'm going to say the *Golden* Pheasant?' Liam stammered.

'Holy shit!' the publican exclaimed. 'You're absolutely right. First one in thirty years!'

'Drinks on you, I guess, then, sir?' Liam deadpanned. 'How about that lucky Golden Pheasant?'

'Weirdly,' he explained to Kate as they lay in his bed many years later and she giggled at the thought of the Golden Pheasant, 'he was so taken with me and my wild Golden Pheasant guess, he decided to reward me further.'

'And what, pray tell, kind sir, was his reward?' Kate said, knowing this would be good.

'Well, you'll like this. He brought me out the back of the pub because he wanted to show me his collection.'

'His collection? Of What?'

'Well, here's the thing. His collection of ferrets.'

Kate nearly choked laughing. 'Ferrets! That was his reward? Are we talking live ferrets or stuffed ferrets? I mean, was he some sort of taxidermist?'

'Oh no, definitely live,' Liam assured her. 'I did not know what to say. He told me almost no one got to see the ferrets. They were running around in a very large cage in the corner of the lounge room that adjoined the pub. He took one out and let it crawl up his arm and said that I could pat it if I liked, because I was special. Because I guessed the Golden Pheasant. It was only me who had ever, ever guessed that Golden Pheasant.'

'Well, it's only right and proper that you should have received your ferret reward, then, Liam,' Kate said. 'There was clearly nothing for it but to show you his ferrets. Only you, mind, Liam Carroll. Guesser of the Golden Pheasant.'

'Only me.' He pulled the quilt over their heads like they were in their own special tent and kissed her on the tip of her nose.

—

Where is the Guesser of the Golden Pheasant now? Is he trying to find her, along with the police? Will his dumb luck or his kooky sense of humour or the sheer strength of his life force guide him here?

Please come here, Liam Carroll. Get me out of this place. Hide me under your duvet and kiss me on the nose. I need you.

She stands up, her knees making clicking sounds as she does, and looks out through the cage.

'Liam! LI-AM!' she yells down through the valley, and it echoes back at her. It hurts to expend that much energy. Her voice doesn't sound like her voice at all. It's reedy and pathetic.

Why is she wasting her breath, anyway? Liam's not here. Liam can't hear her. No one can.

Once her ears adjust to the sound of the cars rumbling, she can hear the water running in the Nepean below. The stained concrete underside of the bridge stretches out overhead. She can see a curious collection of strange dark brown things hanging down from it. What are they? Bats? But they aren't living. They're covered in parts by thick spider webs. Are they fungi? Or wasp nests? Or some sort of stalactite? Can stalactites form from man-made structures? And why are they a different colour, if so? Some sort of mineral deposits?

If it's wasps, she thinks she'll pass out. Kate is deeply allergic to, and terrified of, wasp stings. She had several as a child. The first time, her arm blew up like it had an AFL football stuck under the skin. The next time her leg swelled up like she was an elderly woman with severe oedema. The doctors have told her next time she is stung it will be much worse.

She has looked up at the tunnel going under the bridge a few times. She wonders what is on the other side. Could she perhaps get out? Or will it just be the same thing at the other side, another cage with another keypad with another eight-digit code that she doesn't know?

She's just too scared to go in there. She thinks again about those two boys who fell into the pylons. She's sure the entrances have been secured shut now, but the thought of it freaks her out so badly. The thought of being in the same place that those two boys must have been, for God knows how long before they died, is just too terrifying.

—

Kate has always been afraid of ghosts, ever since she was little. She used to wake up to a sensation that some force was pushing her back down onto her bed and she always just assumed it was the undead living in her cupboard.

Here, now, she senses the history of so much death. Michael King once told her when they were driving over the Pheasants Nest Bridge that this was a place where people in this part of Sydney came to suicide. She remembers looking over the side of the bridge into the ravine and thinking how desperate one would have to be to want to cut life short in such a terrible way.

She remembers that documentary, *The Falling Man*, about one of the jumpers who chose to escape the flames of the World Trade Centre after the hijackers had ploughed their plane into it on September 11. The documentary was about trying to discover the identity of the man whose leap had been captured in an iconic newspaper photograph from that day. In the image, with the vertical lines of the tower behind him, the man seems almost peaceful and weightless after making such a horrendous decision—to choose the manner of his death, inevitable as that death was.

Kate had not been able to sleep for weeks after watching that documentary. The image, once seen, was forever burned into the retina. The story was so unspeakably sad because, of course, the man was not the only one who had chosen to jump to his death. She had thought about it when Michael told her about the Pheasants Nest jumpers.

And she feels the jumpers are around her now, watching her. She feels their resignation and their sadness. And while, in some senses, it makes her feel very afraid, it also somehow makes her feel paradoxically less lonely.

She thinks of Auntie Maggie, who would know exactly which saint Kate ought to pray to. The small matter of Kate not hitherto believing in God or saints seems churlish now.

Patron saint of, let's see, what? Kate wonders.

Impossible Causes. Being locked under a bridge in a cage in the cold when no one knows where you are, after having been raped and kidnapped by a stranger is definitely *an Impossible Cause. St Rita of Cascia. Patron Saint of Impossible Causes.*

Auntie Maggie called her 'Patroness'. St Rita always scared the hell out of little Kate because she was depicted with a partial stigmata wound on her forehead—thought to echo Christ's suffering from the crown of thorns. In the mass cards and paintings, there would be a ray of light shining from, presumably, Heaven, to the open wound on her forehead. Her face always looked in rapture.

Rita of Cascia had a terrible life, with an abusive, unfaithful husband who was ultimately murdered. She had two sons, but they died of dysentery. She entered a convent. She also was the saint for battered wives and infertility and loneliness and bodily ills and wounds.

Kate remembers Auntie Maggie making her chant the prayer to St Rita in the little parlour at the back of her flat. What was her aunt's impossible cause? Auntie Maggie was so innocent. Perhaps an ever-pregnant sister with persistent mastitis, or a brother whose family was behind on the hire purchase furniture payments?

Or a particularly unfortunate run at the weekly bingo tournament at the end of the road?

'O powerful St Rita, rightly called Saint of the Impossible,' Kate recites now, remembering her aunt's clasped, blue-veined, arthritic hands, and glad eyes gazing skyward. 'I come to you with confidence in my great need. You know well my trials, as you yourself were many times burdened in this life.'

As Kate says the prayer, she imagines a quizzical St Rita gazing back down on her and clicking her saintly tongue, a trickle of blood oozing slowly from the partial stigmata on her saintly brow.

But child, you have strayed, you have strayed for many years. Your cause, I see, is definitely impossible, but I cannot help a sinner.

'Fair play to you, St Rita,' Kate whispers, crying. She looks down at her blueish fingers. 'Fair play to you.'

She hears a rustling sound and freezes as she notices a red-bellied black snake inching its way alongside the cage into the sunlight. Surely it's too cold for snakes! But it's been a mild and dry winter, so perhaps they're out early this year.

Her wasp and spider phobias are possibly only trumped by her fear of snakes.

Please, St Rita.

Alas, child, it cannot be helped.

Kate nods and wipes another tear away.

—

Both of Kate's parents had a northern European fear of reptiles and creepy crawlies. When they first moved to Australia, Mary Delaney called Billy home from work because she had found a skink in Kate's bedroom. She had stuffed newspaper under the door and forbade Kate from going anywhere near the room.

'Jesus, Mary and Holy Saint Joseph, Billy Delaney, you'd better get home now,' she remembers her mother yelling into the plastic orange telephone that sat on the hall stand.

Kate has never forgotten watching her father kill the poor little thing with a meat cleaver, which sliced its tail off. She watched in horror as the tail continued to wriggle for some minutes after it had been removed from the body.

Billy Delaney had an almost pathological fear of snakes. He would wake up in the night, screaming, thinking that there was a snake in the bed. He had sprained ankles and grazed elbows jumping out of the bed, waking a terrified Mary, who wouldn't be able to go back to sleep.

Kate had inherited the phobia and did exactly the same thing. Poor Liam had woken up to Kate's screams on many occasions, having to calm her down and convince her, as she shook and cried, that there was no snake or spider in the bed.

'It's okay, baby, it's okay,' Liam would whisper, stroking her hair, after shaking out the duvet and all of the sheets to prove to her that there were no beasties lurking within them.

She would fall asleep in his arms, and he'd lie there, eyes jammed open, wired and mildly traumatised by her screams. She would bound happily out of bed the next morning and he'd look like he'd just landed on a flight from Heathrow.

She can't take her eyes off the snake. She daren't make a noise nor move a muscle. What if someone stops at Pheasants Nest while it is there? She won't be able to bang on the cage lest she startles the snake, and it comes for her. It lies there, soaking up the morning rays, seemingly oblivious to the fact that she is staring at it only metres away and she is terrified. The risk is, of course, almost comically low. The cage runs right down to the ground, but Kate's fear is so irrational that she imagines the snake slithering up the cage and over the spiked top, to come and join her in her prison.

'Most snakes aren't interested in attacking people, Kate,' Liam would say right now.

'Yeah, yeah, yeah, "They're more afraid of you than you are of them,"' Kate would chime in reply. 'Except I don't have venom and I don't bite snakes (nor anyone else besides the kid in Year Five who tried to kiss me on the playground) and if I did, the snake wouldn't die from a Katebite now, would it? The snake wouldn't be rushed to hospital, requiring anti-venom derived from poison extracted from other Irish girls called Kate.'

'Well, that is true, my love, but if you leave them alone, they'll leave you alone. Roughly one to two people die of snakebites in

Australia every year. We don't have aggressive ones like rattlesnakes here. You are more likely to die from a car accident. Or the flu. Snakebite deaths are, my darling, vanishingly rare.'

'Vanishingly rare? You read that somewhere, didn't you?'

'I have been swotting up on snakes since the last time you nearly scared the living daylights out of me by waking up screaming and insisting there was one in the bed. Yes, I may have plagiarised "vanishingly rare". Nonetheless, the fact remains, it's unlikely to be a snake that finishes you off, Ms Delaney.'

'Vanishingly rare,' Kate says to herself now, over and over as she watches the red-bellied black snake sun itself. 'Snakebite deaths are vanishingly rare.'

25

DNA

ONLY A FEW kilometres away, Liam Carroll has returned to the crappy motel. Exhausted, he and Sylvia trudge down to reception and get some cans of cola to try and keep themselves alert. The woman at reception asks them if they would like a guide to the local restaurants.

'Sure!' chirps Sylvia.

'Okay, well, my recommendation would be the Italian just down here,' the woman says, using a felt tip pen to mark a little cross on the map of the region she has unfolded. 'You just turn right, and head straight down the road. It's a decent walk, but I guess you can work off your food. Now, you should know, they make pizza, but it's *European*-style pizza.'

'European-style pizza?' Liam replies, furrowing his brow, imagining some sort of Germanic situation.

'Yes, it's not like our pizza—you know, not like Pizza Hut or Domino's—it's very thin and has, you know, buffalo mozzarella on it. Apparently, it's just like the real pizza you get in Italy, instead of Australian pizza.'

'Well, it sounds perfect,' Sylvia says, elbowing Liam in the ribs.

'European-style pizza,' Liam manages, wearily. '*Who knew?*'

The woman behind reception beams and winks at him.

When she gives him the key to his room, which she assures him is the best in the motel ('She's got the hots for you, Liam,' Sylvia giggles), he finds it up a flight of stairs and along a walkway with a rusting balcony. He notices that all the way up the stairs and along the walkway is a trail of what looks to be drops of dried blood. Charming.

He slumps onto the bed, stretching out on slightly pilled polyester sheets with a nasty acrylic quilt. He shudders as he wonders what the forensics blokes D'Ambrosio has been working with would find if they shone one of those UV lights on this whole room. The place is so damp he can't hang his clothes in the wardrobe, so he'll have to hang them on the backs of chairs. When he gets up in the morning, he'll find the fine gauge knitted jumper he was going to put on had a slick of condensation on it.

That night, B-double trucks thunder along the freeway. The room has a split system heating and cooling system. This means it is either arctic cold when it is off, or baking hot when it is on. Similarly, the shower ranges between freezing and boiling. He tries before he goes to sleep to iron one of his shirts and the iron leaks limey water all over the fabric.

Unlike most motels, there are no bottles of water in the room and he is not keen to drink the tap water. The towels are beige and look almost miniature, designed for small children. In fact, everything in this motel room is beige. Fifty Shades of Beige.

He falls asleep blankly watching reruns of a comedy show, cradling a lager from the six-pack he'd picked up at the bottle shop. He wakes up moments before the thing is about to spill all over his pyjamas and the bedding, and struggles to get back to sleep.

—

Scratchy sheets or otherwise, the next morning, Liam doesn't want to get out of bed. He has been dreaming about Kate through the night, right up to this morning, and she seems so real and so near. In fact, she is quite near, but he doesn't know that. He doesn't want to wake from the dream, even though towards the end of it, he is slowly gaining consciousness and realising that he is in a dream, and willing himself back into it.

He doesn't think she's dead. Or at least, he can't think she's dead.

He has that song by the Magnetic Fields in his head, and he's lying face down on his pillow, singing it in a tiny voice in his head.

I don't wanna get over you. He's always loved how the protagonist in the song muses about all the ways he could try to get over the woman he loves—take Prozac to make him smile at a sweet new girl who is not terribly bright. But why would he? He doesn't want to get over her.

His favourite lines of the song make him smile, despite himself, because Kate loves them so much, too—that he could make his career out of his misery and read Camus and smoke clove cigarettes and drink Vermouth. Which would be, the protagonist muses, 'a scream'. But why would he? *I don't wanna get over you.*

The lyrics remind him of the sort of guy he thought was unbelievably cool when he was a teenager and sneaking, underage, into jazz clubs, feeling terribly sophisticated and chuffed with himself. He laughed with Kate at how she'd done the same and how they were more or less caricatures. She'd even worn a beret.

He can't imagine what it would be like to try to get over her. Or how he ever could.

Kate and Liam used to joke about being type-A personalities. About how they struggled to just allow other people to get things done when they wanted to take over and get it done themselves. *Duces of Fair to Middling Schools, Unite and Take Over.*

He wishes he could somehow make the DNA process hurry up. That someone would put him in charge of the police case.

Even though he is not a police officer and would, admittedly, have absolutely no idea where to start.

I don't wanna get over you.

He blows his nose and forces himself to get up. He texts Sylvia and asks her if she wants to go for breakfast.

You bet I do, kiddo!

She drives him a bit mad at times, but he can see why Kate loves her so much. She is so relentlessly cheerful, but not in a cloying sense. She makes fun of people and situations and herself in a good-natured way. It's like she's constantly tap-dancing, helping to keep him from completely losing his mind.

He's getting out of the boiling/freezing shower, drying himself off with the miniature towel, when his phone starts to ring.

He slips on the beige bathroom tiles as he reaches for it and bangs his shin so hard, he wants to pass out with the pain.

'Sergeant D'Ambrosio? Arggh! FUCK!'

'G'day, Liam. You okay, mate?'

'Yes, I just slipped on the tiles in this godforsaken motel room and banged my shin.'

'Oh, that's the worst. Just wondering if you could come down to the station this morning. I've got some news for you, but it's better delivered in person.'

Liam gulps. 'Please tell me she's not dead.'

'No, it's not that. We've got a DNA match, mate.'

'Holy crap. Okay.'

Liam hangs up the phone and wrestles himself into some clothes and knocks on Sylvia's door. He notices that she has applied exaggerated winged eyeliner and orange lipstick and if he was less frantic, he'd wonder why she has chosen, in a situation like this, to go to the trouble.

'Okay, our breakfast plans have been a bit scotched. Let's get something to eat after we head down to the police station,' he says.

'How come?' Sylvia says. 'Is there news?'

'They've found a DNA match. He didn't want to tell me on the phone.'

Sylvia bites her lip so hard a little bit of blood oozes up through the matte orange lipstick.

'Ouch! Christ,' she says.

'We're all in the wars this morning, Sylvia,' Liam says, rolling up his jeans to show her an already impressive bruise.

'Okay, snap.'

—

At the police station, Peter D'Ambrosio walks out to meet them in the carpark.

'G'day, team,' he says. 'C'mon inside. Nice outfit,' he says to Sylvia, who, along with the winged eyeliner and orange lipstick, is wearing platformed boots, a pair of silver lame hotpants with magenta opaques and an oversized black knitted turtleneck that has three sleeves and cost eight hundred dollars on sale.

'Thanks, Sarge,' says Sylvia, smiling sweetly and arching an eyebrow. 'As it happens, you've got very winning taste.'

'You'd find if you got to know me, Sylvia, that there are many surprising things about Pete D'Ambrosio. I know my Issey Miyake from my Comme des Garcons.'

Sylvia colours and Liam shoots a look at her. Does he detect a frisson between these two? Between three-seasons-ahead Sylvia Estrellita and a cop from regional New South Wales with sad eyes who talks about himself in the third person? Surely not. Liam cocks his head and raises an eyebrow. Sylvia glares at him and presses her lips together, tightly, as if to say, *Shut the fuck up, Liam.*

D'Ambrosio doesn't notice, or at least, if he does, he pretends not to.

'Okay, guys, I'm not going to tell you how to feel about this, but I want you to know that it's promising that we've got the DNA,' D'Ambrosio says as they sit, again, at the Laminex table under the fluorescent lights that make them all look like ghouls.

'I sense a "but" coming,' Liam says, his eyes narrowing.

'Well, it's not a "but" as such,' D'Ambrosio says. 'It's just very difficult news—both for me to deliver and you to digest.'

Liam puts his head in his hands. What the fuck now? Sylvia puts her hand on his shoulder.

D'Ambrosio's eyes start to shine again. 'The DNA comes from a known sex offender,' he says. 'A man who was jailed some years ago for violently raping a stripper.'

Liam starts to involuntarily shake. Sylvia's lip starts to tremble.

'As far as we are aware, he is not a huge recidivist, but there is a very good chance, given his past and the fact that Kate is missing, that, well, there is a strong chance that what Kate has experienced could amount to—' he pauses and looks at the floor '—sexual assault of some kind.'

Sylvia lets out a strange little sound that is somewhere between a gasp and a squeak.

'And whatever happens,' D'Ambrosio continues, 'I suspect nothing is going to be the same for her. What we are most concerned about at the moment is that this man, who I hasten to add has never committed a homicide, might do so because Kate is the only witness to his crime against her. And he's probably going to know by now that this has become a high-profile case. He's probably heard things on the news like everyone else has. That might spook him a bit. He's been out of gaol for a couple of years, you see.'

'No,' says Liam. It's all he can manage to say. 'No.'

'I understand that this is absolutely horrible news for you to wrap your head around, Liam,' D'Ambrosio says softly. 'I'm terribly, terribly sorry to have to tell you this. And you, too, Sylvia.'

Sylvia has her head on the table. Through the horror of the moment, Liam notices that the third sleeve of the turtleneck is lying on the Laminex, too, in want, almost, of a third arm, and he is struggling to focus, instead wondering, *Why? Why the hell a third sleeve, Sylvia? Why the hell a third sleeve in this, of all situations, Sylvia?*

'Poor Tiger,' Sylvia says, over and over. 'My poor baby Tiger.'

'I know, it's bloody awful,' D'Ambrosio says. 'I'm so sorry. The world is a pretty messed-up place. But we need to focus on the positives, for now.

'The first positive is the fact that he has form—that means we know who he is. If this was the first time he'd chosen to offend, it would be very, very difficult for us to determine who he was from that DNA sample. The second positive is he's a bloody idiot for dropping those gloves and for not doing anything about the blood at the scene.'

Liam sniffs and nods. 'So, what happens now?'

'Okay, although we know who he is, because we don't have any CCTV or anything like that of him, what we have to do now is release a photofit image. We're not allowed by law to release a real photo. And we've got to hope to hell that someone recognises him and has seen him. Fortunately, he's a fairly distinctive looking guy.'

D'Ambrosio pushes across the photofit image of a muscular man with angular features and pale blueish-green eyes and hair that looks like it's been tipped by the same hairdresser as Shane Warne in the nineties.

'This is what we're putting out. Now, this man doesn't look vaguely familiar to either of you, does he?'

Liam shakes his head. He's pretty sure he's never seen this piece of scum.

But Sylvia takes a sharp intake of breath. 'Oh my God,' she says, her stomach dropping to the floor. 'We saw him.'

'Who saw him, Sylvia?' D'Ambrosio says slowly.

'We all did. That's Saggy Arse Guy.'

'Sorry? Saggy arse guy?'

'Yes. We saw him. The night that Kate disappeared,' Sylvia sputters. 'He was at the bar. Monkey Bar—that's where we were. And he tried to crack onto Kate. And he said she had a nice arse. And Kate hates guys like that. You know, she gets all feminist, and so she should, but she likes to have a go at them, and so she circled back behind him and made a crack about his saggy arse. And he was filthy about it, and anyway, we all just grabbed our things and ran.'

'And did you see him again that night, Sylvia?' D'Ambrosio asks.

'No! We thought we'd lost him. We'd all had a few drinks and we thought it was pretty funny. We picked up our things and ran off to another bar. I didn't see him follow us or anything. But that's the guy. I remember, because I remember thinking he was a bogan and it made me kind of laugh that he thought he'd ever be Kate's type.'

'You never told me this before, Sylvia,' Liam says.

'Well, I never thought it was relevant. I seem to remember I did mention it briefly when that Dooley cop down in Melbourne took my statement. But it was around about the time that they were trying to fit you up with clocking Kate over the head with a religious statue.'

'Thank you for this information, Sylvia,' D'Ambrosio says.

He gets on the phone and calls John Dooley.

'Mate, it's Peter D'Ambrosio. Yep, good, good. Don't know if it's been filtered back to you blokes yet, but we've just got a DNA match this morning. Yep. Yep. Known sex offender from up here. Yep. Must've been living or staying down there. Now, listen, I've just shown the photofit image to Sylvia Estrellita. Yep, the best friend. I don't know if you remember, but she mentioned to you that there was a bloke that night that Kate had a crack at, something about a saggy arse? Rings a bell? Yep. Only briefly. Yep. Well, Sylvia reckons that's him. Can you pull out the CCTV for Monkey Bar and the Old Tate again and see what you can find? I'm emailing you his file details now. Yep. Aw-kay. We'll get the photofit out to the media here if you guys could do same. Yep. Thanks a lot. Talk later.'

26

BINGO

JOHN DOOLEY FEELS a wave of guilt come over him. When Sylvia Estrellita briefly mentioned that thing about the guy who Kate had taunted about his saggy arse, he hadn't really paid attention. He goes back to his notes and sees it there. He hadn't followed up on it. At that stage he was absolutely convinced that the boyfriend had done something to her. He had allowed his feelings about that annoying hipster lawyer, his preconceptions about the omnipresence of domestic violence—how it traversed the boundaries of social class that were more clearly delineated in other categories of crime (Those preconceptions are almost always true! They are almost always on the money! It normally IS the boyfriend)—to get in the way of proper policing.

The fact that he, a stickler for the rules with a penchant for precision, made an error like this on a case that has turned out to be as big as this one makes Dooley bristle with hot shame.

His colleagues had done a door knock of the shops across the road from Monkey Bar and gathered up as much CCTV as they could find. The technical information officer (known as the TIO) had entered the CCTV clips in the computer system log and separate USBs had been kept. Dooley had watched the vision after it had been copied into the system. He remembered seeing Kate and her friends running out of Monkey Bar. He hadn't thought much of it, just a bunch of half-cut girls on a night out having fun.

There is nothing logged on the system after the Monkey Bar. He sits and stares at the screen for a while, drumming his fingers on the desk. It's weird, he thinks, that there wasn't any vision from outside or over the road from the Old Tate. He rings Tony Scala, the TIO.

'Hey Tony, it's John Dooley. Yep. Yeah, you saw we got a DNA match to a bloke with rape priors. Yep. Just wondering, we definitely didn't get any vision from outside the Old Tate, did we?'

Tony Scala says they did get some vision.

'But Tony, there's nothing logged. There's nothing in the system.'

'Well, John,' Tony replies, defensively, 'I can assure you that we did—I remember putting the USB in the file.'

Dooley's heart starts pumping. 'Tony, you didn't log it. You didn't log it.'

Tony goes silent on the other end of the phone. He finally starts to speak, but Dooley hangs up on him. Dooley runs back into his office and empties the evidence envelope onto his desk. The USBs scatter across the Laminex surface. He picks through them and finally sees one with a tiny label. *Old Tate*. Dooley's stomach falls. He puts the USB into his computer and the CCTV flickers on.

He watches it again. The vision is grainy and slow. The girls' heads bobbing and down, laughing. Their legs clop-clopping on the pavement as they run out of shot.

Nothing happens for a long time. Then, suddenly, a muscular figure with blond hair walks into shot. Dooley feels the coarse ginger hairs on the back of his neck stand on end as he watches the man standing outside the window at the Old Tate for a long time, peering in. You can't see what he's looking at. After some time, Dooley watches the man disappear into the shadows. Out walks a tall redhead in a miniskirt and long sixties-style boots. The man stays out of view and lets her walk for a while, and then, after enough time has passed that it's not clear he's following her, he walks in the same direction, out of shot.

That's the last CCTV they were able to secure for that night. She had then walked along a stretch of residential properties with no cameras at all. There were no cameras to pick up the *Bam. Bam. Bam.* No cameras to film The Guy clutching her arm so hard it bruised. No cameras to record him pushing her violently into a laneway. But still, for this to be missed, well, it's still a lot.

John Dooley sinks back on his chair.

He edits up a clip of The Guy and emails it to Peter D'Ambrosio with the subject line BINGO.

—

Police Media in Victoria and New South Wales are given the photofit and the CCTV to distribute to all television channels and newspapers.

Keri Kane gets a tip-off from her contact at Victoria Police that they're going to release some pictures of a suspect. She runs breathlessly up to the news desk to let everyone know.

'So much for your boyfriend theory, then,' Marina Chang plucks up the courage to quip. 'Your sources really were "impeachable" after all.'

'Look, that was really early days,' Keri quickly counters, flicking her hair and ignoring the barb about her slip of the tongue. 'And I'm not the only person who was running with that information.'

'Kinda defamatory, though,' Marina replies. 'Of, without putting too fine a point on it, a lawyer. And as I said at the time, a really bloody nice one, too.'

Keri ignores Marina and shows the chief of staff an email she's received with the photofit and the CCTV of a shadowy blond muscle man standing outside a bar, looking in.

'This is what they want us to put out,' she says. 'They're saying he's got priors.'

'Glad to see they're finally doing their jobs,' Marina returns.

Marina walks into Sean's edit suite. 'I can assure you, Peter,' Sean deadpans, 'my sources are *impeachable*.'

Marina grins. But then her face falls. 'God, I hope she's still alive.'

'Yep, me too,' Sean replies. 'That poor, poor girl. So scary.'

All of the commercial TV channels begin to run the photofit image and the CCTV on high rotation. The Guy's likeness is plastered on the front of every newspaper up and down the eastern seaboard.

Liam Carroll gets a text message from Suzie Monroe, his dodgy doctor defendant lawyer nemesis.

Oh god, Liam. Oh GOD. You must be reeling. Suze ❤

Liam feels his blood pressure starting to rise. Suzie Monroe does schadenfreude better than almost anyone he has ever met.

I'm hoping for the best, Suzie. I am buoyed by the fact we now have some information that will hopefully lead us to finding Kate.

Of course, Liam. Of course. Not sure if you're at work at the moment but if so, we have a statement of defence in my client Dr Moralis's case. Anyway, I'm sure you're super distracted, but please turn your mind to it when you have a moment. Or please advise who I should be sending this to. 🙇

'Super distracted.' That is certainly one way of putting it. God she is a horror.

Dr Moralis wrongly intubated Liam's client's baby, putting the breathing tube in the child's gullet instead of her windpipe, leaving the infant with profound brain damage. The parents were deeply religious and now spent twenty hours of every day caring for the child. The baby, now preschool age, would never speak nor walk. She just gazed skyward, looking permanently and heartbreakingly rapt. When Liam went to visit the family at their home, he had to excuse himself to go to the bathroom and sob uncontrollably.

Suzie. Please have some sensitivity. This is not the time to discuss Dr Moralis—who, by the way, the record would show, catastrophically disabled a baby girl. My girlfriend is missing, and the DNA has been matched to a known sex offender. Have some sensitivity.

He sees the three little dancing dots indicating a message is about to land. He pauses for a moment. And then he thinks *fuck it* and dashes off another text before she can send hers.

Incidentally, not long before she disappeared, Kate noticed I had a case against you and she reflected that you have the most realistic-looking fake Birkin bag she has ever seen.

She was surprised you couldn't afford the real thing, but applauded your thriftiness and your discerning eye.

Best, etc.

The three little dots that indicate an impending reply pop up, then disappear, pop up, then disappear. She's trying to craft a response. How does one respond to someone who has burned them so savagely, but is the boyfriend of a missing woman who has been kidnapped by a convicted rapist? There is no response. There is no return fire. The three little dots stop dancing before Liam's eyes.

Liam Carroll doesn't receive another text message from 'Suze'.

She will make his life hell when he finally does get back to work. But it is worth it for this little golden moment.

Kate Delaney would be so proud. The Carredashians would clink their champagne flutes in honour of their boy.

If Suzie Monroe dares to text him again, he'll mention lumpy dermal filler. Just try and stop him.

—

As images of The Guy flicker in an endless loop across television screens and online, The Guy himself is hiding out at a caravan park. Before they started running these pictures of him, he'd bought himself a swag and some camping supplies. He'd also got a new burner mobile phone with a prepaid SIM card. He'd then fanged it, without delay, over the border to the Sunshine State.

He's staying in a quiet campsite in south-east Queensland. It's off-peak, so there's hardly anyone around, bar a few Israeli backpackers who are too busy with constant partying to pay attention to their neighbours or watch the news. He keeps himself to himself and wears a beanie and sunglasses most of the time.

But he's now seen the CCTV and the photofit in news reports. He's filled with dread. He can't do more time. They'll flay him alive for this one. A pretty journalist who is the biggest news story in the country. He'll get a really long sentence. The blokes inside will go after him because rapists are not well-liked in prisons, on account of the fact that so many criminals were victims of child sex offences themselves when they were kids—hence why they went off the rails and ended up on drugs and whatnot. Prisons are full of people who were once victims of these crimes. He'd left Goulburn gaol promising himself never to darken that door-step again. He won't darken it. He won't.

The Guy checks himself into a fancy Surfers Paradise hotel under a pseudonym and requests a room that's on a high floor with good views. He orders a club sandwich with fries, a banana split and a bottle of champagne. He buys a porno on the hotel's television system. He finishes all of the pop, necking it straight from the bottle. He pulls a few cones and jerks off to the porn. He feels so alive. Smoking dope inside a hotel room? Who gives a fuck? You only live once.

And then he walks out to the balcony of his twenty-fourth-floor room, stands on the ledge, looks out to the beautiful vista of the Pacific Ocean. The orange sun falls slowly behind the silhouetted skyscrapers. He jumps.

27

HELLS BELLS

JUDY KING IS on her lemon leather recliner, staring blankly at the telly, when a news update flashes up onscreen.

'And now we're going to hear live from Keri Kane, who has rushed up to the Gold Coast in Queensland for the latest on a man believed to have abducted high-profile Melbourne journalist Kate Delaney. Keri, what can you tell us?'

'Well, this story that has stopped the nation has taken a very dark turn. As you know, pictures have been circulating of the man who police believe could have had some answers about the whereabouts of Kate Delaney, based on DNA samples from gloves and a property in the New South Wales Southern Highlands. Well, I'm standing outside the Orbital Hotel here in Surfers Paradise and you can see, just over to my left here, we have police tape and there is a tent that is believed to be covering up a man's body.

That's right, a man's body has been found. It's believed the man jumped from a balcony of a room on the twenty-fourth floor of the Orbital here, and it's believed that this is in fact the man who was in those CCTV pictures that we're showing you now.

'The devastating aspect of this is, of course, that if this man did have some information about Kate Delaney's whereabouts, he is now dead and can't assist police and we are no closer to finding out what has happened to her, and whether, in fact, she is still alive. Back to you.'

The newsreader, who has always reminded Judy King of a Ken doll, shakes his head and says 'Thanks, Keri. Keri Kane there, reporting from the Gold Coast on this tragic situation. We'll of course bring any further information to viewers as it comes in'.

Hells bells, Judy thinks, resolving to tell Mandy when Mandy gets back from the Blue Mountains.

Mandy has taken herself to a silent retreat where she is forbidden to speak or access any phones or computers. It was advertised as a way of finding profound inner peace. Mandy has been in turmoil since she found out about Kate, who has been missing for nearly a week. It has brought back all the grief from when she lost her only brother. She feels powerless and overwhelmed. She booked the retreat months ago and was going to cancel, but she would have lost her fifty per cent deposit and she is really strung out. She decides to go to the retreat for a couple of days to try to unplug, but is due back in Acacia Hills tomorrow.

Judy goes to the fridge and pours herself a sauvignon blanc. *Hells bells.*

Peter D'Ambrosio is sitting at his desk when he gets word from Queensland Police that they have found The Guy's body on the street below the Orbital and that he has topped himself. But Kate. Where is Kate?

The room starts to spin. The phone suddenly feels very heavy. D'Ambrosio's face goes numb. He stands up to walk out and tell one of his colleagues, but he feels like he's wading through treacle. His legs buckle underneath him like rubber bands. There's a ringing in his ears that sounds like hundreds of cicadas have suddenly emerged from hibernation.

He starts seeing them, again. The dead people. The jumpers. The people he's pleaded with not to step off the Pheasants Nest Bridge. He tries not to think of the fact that he, Peter D'Ambrosio, a cop who prides himself on his empathy and kindness, has never been able to talk one of them out of jumping from that bloody bridge. *Don't do it, mate, I can help you. Don't do it.* He sees their faces again now. The people he sees standing at the end of his bed, every night, their hollowed-out eyes and their blank stares. The bodies on the rocks in the ravines. The crow taking the eye. His Scottish papa's song.

He's been hoping that finding Kate Delaney might put those memories to bed. But it seems he's failed. Again. Peter D'Ambrosio takes himself to the old walk-in stationery cupboard at the back of the cop shop. And he sits on the floor, clicking his four-colour retractable biro—*black, blue, red, green, black, blue, red, green, black, blue, red, green*—and shivering. In his pocket, his phone rings, more or less non-stop.

—

Outside, in the foyer, Liam Carroll and Sylvia Estrellita are pacing again. Sylvia is weeping, uncontrollably, her perfectly winged eyeliner now a hot charcoal mess. Some news crews have followed them from the car to the entrance of the police station.

'What do you think about the fact that Kate's kidnapper is dead, Liam?' a reporter shouts at him. 'Do you hold out any hope?'

It takes every fibre of his being for Liam not to turn to the guy, hold him up against the wall by his collar and tell him to fuck right off.

Sylvia gently pats him on the shoulder and sputters, 'Come on, let's see what they have to say.'

In the foyer, Liam begins arguing with Horvath at the front desk.

'Look, I'm really not sure where he is,' Constable Horvath stammers. 'I promise you that as soon as I find out where he's gone, I'll let you know. He's just not answering his phone. He must be really tied up with the case.'

'Tied up with the case, Constable Horvath? Tied up with what case? What case? The suspect threw himself off a hotel balcony last night. You guys don't have a case anymore. You don't have any idea where Kate is. She could be anywhere. And the remains of the only person who had Buckley's of helping you with that information are splattered all over a bloody street in Surfers Paradise.'

28

STRANGER DANGER

UNDER THE PHEASANTS Nest Bridge, Kate Delaney has reached that stage of hunger where she is beginning to hallucinate. It's been five nights under that bridge. She's lying on the little steps, so cold. Mary used to talk about being cold in your bones. The sort of cold where it takes all night to get warm again. That sort of cold hurts, so much. She can't wrap the blanket tightly enough around herself. She keeps folding it over her feet, and then they pop free again, a blast of wind hitting them each time. She's given up blowing hot air into her hands because she can't feel her hands anymore.

The Burger Rings packet is now empty bar a few crumbs at the bottom. The Iced Vo-Vos are finished. The apple feels like weeks ago. She has a few sips of water left and then the bottle will be empty. She's finding it hard to focus on what's in front of her. The bats/wasp nests/stalactites hanging from the underside of the bridge definitely haven't moved, so she's landed on stalactites.

She wonders if this means the bridge is unsafe. Is it about to collapse on her? Will she now star in two stories, not just one? A high-profile kidnapping and then a tragic bridge collapse. She figures Cameron Patrick will give her one day to recover after being pulled out of the wreckage before she has to file her first-person piece.

If it wasn't for the sharp sting of the cold wind creeping through the cage, the ache of her sores, the hunger, she'd still struggle to really comprehend that she is a victim of an abduction at all.

It seems like such an odd and implausible thing. *Woman snatched from street.* She remembers patiently explaining to Mandy King in a slightly exhausted tone that she's now ashamed of, that all the records showed that stranger danger abductions were unbelievably rare. She had looked into Bureau of Crime Research statistics and you were, she found, more likely to have been the victim of a freak violent crime in 1930s Sydney than you were to become one now.

'Everyone talks about the good old days, Mandy,' she had said, ever-so-patiently, 'but the good old days were scary times. You and your kids are much safer now.'

The conversation had taken this dark twist because Mandy could be, at times, a shocking helicopter mother. She was jittery and overprotective about her kids, using baby monitors until they were at school, fitting out the backyard in spongy rubber so they didn't hurt themselves if they fell over, banning them from watching the news, making excuses not to let them have sleepovers, obsessively locking and relocking the doors at night, not turning her head for a moment when they were out and about.

Kate thought this to be complete nonsense. She had the dismissive confidence that the childless possess until they finally become parents themselves and spend the first few weeks terrified that the baby will die, madly googling Sudden Infant Death Syndrome and choking hazards.

Until The Guy took her that night, Kate had always rolled her eyes at the idea of stranger danger, thinking it was an exaggeration cooked up by conservatives on law and order campaigns. *Everyone knows that women are far more likely to be murdered in a domestic violence incident. Everyone knows that children are more likely to be abused by a relative than a creepy stranger.*

—

As it happens, The Guy wasn't the first stranger who had preyed on Kate Delaney. The first one came across her in Dublin, when she was a pig-tailed five-year-old playing at the treeless local swing park with a couple of friends, back in the days when five-year-olds played at parks unsupervised.

Kate had, for reasons she couldn't explain even to her five-year-old self, not bothered to put on underwear that day. She was wearing a navy and red dotty dress with an embroidered collar and a full, above-the-knee skirt that Auntie Maggie had bought her. It had reminded young Kate of something from a story book. Mary thought it was hideous and kept burying it at the back of Kate's wardrobe, but Kate had dragged it out that morning and smoothed it over her little body in front of the mirror.

As she was careening back and forth on the metal swing, gazing up into the slate-grey sky, the wind caught the dress and a couple of mohawked teenage punks had noticed and joked about showing them her fanny. Shame had jolted through Kate, and she pretended not to notice as they chortled. The punks were just bullies, but there was also a man who had been slinking around the sidelines of the park.

She can still remember him now. She'd still pick him in a police line-up. He was wearing brown and beige houndstooth trousers and a wash-and-wear polyester shirt the colour of buttermilk, and he had tinted, clear-framed coke-bottle glasses. Thinking back, he really did present as a paedophile from central casting. He could have worked on his look.

'Howarye?' he said, his hands on the iron bars of the fence. 'Wha's the craic?'

He told Kate and her friends that he had Tayto crisps and Club Orange and Christmas selection boxes, and would they like to come with him?

The children had been warned about stranger danger and knew not to go, but they stood motionless, gawping, sort of mesmerised by this cobra in worsted wool, rising out of his kiddy-fiddler snake basket with heady promises of crisps and minerals. He made them feel simultaneously afraid and unable to avert their gazes.

'C'mon, ye little messers,' he kept saying, holding out his hand. 'You'll be sorry, wha'?'

He was particularly fixated on Kate, who felt by then like she had a giant sign on her head saying I DIDN'T WEAR ANY KNICKERS TODAY. Mary Delaney would have had a fit if she had known.

It was one of the first times that Kate Delaney had found her inner firebrand. She summoned every ounce of courage in her tiny body, punching through the shame of no knickers and her natural shyness.

'You're a Bad Man! I'm tellin' my Mammy!' she yelled at him. And then she started to scream, loudly, in the highest pitch she could muster. Coke-Bottle Glasses Man's eyes widened, and he started madly looking around the stubby field to see if anyone else was watching.

The three five-year-olds saw their opportunity, held hands and made a run for it. There was no way the man, who seemed to have a gammy leg, could keep up, even if he did want to risk chasing after screaming children in daylight. They ran all the way home and never said a word to their parents. They never spoke of it to each other again either. Kate had kept it secret until she was an adult. Her parents were horrified she had never disclosed it to them, and she had ribbed them about allowing a five-year-old to go to a park without an adult present.

—

But that Stranger Danger incident was different, she now reflects. That dangerous stranger was trying to entice her and her friends. He gave them an out. He didn't just grab them. The Guy had not groomed her, nor spoken to her in any way after the 'saggy arse' comment. He had just taken her off the street and savagely raped her.

And Kate is now the horrifying prospect that keeps parents like Mandy King awake at night, that makes women out walking clutch their keys in a strategically defensive position and keep their phones poised and out of their handbags. She is the statistical anomaly.

How will they write up her story? What will be her newspaper lead? How will they avoid clichés?

Trying to keep herself alert, she starts writing the script of a nightly current affairs story.

'It's the early hours of Sunday morning in Northcote, and a man is following a woman who has been out for drinks with her friends,' the reporter's voice says, over a stylised re-enactment of feet walking up High Street.

'Kate was so happy that night. We all were,' one of her friends like Adie or Sophie say, thought-tracked as the walking scene re-enactment continues.

Then it comes to Adie/Sophie in the interview with the reporter, in sync, teary: *'I just can't believe that she's gone.'*

Cue dramatic production music. Cue Kate's Most Flattering Picture, dutifully distributed to the media by Sylvia, because, as Sylvia's always said (and Kate agrees, wholeheartedly), unflattering photos are tantamount to a war crime.

Reporter voiceover: *'Before this terrible night in Northcote, Kate Delaney was one of Melbourne's most decorated newspaper journalists.'* (Maybe a bit of a stretch, but she'll take it.)

Cue Cameron Patrick, in his office, shaking his head: *'She was perhaps the most talented reporter of her generation.'* (Again, a stretch, but they always say this sort of shit when someone dies and again, who is she to argue? She'll take it.)

Reporter voiceover: *'But now, she's joined the ranks of the victims whose stories she once told.'*

Cue pictures of Liam and Sylvia walking out of a police station in slow motion. Et cetera. Et cetera. Et cetera.

Kate Delaney feels that from this moment forward, if she ever gets out of this cage, she won't be smug and presumptuous with anyone. She won't roll her eyes at Mandy, if she ever sees her again. She won't be sarcastic. She'll tolerate sundried tomatoes in regional cafe sandwiches. She won't frown at bad shoes or cheap suits or mentally take a red pen to poorly executed social media commentary. She'll always use her powers for good.

Who is she trying to kid? She is fading away, here. She closes her eyes. It hurts too much now, to keep them open. Under the Pheasants Nest Bridge, the cage keeps fading to black.

29

I CAN'T

IN THE SMALL backyard behind her brick-veneer unit in Melbourne, Gloria Estrellita is standing on her little patch of lawn, her kitten heels sinking into the grass, little divots of soil flying into the air each time she moves. Before her is a dead chicken she's preparing to bury in the turf. In a moment she now concedes may well have been madness, Gloria decided to buy a couple of chickens after seeing a documentary Sylvia had made her watch on the evils of the egg industry. 'But Nanay,' Sylvia said, rolling her eyes, 'I made you watch it so you would buy free-range organic eggs, not so you'd buy chickens to scarper around the backyard!'

But Gloria wouldn't listen, and now she is trying to bury the headless carcass of Hope, named after the beautiful and long-suffering Hope Brady, Gloria's favourite character in *Days of Our Lives*. Hope's luck ran out after one of the foxes that prowled the neighbourhood got in through a hole in Gloria's patio fence. For someone who had planned on raising fowl, Gloria had made scant preparations for their security. She now sinks to her knees and starts digging in the dirt with a trowel that is simply not up to the task. She wishes Sylvia was here to help.

Instead of Sylvia, she can hear the sound of her daughter's Russian toy terrier jumping up and scratching on her decorative fly screen, yelp-yelp-yelping. She hasn't let Boris out because she fears what he might do to the headless chicken, not to mention the live one.

Operation No Hope duly executed, Gloria Estrellita clack-clacks down the hallway, and scoops Boris into her arms. Her Button has spoiled this stupid dog. He'll only give her peace when she picks him up.

She settles into the lounge-room sofa with Boris. He looks up at her and cocks his little head and she smacks her tongue against the roof of her mouth and sighs at the grass stains on her teal capri pants. Gloria's television blares with news, but still there is no sign of that poor darling Kate. Sylvia only answers Gloria's calls from time to time. 'I can't speak to you, Nanay,' she says in a voice that Gloria doesn't recognise. It's lower and quieter. It's not her Button's voice. 'I can't speak anymore. I can't.' Gloria Estrellita's chest tightens, and she turns over to the soapies and makes a sign of the cross on her chest.

—

Sylvia Estrellita is in the crappy motel room, curled around the pillow in the foetal position, not wanting Liam to see her, because she's finding it increasingly impossible to keep trying to cheer him up. The damp is rising into her bones. She's under the blanket, wearing an alpaca jumper, with that cashmere wrap she brought for Kate wound tightly around her, but nothing makes her warm. Her thoughts are constantly invaded with thoughts of Kate's assault. As if Kate's body is her body. Survivor guilt hovers in her every thought. She is just so, so cold.

—

Liam Carroll can't feel the Southern Highlands freeze. He can't feel anything. He's sitting on the concrete outside the cop shop. His phone shows twenty-four failed calls to Peter D'Ambrosio and John Dooley has stopped picking up, too. Every time the automatic doors burst open, he turns with a start, but every time, he's disappointed. A young mum wheeling a pram. A country solicitor in a shiny charcoal suit. Two traffic cops on their smoko. From time to time, his joints creak as he pulls himself up and walks through the entrance to the front desk, but every time Horvath just looks back at him and gently shakes his head.

—

Peter D'Ambrosio is still in the stationery cupboard, holding his pen. He's remembering, with a little sting, how he first wanted to be a detective in Year Five of primary school after his teacher set a task where they had to solve a mystery. Young D'Ambrosio solved the mystery first. He can't for the life of him remember, now, what that stupid mystery was. But he remembers the burst of pride when his teacher, Mrs Hegarty, gave him a gold star, a scratch 'n' sniff sticker that smelled of bubble-gum and said TOP WORK! and a Caramello Koala. It was the first time that Peter D'Ambrosio ever won anything. But solving mysteries became something that Peter D'Ambrosio could do. He wanted all the gold stars. If a constellation was the collective noun for stars in the night sky, what was the collective noun for gold stars? A shimmer? A shower? A glimmer? But who was he kidding? All he had now was a four-colour ballpoint pen and a calloused thumb. *Click. Click. Click. Click.*

—

Under the bridge, in her reverie, Kate Delaney can see Liam Carroll coming towards her. They're in the centre of the reading room at the State Library. She kisses his soft lips. He runs his hands through her hair.

'I always loved your hair, Kate Delaney. You've got great hair,' he says to her, like he always does.

She presses her forehead against his. He takes her in his arms, and they start to dance. As he's whirling her around, she looks up, the magnificent white dome spinning around and around above the terraces of books.

'One million books,' Liam once told her, when they were pretending to read, but really stealing glances, wanting to jump on one another. 'This room is designed to store one million books. Can you imagine how many thoughts are in one million books?'

It's night-time and she can just make out the stars through the windows and porticos above. The green glass lamps on the wooden desks that span out from the centre whiz by. The room is empty but for them. Just two nerdy kids from forgettable schools in forgettable suburbs, spinning around an octagonal Edwardian room. She can hear The Church, somewhere, playing 'Under The Milky Way'.

And it's something quite peculiar
Something shimmering and white
It leads you here
Despite your destination
Under the Milky Way tonight.

But when she forces open one of her eyes, all she can see around her is a dark cage, all she can hear is wind whistling.

She can feel the eyes of the jumpers, who now perch in the trees. The pain of all the lives that ended too soon. So palpable here, that pain could run a Soviet power station. The pain of decisions that wouldn't have been made on other, better, days. The words they tried to say or wished they had said to the people in their lives.

Stop hurting me.

Why don't you believe me?

I was only eight.

I didn't mean it.

I've run out of options.

I'm sorry. I love you.

I'm so proud of you.

I tried.

I can't.

On cue, some spinifex tumbles past to the left, like it does in all the Australian horror flicks. In the distance, she can hear the sound of the gang gangs calling like creaking gates. Kate Delaney wants to go back to the dancing. She closes her eyes again and slips gently away out of consciousness.

30

PHEASANTS NEST

WHEN MANDY KING wakes up, lying on pristine, high-thread-count bed linen, her pillows feel like clouds. Last night's incense has burnt away to leave a pleasant aroma of calm. She's only been at this retreat for two days, but she feels so much better.

She really, really needed this time out. Mandy King hasn't had a holiday on her own in years. Her brief respite from the kids' chaos and Judy's monotonous chattering about nothing much has been a tonic. She hasn't had any booze and has been drinking lemongrass and ginger tea and eating food that the instructors describe as 'clean'. Apparently, Mandy's food has been dirty until now. The food at the retreat involves a lot of kale and samphire and salt-reduced tamari and bone broth. The bone broth makes Mandy chuckle a little. Her body, the instructors have cautioned her, is a temple, and she needs to tend to the temple's gardens and waterways more carefully. Mandy, forbidden from any conversation, has just nodded serenely.

She feels like a whole new Mandy King.

She is wearing a tiered floaty purple paisley dress she bought for the occasion at Tree of Wisdom and has had her hair braided into cornrows. She has bought little silver toe rings and a rose quartz pendant from the shop at the retreat. She's had her aura done (although still doesn't quite know what that means, and doesn't care). The skin on her arms and legs glows with body butter and her body is still humming from the massage she had yesterday. She smells like pine spruce and freesias. Her mind feels at ease. She should do this more often.

At eleven am, she gets in her little Mazda and glides home to Acacia Hills, determined to live a more mindful existence from now on. She hasn't entirely worked out what that entails, but she is intent on giving it a solid try. She plays calming wellness music all the way up the freeway. It's punctuated with bird calls and wind chimes and chanting.

'Hello, darling,' Judy says, when she gets in the door. 'You look very relaxed. Have you heard the latest?'

'What latest, Mum?'

'About Kate. Well, not about Kate, but the man they think took her. He's killed himself, I'm afraid.'

'What?' Mandy says.

She pulls out her phone to find the story online, but it's out of battery. She runs over to the kitchen bench, plugs it in and waits for it to charge up before madly googling.

His face takes up the full screen. His blond-tipped hair, his pale seawater eyes that crinkle up at the sides. His knowing smile. His ripped, veiny arms. The yin and yang tatt on his bicep.

Mandy King runs into the bathroom and is violently ill.

'What's wrong, Poppet?' calls Judy.

'It's *him*, Mum,' Mandy says, wiping vomit from the corner of her mouth. 'It's him.'

'Who, love?'

'Him.'

Judy never met The Guy because Mandy had wanted to keep him away from her kids until the relationship got Really Serious. But that had never happened. And Mandy was relieved, when it all broke off, that she hadn't complicated things for her children by introducing someone who would just leave their lives in the end anyway.

Mandy runs to get her handbag and keys. 'Mum, I'm going out.'

'Where are you going, love?'

'To find Kate Delaney.'

Judy King purses her lips, clicks her tongue and turns back to the episode of *Judge Judy* she's watching on the television.

'You think you are all that,' Judge Judy barks at the woman cowering in front of her in the courtroom. 'I can tell you what someone should have told you years ago. You are NOT all that! Case dismissed.'

'You are NOT all that,' Judy mumbles under her breath as the TV judge slams her gavel down on her bench. She clicks her tongue. '*Tickets.*'

—

Mandy jumps in her car and tries to remember the name of that Filipina girl who had been Kate's best friend, whom she had seen on the news a few days ago with some guy who seemed to be Kate's new boyfriend.

Sonia? No. Dammit, what was her name? *Sophia?* No.

Sylvia! Sylvia.

She digs her phone out of her bag, plugs it into the car charger and scrolls through the list of names, while trying to keep her eyes on the road. She had to call Sylvia a couple of times around the time of Michael's funeral because Sylvia was helping Kate, who was a mess. Mandy remembers that Sylvia was a nice girl. She was kind to Mandy. She was funny and kooky and the sort of girl you wanted to be your friend, even if the instant you saw her, you immediately felt self-conscious and realised your outfit was unimaginative and suburban and at least three seasons behind.

There she is. *Sylvia Estrellita. Kate Friend.*

She puts the phone on speaker on her lap and calls a couple of times. But it rings out. She figures Sylvia probably thinks she is being a nosy parker. One of those annoying people who likes to get in on the grief action. She remembers those sorts of people driving her crazy after Michael died. It was hard to get a proper rest with all the neighbours ringing on the doorbell and coming to sympathetically nod.

She waits until she pulls up to a set of lights, and sends a text message.

> Sylvia, I'm so, so sorry about what's going on. It's Mandy King. Michael's sister. I'm only calling because I have some really important information. Call me ASAP.

Sylvia has convinced Liam to come back to the hotel because D'Ambrosio can't be contacted, and Horvath isn't giving them anything.

She is still lying under the synthetic beige coverlet, trying to stop sobbing. But every time she does, she thinks of something to do with Tiger, and she starts up again. Her phone is on the coverlet next to her, but she hasn't realised it has clicked on to silent. She has not heard the phone ring at all.

She knows she needs to pull herself together for Liam. She decides to do what always brings her a great sense of calm and equilibrium in time of crisis: internet shopping.

When she picks up her phone, there are multiple missed calls from the same number she doesn't recognise.

She goes into messages and sees the text from Mandy and calls her immediately.

'Hi, Mandy. Yes, long time no see. Yes, I know, it's so bloody awful. Poor Kate. What's up?'

'Sylvia, I feel absolutely terrible,' Mandy begins. 'But I know that man. Or at least, I knew him. That man on the TV, that killed himself. The one they think took Kate.'

'Holy shit, really?' Sylvia says.

'Yes, really.'

'I have a feeling I know where Kate is. Are you guys still in New South Wales? Did I see you going into a cop shop?'

'Yeah, that was us—me and Liam, Kate's, uh—' she says, feeling guilty about saying it to Michael's sister. 'Kate's, you know?'

'Her boyfriend?' Mandy asks. 'Yes, it's okay that she's got a boyfriend. It makes sense that she would. She has to live her life. Listen, Sylvia, if you're not too far, do you want to meet me at the Pheasants Nest Bridge—you know, the big one on the freeway? You can pull over to the side of it, before you get on to the actual bridge, heading north. I'll see you there. I should be there in fifteen or so.'

'We're very close by,' Sylvia says. 'We'll get in the car.'

Sylvia goes and pounds on Liam's door.

He opens the door, rubbing his puffy eyes. 'What's going on?'

'Let's get in the car,' Sylvia says.

'What do you mean?'

'Get in the fucking car, Liam. Get in the fucking car!'

Constable Mark Horvath is standing at the door to the stationery cupboard at the back of the cop shop. It's locked.

'I know you're in there, Sarge,' he says.

Peter D'Ambrosio says nothing.

'Do you think you could come out?'

'No offence, Mark, but go away. Let me just have a minute.'

'But that minute's been a few hours now, Sarge. You must be hungry.'

'I'm not hungry. Listen, I just need to be on my own for a bit. I didn't want anyone to find me in here.'

'I know. I won't tell anyone that you're in there or how long it's been. It's a quiet day so I don't think anyone else has noticed. I've just seen you head in here before sometimes, I expect when things get too much.'

'Mmm.'

'I just want you to know that there's pretty much no one else in this place like you. No one gives a shit like you do, Sarge.'

D'Ambrosio's ears start to ring again.

'Fat lot of good it's done that girl.'

'None of what happened was your fault. Vic Pol are the ones who fucked up the CCTV.'

'Hmm.'

D'Ambrosio suspects he's acting like a petulant idiot. On the one hand, it's mortifying and probably deeply unprofessional that he's exposing himself like this in front of this young constable. Sworn officers don't hide themselves in stationery cupboards. Sworn officers don't show emotional vulnerability in front of their juniors. It won't do.

On the other, the ringing is just too loud. His stomach is doing that washing machine thing it does. His fingers are tingling. He still can't feel his face.

'You know, you're the first bloke around here who showed me it's okay to feel. Like we *should* feel,' Horvath says. 'The shit we see. We should feel. It would be so weird if we didn't.'

'That's a very millennial view of the world, Horvath.'

'Well, I am a millennial, Sarge.'

'True that.'

D'Ambrosio reflects that, with all their irritating tendency towards work-to-rule and their mental health days and their social media oversharing, millennials don't put up with shit the way his generation always has. They're righteously indignant. They demand better. It could be a legacy of overwrought parenting where kids were given agency and asked for their opinions, instead of, as he experienced, being seen and not heard and reared by a combination of mild fear and benign neglect. But he has to hand it to them for standing up for themselves.

Whereas for so many years, like so many of his colleagues, he's just kept going and going like an old Clydesdale, and expecting he will until the scabby horse can't go any more.

And he hides in stationery cupboards, and pastes tin foil on his windows and spends his weekends horizontal on his sofa, so exhausted that even when he's lying on the remote control, he just leaves it there and takes another swig of his beer. He's so spent that on weeknights he just crashes on that stupid sofa at the station with the dried noodles down the back of the battered cushions.

Stupid, stupid, old Clydesdale. Just keep going until you're done. Until someone sends you to the knackery.

'We can't always make it better, Sarge.'

'Yeah, thanks, Oprah,' D'Ambrosio says, before realising that this kid probably barely registers who Oprah Winfrey is.

'You know I speak the truth,' Mark Horvath says, raising his hand and again knocking softly on the cupboard door.

D'Ambrosio puts his head in his hands and rubs his eyes vigorously. Just this time, this time, he had been wanting matters to pan out differently or, even, God forbid, well. Was it so much to ask to have them pan out well?

He wasn't able to stop a bankrupt farmer from jumping off that bridge right there in front of him. He wasn't there to take the wheel from a nineteen-year-old driving along to blaring music while his mates pulled cones in the back of the car, only to take his eyes off the road and end up in pieces at the bottom of the ravine. He didn't get to a house before a pregnant woman's de facto king hit her dead, in front of the kids.

But this girl's disappearance doesn't have any of the split-second rotten luck, or the grim inevitability, of those things.

Kate Delaney is the sort of girl who, all the signs say, is not supposed to disappear.

He flips open his phone cover and searches up her name. He sits and looks at the flattering photo Sylvia Estrellita made sure went out on the socials. The flattering photo he can't bear the thought of being in an oval frame on the front-page splash of the tabloids—an oval frame that means she's dead. That means he didn't get to her on time.

'Please, Sarge. Come out,' Horvath says again. 'C'mon.'

D'Ambrosio sighs and starts to get to his feet. His knees creak in an altogether too middle-aged way. He needs to get back to Pilates, but who is he trying to kid? He probably won't.

—

As he begins to stand up, D'Ambrosio hears the sound of rubber-soled steel-capped boots running in the hall. And Michelle Wang's voice, raised with a sort of urgency that he hasn't heard before. An urgency that defies her usual eye-rolling cynicism.

'Mark, Mark, where's Pete D'Ambrosio? Quick, where is he?' he hears Michelle say, her words catching with breathlessness.

'Uh, he's, um, well . . .'

'Here!' comes a voice from the stationery cupboard.

D'Ambrosio scrambles to his feet and bangs his head on the corner of a sharp metal shelf as he does.

'I'm here,' he says, opening the door and cursing what he knows will be an ugly shiner right in the middle of his forehead. 'I was just looking for some stuff in there. What's a man got to do to find a bloody stapler around here?'

'M'kay,' Michelle says, in that way she has, that tone that says she doesn't believe him and always makes him feel like a pathetic old fart. But she doesn't have time to take the piss out of him now.

'We just heard from triple-zero, Sarge. You need to get to the Pheasants Nest Bridge. Right now. Apparently, Kate Delaney might be there. That bloke, that bloke that topped himself in Surfers, he used to bring girls there. Or *a* girl, at least. And she's called to say we should go there.'

The ringing in D'Ambrosio's ears just stops, suddenly. His heart starts to beat so fast he can almost hear it.

'What?'

'Why don't I fill you in on the way over there, Sarge?' Michelle says, waving a report. 'We don't have enough time to sit here talking about it.'

'Sounds like a plan, Michelle,' D'Ambrosio says, nodding and regaining his composure as he does. 'Sounds like a plan.'

Constable Mark Horvath rests his hand on D'Ambrosio's shoulder.

'Good man,' says D'Ambrosio, and gives him a quick and almost imperceptible look of thanks.

'I might hop in the car, too,' Horvath says. He sees the fevered look in D'Ambrosio's eyes and he's desperately worried about what they might find at that bridge. Michelle Wang is a very competent police officer, but empathy isn't always her strong suit.

The three country cops race out to the sally port and into the waiting car.

'Put the siren on, Constable,' D'Ambrosio says to Michelle Wang. 'Are the ambos on their way, too?'

Horvath looks from the back seat at his superior to see that, on each hand, D'Ambrosio's two fingers are crossed and folded up underneath his thumbs. His hands are a reddish purple, and his knuckles are white.

The young constable puts another tentative hand on his boss's shoulder and D'Ambrosio pretends not to notice.

Michelle Wang nods. 'On it, Sarge.'

—

The Pheasants Nest Bridge isn't too far from the motel where Liam Carroll and Sylvia Estrellita have been staying.

'What's this about, Sylvia?'

'I don't really know, to be honest, Liam,' Sylvia says. 'Mandy King is the sister of Kate's ex, Michael. Kate has barely seen the family since he died in a car accident.'

'Oh yeah, from what she's told me, they're kind of nightmares.'

'Well, to be fair, Mandy's actually very inoffensive and pretty sweet, but the mum is a complete horror show,' Sylvia says. 'But yeah, Mandy rang me out of the blue a few minutes ago and said to meet here. She said she knew the bloke who topped himself. She didn't say why or how. She just said to meet her here. She didn't sound like she was on handsfree on the mobile, so I think she just wanted to get off the phone and explain when she got here.'

HIGH WIND AREA. PROCEED WITH CAUTION, says a sign on the side of the road. And it's true. It feels like the car's being battered with the force of it. Sylvia just keeps driving. She's dispensed with her usual jokes and pleasantries and has a demonic look in her eye Liam hasn't seen before.

The sign looms in front of them. NEPEAN RIVER. PHEASANTS NEST BRIDGE.

'I think this is us,' Sylvia says, swerving to the left without warning and jerking them both suddenly sideways.

Liam winces as he bites his tongue.

They get out of the car and sit down on a roadblock to wait for Mandy. Liam tries to swallow, his mouth dry and papery, as he catches sight of the faded carnations stuck to the road barrier, the cursive RIP on the stained, graffitied concrete, the little memorials for the dead. He gulps and tries not to catch the eyes of the young man in the photograph, who is smiling bashfully out from a frame in the middle of a simple concrete cross. IN LOVING MEMORY. And in the cement, that word, etched. MUM.

Liam feels the old pang of grief well up inside him. Mum. *Teddy times*. Everything is pain.

Sylvia is tapping her gold cowboy boots on the gravel almost maniacally, looking at her watch and wondering what is keeping Mandy.

The late winter sun that has been out for a couple of days has disappeared behind the clouds. The sky looks like a fluffy grey continental quilt and rain has started to mist over them.

A little silver run-around suddenly screeches to a halt and a small blonde woman with cornrows, round brown eyes and a purple paisley dress slams its door shut and runs over, breathlessly.

Mandy grabs Sylvia and almost squeezes the life out of her. 'So good to see you, Sylvia,' she says, catching her breath, then turns to Liam. 'Hello,' she says, shyly. 'I'm Mandy King.'

'I'm Liam Carroll,' he says. 'Nice to meet you, Mandy.'

'Come on.' Mandy pushes through her shyness and intimidation and takes Liam's hand on one side and Sylvia's on the other.

'Where are we going?' Liam asks.

'We're going to get Kate,' Mandy replies, nodding vigorously. 'This is where *he* used to come. This was *his* place.'

'Whose place?' Liam asks.

She's talking without pausing for breath. 'He was a bad man. I didn't realise it, well, not at first. He loved this place. I've got no idea why. I mean, look around, it's pretty creepy, right? He tried to hurt me here. I told him I wouldn't let him.' She nods her head vigorously as she's talking, and presses her mouth into a little, firm, white line.

'What bad man?' Liam asks again. 'Mandy, what bad man?'

'The man who jumped out of that hotel at Surfers. I'm sorry. I didn't know. I mean, I only just found out that it was him.'

Liam looks at Sylvia. He feels like he's going to throw up.

'What did he do to you? How did he try to hurt you?'

Mandy stops and just stares at him for a few seconds and shakes her head. 'Come on, let's not talk about that. I don't want to talk about that. You don't need to know about that. Not now. Let's keep moving.'

Liam shudders.

The sky stops spitting for a few seconds and it looks like the sun might appear. But then the clouds above the Southern Highlands open up with a sudden violence and bucketing down on them is what Kate's Auntie Maggie would have called 'wet rain'.

'Watch your step here, it's slippery,' Mandy says, dodging broken glass.

She brings them down a winding path through the shrubs, past the ratty old ice-cream container and the bubble wrap, the dirty nappy, the dildo and the red-bellied black snake, which has by now retreated from the rain, looking out at them from a narrow slit in a hollow log.

They turn around to the right, back up towards the bridge.

Liam glances down at the Nepean splashing on rocks at the bottom of the gorge below and starts shivering. The ghosts of the jumpers are all around them, watching from the branches of the trees, with the gang gang cockatoos. He doesn't know their stories but, somehow, he feels them. He feels the overwhelming sense of despair that hangs in the valley.

'I don't like this fucking place, Chicken,' Sylvia says, wrapping a floor-length alpaca cardigan around her little body.

'Yeah, I don't much like it either,' says Liam.

Mandy remains focused on the task.

'Here we go. This is us,' she says. 'This is us.'

Liam and Sylvia look up to see a dark anteroom attached to a cage nestled in the underside of the bridge.

And slumped over on a little wooden stoop of the cage, grazed legs off to the side, an empty packet of Iced Vo-Vos at her feet, is Kate Delaney.

—

'Tiger!' gasps Sylvia.

Liam runs up to the cage and Mandy and Sylvia stand back. The rain is falling so hard he can barely see. The ground has gone muddy under his feet and he's slipping as he goes towards her.

He begs the universe for her to be alive.

He bangs on the cage, repeatedly. 'Kate! Kater! Katie . . .'

She doesn't move.

He turns to Sylvia and Mandy. 'Ring D'Ambrosio, ring Horvath, ring Dooley. Ring the ambos, ring triple-zero.'

'It's okay, I already rang triple-zero,' Mandy says, and as she speaks, sirens begin to sound, and lights begin to flash from above them on the bridge and the freeway.

There's a slamming of car doors and, from the roadway, they can see D'Ambrosio running towards them with Horvath, a young female cop and some cardigan, as he'd put it, from Roads.

'Where is she? Where is she?' D'Ambrosio spits out between breaths as he reaches them.

Sylvia and Liam and Mandy all motion to the cage.

Both D'Ambrosio and Liam notice, at this moment, all the signs saying the area is *under 24-hour surveillance* and turn, with narrowed eyes, to the cardigan from Roads, who shrugs.

'Not my job,' says the cardigan, waving his hands.

The cardigan asks Liam to step aside, and he punches eight digits into the keypad on the door to the anteroom.

The door springs open.

Some ambos come running with a stretcher that has one of those silver blankets Liam has seen on the news, in stories when people are rescued *after all hope was thought to be lost following seven terror-filled nights in the snow.*

They put the stretcher next to the unconscious Kate and carefully ease her onto it.

—

Her legs look like bones. Her little Mary Quant–style mini dress is ripped and hitched up—a paramedic pulls it down for modesty. She's all cut and grazed. Her skin is the palest blue. Her lips are purple. Her usually glorious red hair is all matted. She reminds Liam of a gothic ragdoll that's been left, forgotten, by a preschooler at the bottom of a toybox.

The paramedics hoist up the stretcher onto a trolley that someone has wheeled down the hill. Suddenly there are people everywhere.

D'Ambrosio is standing over Kate, staring at her intently, his face numb and his heart feeling like it will beat on out of his chest. He has the beginnings of a large egg-shaped shiner in the middle of his forehead.

'Don't ask,' he says to Liam.

Liam wasn't going to ask. He doesn't care about D'Ambrosio's shiner. He just wants Kate to wake up.

'Come on Kate, come on Kate, c'mon Kate, come back to us,' D'Ambrosio's saying, while one of the paramedics is doing vital signs. But in his mind he's saying, *Don't let us down, don't let me down.*

They're all crowded around her, someone's doing CPR and Liam can't get anywhere near his girl. She's unconscious but he hears someone say they've got a pulse. It's absolutely pelting down now and they're trying to cover her before they can get her up to the ambulance.

Mandy and Sylvia are standing in the rain, holding hands, too afraid to speak.

'Please let me talk to her,' Liam begs them. 'Please, please, just let me talk to her.'

The frantic paramedics ignore him, but Peter D'Ambrosio quietly but firmly signals at them to let Liam in. They part slightly to give Liam the room to walk alongside the stretcher, next to her face.

He strokes her brow. 'Wake up, Kate, wake up,' he says. 'Wake up for me. It's Liam. Wake up for me, sweetheart.'

The paramedic tells Liam he's going to need to move away, they need to work on her and get her up to the ambulance and out of the rain.

'You can ride in the ambulance with her, mate,' D'Ambrosio says, resting his hand on Liam's arm. 'She needs you.' He takes one of his mum's hankies out of his anorak pocket and loudly blows his nose. He uses his sleeve to wipe his eyes. 'She needs you, mate.'

On the stretcher, Kate Delaney is starting to stir. The voices are at once all around her and far away, like a swarm of bees, buzzing in and out. Exhaustion smothers her like a weighted blanket. But she can hear a voice that belongs to Liam Carroll. Guesser of the Golden Pheasant. He has come. He has found her.

Liam notices the smallest movement in her chest and her hand seeming to stir.

'I'm here with you now, Kater.'

He kisses her eyelids. They're all slippery and soaking wet from the rain.

'I love you, Kate Delaney.'

Her eyes flutter open, and she looks at Liam, and then around at the paramedics; at Sylvia and—is that Mandy King?—standing sodden and holding hands; at a shabby detective with kind eyes standing over her and telling her to live; at the water teeming down over the Pheasants Nest Bridge from the sky.

'Someone had better get the Child of Prague,' whispers Kate Delaney to Liam Carroll, 'to stop that rain.' Her chapped lips crack and she manages the smallest of gap-toothed smiles.

The paramedics push the stretcher into the back of the ambulance, and Liam climbs in and sits alongside her, holding her hand.

The door slides closed, the siren blares on, the red lights flash; the ghosts of the jumpers shrink back behind the trees and the rain falls hard. The ambulance disappears over the horizon.

ACKNOWLEDGEMENTS

I WANT TO thank all of the people who supported me during the past few years that led to this book—personally as well as professionally. My beautiful family, first and foremost. I love you all. To Nick and the kids for again lending me to the writing process that you know brings me such joy. To my darling pals, Louise Adler, Karen Rieschieck and Andy Burns, who read parts of this book in the early stages and spurred me on to keep writing. To Sally Rugg and Mary Fallon, who were each, in different ways, an enormous support to me during the challenging time in my life that this book was written. To the detectives serving and retired, who helped with the research. To Toby, for having the most ridiculous stories that were just begging to be told to a wider audience.

To my indomitable agent, Jeanne Ryckmans. To Jane Palfreyman, who understood this book from the beginning, and to all of the top-class team at Allen & Unwin.

To all of the real-life people I've met over two decades in journalism who helped inspire parts of these characters or parts of their stories—kind cops worn down by tragedy, friends who make me laugh like a drain, lawyers who go into battle on behalf of the vulnerable, people who waded through trauma, and those who know and have known love.